"You refuse to have feelings for a woman, don't you?"

Molly wearily pushed open her door and made her way to the house. It wasn't large, but it had a cozy cottage look, and she could envision paint and flower boxes filled with impatiens.

Hunt stood very still with his back to her, his hands low on his hips as he faced a shadowed doorway. Their two bags sat in the middle of the living room. Even in the dying light of early evening, she could see that he was keeping his fury restrained.

"What is it?" she whispered.

"There are two bedrooms, but one doesn't have a bed. That's what it is."

For a second she missed his point, then it hit her. "At least they're twin beds."

She grinned, amused and a little flattered that the arrangement had caused him such turmoil. Suddenly he seemed vulnerable, and for Hunt, she guessed, that wasn't a pleasant experience. "You're afraid, aren't you?"

ABOUT THE AUTHOR

Dee Holmes, a much-published author of both fiction and nonfiction, won her first major award—a RITA—back in 1991 for her first novel. Happily married, Dee makes her home in Rhode Island and is the mother of a grown-up son and daughter.

Books by Dee Holmes

HARLEQUIN SUPERROMANCE
699—HIS RUNAWAY SON

PROTECTING MOLLY McCULLOCH
Dee Holmes

Harlequin Books

TORONTO • NEW YORK • LONDON
AMSTERDAM • PARIS • SYDNEY • HAMBURG
STOCKHOLM • ATHENS • TOKYO • MILAN
MADRID • WARSAW • BUDAPEST • AUCKLAND

ISBN 0-373-70732-0

PROTECTING MOLLY McCULLOCH

This edition published by arrangement with Harlequin Books S.A.

® and TM are trademarks of the publisher. Trademarks indicated with
® are registered in the United States Patent and Trademark Office, the
Canadian Trade Marks Office and in other countries.

Printed in U.S.A.

PROTECTING
MOLLY McCULLOCH

CHAPTER ONE

MOLLY MCCULLOCH in the arms of a gangster?

Hunt Gresham stared for a full thirty seconds without blinking. Standing on the tiny balcony off his bedroom, holding a half-finished bottle of beer, he'd been unable to drag his gaze away from the open windows of her apartment across the courtyard. God, he had to be seeing things.

Molly was young and attractive with long cinnamon-colored hair that she wore in a single thick French braid. Hunt thought the braid emphasized a carefree youthfulness. Or maybe he just associated braids and kids. Molly, however, was no kid.

Since their collision a few weeks ago in the courtyard that separated their apartments, Hunt had deliberately avoided her. Not because he didn't like her, but because he was afraid he might like her too much.

Complications and involvement with a woman— any woman—wasn't on his list of retirement plans. In fact, it wasn't on a list of *any* of his plans. He'd chalked up his imagination overload to an aberration, or given that he was nearing forty, an approaching midlife crisis.

If Molly had been hugging a professor, or a grad student whose exposure to the seedier side of life had been limited to TV—that he could buy. However, Molly even knowing Vern "The Spider" Wallace, let alone being a girlfriend, astonished him.

Now her arms were so tight around Wallace, Hunt thought she'd never let him go.

He damned his curiosity. Or maybe it was nosiness. Even disbelief.

Whatever it was, he went into his bedroom and dug a pair of binoculars out of a box he still hadn't unpacked. He'd moved to the Massachusetts college town of Woodbriar a month ago, in late July. Because he was a criminologist—and because his sister, Denise, was the lecture coordinator—he'd been invited to give a series of law enforcement lectures at Woodbriar College.

Earlier in the year, he'd taken early retirement from the Boston Police Department. It was a decision he'd toyed with for two years after his wife's death from breast cancer. He'd been devastated. The relentless passion for justice that made him a tough and thorough cop had been lost when Kristin died. That loss had slowed his reflexes and muddied his instincts. A few run-ins with Internal Affairs had strained his relationship with other cops and with the department. Then had come the mistaken release of a small-time thug who had been a key to a year-old investigation of organized crime figures.

Hunt had been startled by his own ineptitude; he'd

believed the thug's story and okayed the release, but later, when he relistened to the taped interview, even he could hear the holes in the alibi. He began to wonder if it was simple carelessness or if he had a death wish. "Time to get out and move on," advised his partner, Sean Sullivan. Hunt agreed. A cop with bad judgment was a hazard to himself, but most of all to the men he worked with and the citizens he was hired to protect.

Financially, he was comfortable, and he was looking forward to the slow pace of teaching a criminology course here at the college. His personal life was hollow and sterile, but he preferred it that way. He guarded himself well, absolutely refusing to get involved in anything potentially complicated.

He reminded himself of that resolve as he tried to ignore the questions his mind conjured up at the sight of Molly with a hit man.

"Why in hell do you care if she's involved with Spider Wallace?" he muttered aloud as he removed the glasses from their case. Just because Hunt had concluded from his own limited knowledge of Molly McCulloch that she was the last sweetly innocent woman on the planet? Just because seeing her now with Wallace destroyed that illusion?

"Damn."

He returned to the balcony. The powerful glasses brought her in so close he felt he could have reached out and touched her. She was no longer hugging the gangster. Hunt caught only a momentary close-up of

Wallace before he stepped back into the shadows of the apartment's interior. Molly, however, hadn't moved from the windows.

She wore a pink cotton shirt tucked into a white flared skirt. The outfit was appropriate for a summer tour guide at the local historical society. Nothing about it suggested that she was a woman about to meet her lover. Rather, she was a study in innocence and vulnerability.

Hunt lowered the binoculars but didn't move back into his bedroom, although he knew he should. His upcoming lecture series still needed hours of work and organizing. Yet, despite wanting to make himself blind to anything that even smelled like trouble, here he was watching and wondering.

Don't be an idiot. Turn around and forget what you just saw. He drained the bottle of beer he'd left on the balcony and took an unsteady breath. *It's none of your business who she messes around with.* Hell, it wasn't even his business if she messed around at all.

"Damn."

Disgusted that he couldn't talk himself into forgetting what he'd just witnessed, he stalked back to the bedroom and tossed the binoculars aside. He snatched up the portable phone and punched out Denise's number. Molly and Denise had been friends since Molly had been hired as the college housing coordinator two years ago.

While he listened to the rings, he returned to the

balcony. Molly's curtains swayed in the slight breeze. Neither she nor Wallace were near the windows.

Hunt dropped into a white resin chair and stretched his legs out. His faded jeans were soft and torn, and his stretched-out T-shirt was a faded red. His dark hair was carelessly brushed back, and a shadow of whiskers indicated he hadn't shaved since yesterday. Denise had given him some dress-code hints for visiting lecturers, which he fully intended to comply with, but until classes began, Hunt didn't even want to think about wearing a coat and tie.

Just as he didn't want to think about what he was doing right now.

Finally, his sister answered.

Never one to bother much with chitchat, Hunt said, "Denise, I've got a couple of questions for you."

"Well, hello, to you, too."

"Sorry." Hunt knew she'd been struggling with her two sons, who were peppered with the measles. "How're the boys?"

"Driving me nuts. How would you like to be stuck with two cranky kids, all the wrong video games and no husband to help because he had an unexpected business trip?"

He winced at her strident tone. He loved his sister, but sometimes he thought she was too tough on Clay. Still, even though Hunt had zero experience with kids, he knew his nephews were a handful even when they were healthy.

"Look, if there's anything I can do..." he began hesitantly.

"You?" Denise sounded stunned.

"Yeah, me. I can always bring riot gear to protect myself."

She laughed. "Sometimes I think *I* need some." After a pause, she added, "Hunt, I love you dearly, but unless you have an instant cure for the measles... Oh, never mind. I guess I'll manage. What did you call for?"

Hunt sighed in relief. Honestly, he felt much surer of himself dealing with Spider Wallace. "It's about Molly McCulloch."

"She's too young for you."

"I don't want a date with her, I just want some information."

"About what?"

"Does she have a boyfriend who doesn't live around here?"

"What an odd question."

"Humor me. Odd questions used to be my specialty."

"Is this a cop question?"

"Yeah, you could say that."

Denise sucked in a breath. "Is Molly in some sort of trouble?"

"Probably not. I don't really know." Even to himself he sounded unsure. "It's more than likely there's a good explanation or I'm dead wrong, but just in case... Does she know a man named Wallace?"

"Hmm. Let me think a minute. There's a Wallace Opalmyer in the science department...."

"No. Last name Wallace. He's got short brown hair, big shoulders and a tattoo of a spider on his left forearm." Hunt hadn't seen the tattoo today, but he knew of the identifying mark from police files.

"Definitely not the kind of man Molly would be seeing."

"I just saw her in his arms."

"You're not serious!"

"Very. I was on my balcony, and she and this guy were standing by the windows of her apartment."

There was a few moments' silence, then Denise said, "Molly is twenty-eight and single, and I guess if she wants to invite a guy with a spider tattoo to her apartment it's no one's business."

Hadn't he been telling himself the same thing for the past ten minutes? Yet here he was speculating and worrying. "If this is the Wallace I think it is, Denise, the spider tattoo is the least of Molly's problems."

"You're making this sound very mysterious."

He took a deep breath and plunged in. "The guy looks like Vern "The Spider" Wallace. I never dealt with him personally, but I've seen photos and I know his history—none of it complimentary. He's well known from Suffolk County to the North Shore. Cops have arrested and charged him a few times, but they've never had the witnesses or the solid evidence to get a conviction."

"Wait a minute. Slow down. Arrest? Evidence? Get a conviction? You're saying that Molly is with a criminal?"

"A professional hit man."

After a gasp, Denise burst into laughter.

"I don't recall saying anything amusing," Hunt muttered.

"I'm sorry, but Molly and a hit man…" More laughter. "Oh, Hunt, now I know you're wrong. It's just too ridiculous to be believable. I mean, she was involved in a crusade last spring against violence on television."

Hunt scowled. His instincts about Molly agreed with his sister's, but he also knew what he'd seen. "Maybe she doesn't know what Wallace does for a living."

"Molly's a good friend and I know her to be levelheaded. Maybe you misunderstood what you saw."

"Maybe."

"I can tell by the skepticism in your voice that you don't think you're wrong."

"I'd like to be."

Denise thought for a few seconds. "All right, let's say you are right. Molly has an idealistic streak. Maybe she knows who he is and she's trying to reform him."

"Reform him? Come on, Denise. I'm not talking about some glib-talking lounge lizard. This guy contracts to kill people for money."

For the first time, Hunt heard real alarm in Denise's voice. "Then you have to do something."

"Yeah, but *what* is the question."

"You're the cop."

"Ex-cop."

"That, my dear brother, is beside the point. If this Spider person was holding a gun on her, you'd go."

"That's different. A gangster hugging Molly isn't a crime."

"Who are you trying to convince? Me or yourself? You wouldn't have called me if you weren't worried. In fact, I think I hear a strong streak of protectiveness in your voice."

"Not a chance." He said it too quickly, but maybe his sister wouldn't catch the defensiveness. Protective indeed. It was just a leftover instinct from being a cop. A natural reaction to seeing someone like Molly with scum like Spider Wallace.

"Well, I hear more than a nosy neighbor jumping to dramatic conclusions."

"You hear annoyance that I even called you," he grumbled, furious that he'd allowed himself to worry about a woman he barely knew. He wanted to think it was merely an objective concern. Yet the reality was that Molly wasn't just any woman, and it bothered the hell out of him that she might be intimately involved with a gangster.

Denise said, "Why don't you call her?"

"And say what? How's your love life? Or better

yet, I could ask if Wallace takes his weapon to bed. No double meaning intended.''

"Then pay her a visit. You'll probably find out that you just thought this guy was Wallace.''

"Yeah, maybe you're right." Denise did have a point. At this juncture, Hunt was drawing a lot of conclusions based on a few glances into Molly's apartment. If he'd seen the tattoo, he'd clearly have a stronger reason to be suspicious. However, a visit would seem odd without a valid reason.

Then he recalled with a partial smile that his apartment's air conditioner hadn't been working right. While Hunt was aware that Molly didn't handle the details of on-campus housing and off-campus apartments, she wouldn't think it was odd if he asked who to see about getting the AC fixed.

"Hunt?"

"What?"

"I think you're very sweet to be so concerned about her."

"Sweet, huh."

"I know you don't believe you could ever care about anything or anyone after losing Kristin."

Hunt stiffened. "An off-limits subject, Denise."

Undaunted, Denise continued, "Her death affected you more deeply than even you realize. Clay and I have both hoped something or someone would change that. At least this concern for Molly shows you feel something."

"Denise." His voice was laced with ice. "Back

off. If you were anyone but my kid sister, this call would have been history forty seconds ago.''

"Okay, okay, but I won't apologize, and if you'd let yourself, you'd agree with me.'' One of the kids screeched in the background. ''Coming, Andy,'' she shouted to her oldest son. Then to Hunt, she said quickly, ''I'd better go. The kids are at it again.'' Hunt heard a crash and then a yowl. ''Oh God, that better not have been my new lamp. Let me know what happens, okay?''

''Yeah. Take care of yourself. Clay won't want a frazzled wife when he gets home.''

He pushed the disconnect button and continued to stare at the windows. The curtains fluttered as a slight breeze broke through the August afternoon heat.

He wondered if they were in bed. He couldn't imagine Molly with Spider Wallace; the idea was ludicrous. Or was it that Hunt didn't *want* to believe she'd have sex or be in love with a killer. Not Molly McCulloch—too innocent, too honest and too deserving of better...

Hell, what was he doing? He barely knew Molly except for his meeting with her to arrange for his off-campus apartment. And the afternoon he'd stopped to watch her play tennis. Later they'd had iced tea and talked about their favorite professional tennis players. Then, of course, there'd been that collision when they were crossing the dark courtyard. But those three incidents were the sum total of their acquaintance.

He wasn't counting the night he'd stood in the dark on his balcony and glimpsed her in one of those shorty nightshirts. He'd been so disgusted with himself, he'd stayed off the balcony at night ever since, and he'd made it a point of walking in the other direction when he saw her.

Until this episode with Wallace.

Denise was right. He should go over there and see for himself. It sure wouldn't be the first time he was dead wrong. And this time he wanted to be.

THE HALL OUTSIDE Molly's apartment was dim and cool, but Hunt felt a line of sweat trickle down his back. He'd considered bringing his revolver, but nixed the idea. A neighbor looking to get his AC fixed wouldn't be carrying a gun. The last thing he wanted to do was make Wallace suspicious and put Molly in unnecessary danger.

Taking a deep breath, he rehearsed his excuse and knocked.

He heard footsteps, and when she opened the door, the first thing that went through his mind was relief. She was wearing the same skirt, shirt and sandals. Obviously the two of them hadn't been rolling around in bed. For reasons he didn't want to think about, he was inordinately pleased.

"Hunt! What a surprise. How nice to see you."

"Molly, I'm sorry to disturb you." He glanced beyond her, his gaze sweeping what he could see of the apartment's interior. It was close to five o'clock, and the sun had moved deeper into the western sky. Molly had closed the blinds, throwing the rooms into shadow. Hunt saw no sign of Wallace.

"You're not disturbing me. In fact, lately, I've gotten the distinct impression you've been avoiding me."

"Avoiding you?" He brought his gaze back to her. The question had come out of nowhere, and yet Hunt heard no coyness or even expectation in her tone.

"I know you're busy getting ready for your lecture series, but the last few times I've seen you, you seemed to walk the other way."

Hunt hadn't thought he'd been that obvious. Now he felt as if he owed her an apology. "Just things on my mind, I guess."

"Probably."

They stood there in the doorway, barely a foot of space separating them. How could he have forgotten how pretty she was or how good she smelled? Without wanting to, he recalled their collision in the courtyard. Her body against his as he steadied her, the brush of her cheek across his hand, the flowery scent of her hair. The entire episode had lasted less than thirty seconds, and yet it was imprinted on his memory.

Hunt took a step back.

Molly touched his arm and the coolness of her fingers made his pulse leap.

"What did you want?"

No involvement with you, dammit. None. Zero. Zilch.... "I came about my apartment. The air conditioner isn't working right. It's either freezing me out or refusing to work at all."

Molly frowned. "I'd specifically requested that the owners upgrade the ACs in these buildings. Your apartment was on the top of the list. Gary Hoagland, the man who handles these things, assured me all the units had been replaced or fixed."

Hunt shrugged. "I should have mentioned this sooner, but, to be honest, I've been so involved with my work..."

"Well, of course you have, and besides, this should have been handled weeks ago." She urged him inside. "Let me give Gary a call. At least he can fix it temporarily. Tomorrow I'll find out if we can get a new one installed for you."

"That would be great," he murmured as he followed her into the large living room. It had a lived-in look without being cluttered. Plump cushions on a blue-and-white slipcovered couch. Wicker side tables with matching ceramic lamps. A tree in a tub in one corner, a family of glass squirrels at its base. Overhead a ceiling fan cooled the room. Everything looked and felt normal and low-key.

No sign of Wallace, and Hunt could hardly search the rooms. He was beginning to wonder if he'd imagined the entire thing. He crossed to the windows where he'd seen Molly standing and looked over at his own apartment. No, he'd seen what he'd seen.

Undoubtedly, Wallace didn't want any close-up encounters with Molly's neighbors. Reasonable enough if he was who Hunt thought he was.

On the phone, Molly said, "Gary? This is Molly McCulloch. Hunt Gresham is having problems with his air-conditioning. He's in 3D of the Oaklawn Complex. He's here now. Yes. I'll let you talk to him."

Molly held out the receiver to Hunt, but covered the mouthpiece and whispered, "He sounds a bit under the weather. You know, a few too many beers. If he can't fix your unit, I have a fan you can have for tonight."

Hunt took the phone, explained his problem and, after a short conversation, extracted the promise his air conditioner would be fixed or replaced.

"That seemed too easy," he said after hanging up. "I'm not sure if we made progress or if Gary was counting the number of full beer cans he had left."

"I'll double-check tomorrow to make sure he didn't forget."

Hunt wanted to ask about Wallace. Her demeanor didn't signal any problem. She was calm, sure of herself and smiling.

Hunt was running out of conversation and a reason for remaining. "I really appreciate the help. From my balcony, I noticed you had company, so the last thing you probably needed was a neighbor with a problem."

"Yes, I do have company. Someone very special." Excitement lit up her face. "He's a little shy, and when you knocked, he ducked into the bedroom."

Wallace, shy? That had to be the understatement of the year. Hunt was at an impasse when Molly grinned. "Would you like to meet him?"

It was what he'd come for, wasn't it? "Sure," he said, hoping he sounded casual.

"Help yourself to a cold beer. I'll be right back."

In the refrigerator was what looked like a summer supper for company. Fancy salads, a tray of expensive cold cuts, a cheesecake and a bottle of unopened champagne. Hunt also noted a box of Godiva chocolates.

All Hunt knew about Godiva chocolates was the price tag. Molly didn't strike him as the type who would buy them for herself, and the box was unopened. A gift from Wallace?

He took out a bottle of beer, uncapped it and took a long swig before returning to the living room.

Molly appeared with a reluctant Wallace. One glance, and in those few seconds of eye contact, Hunt knew he was right. Standing just a few feet from him, beside a grinning Molly, was Vern "The Spider" Wallace.

He wasn't a particularly imposing figure—he looked more like a vinyl-siding salesman than a gangster. His hair had been freshly cut, and he wore light chinos and a blue sport shirt. His eyes were disturbing, though. Sharp, cold, assessing, as if their depths masked a thousand secrets.

Yet when he looked at Molly, they softened with affection. Clearly he wasn't pleased Hunt was there, but for Molly's sake, he was trying not to show it.

Molly stepped forward, so much pride on her face that even a blind man would have seen it.

"Hunt, I want you to meet my brother, Vernon Wallace."

CHAPTER TWO

ONCE THE INTRODUCTIONS were made, Molly invited Hunt to stay, but he sensed her heart wasn't in it. Obviously, she wanted to spend time alone with her brother.

Hunt and Wallace exchanged looks, both men too savvy to miss the implication of Hunt's hanging around. And since Wallace had done nothing but come to visit his sister, Hunt had no right to initiate questions or indulge his curiosity. For that matter, he wasn't even a cop anymore. And if he'd never been one, he would be on his way right now without ever noticing the ruthlessness in Wallace's eyes. An iciness that said "Get lost, buster," in no uncertain terms.

Hunt mumbled something about expecting a phone call and retreated with a jumble of thoughts that promised to keep his mind occupied for the rest of the evening.

Back in his apartment, he tried to concentrate on his lectures, but by eight that evening, he gave up. The AC quit—again—and cursing himself for forgetting the fan Molly had offered, he tried to reach Gary Hoagland. No answer. If the maintenance man

didn't show tomorrow, Hunt intended to call someone else to fix the damn unit and pay for it himself.

Wearing only a pair of faded denim cutoffs, he
went to the kitchen, opened the freezer side of the
refrigerator and stood in front of the misty cold air.
Spotting a pint of chocolate chip ice cream, he took
it out, closed the door and, a spoon in hand, returned
to the balcony.

Digging into the cold carton, Hunt ate ice cream
and allowed the summer evening sounds and activity
to drift over him. Car stereos, parents laughing at the
antics of their toddlers, traffic on the nearby street, a
game of catch between two kids in the courtyard.
Hunt watched them, recalling those summer nights
of baseball with his kid brother, Luke. He lived in
the Midwest now, where he'd moved five years ago
to escape the hectic life here on the East Coast. Luke
had married Natalie, his college sweetheart, had three
daughters, two German shepherds and a small-town
medical practice. Dr. Lucas Gresham. Hunt still
couldn't imagine his brother, who almost blew up the
chemistry lab in high school, doing anything as delicate as surgery. But then, before he became a cop,
Hunt hadn't known the difference between an assault
rifle and a shotgun. Now he knew more about guns
and killing and horror than he'd ever wanted to
know.

One learns these things and then one moves on,
he thought philosophically. As he had done when he
retired.

Glancing in the direction of Molly's apartment, he wondered what kind of kid Vern Wallace had been. What had he and Molly done together as children? Probably fought, like most siblings. Hunt and Luke had scrapped often, and they'd teased Denise when they weren't ignoring her.

He finished the ice cream, set the carton on a side table and slid down in the white resin chair, his legs stretched out, the cooler evening air drifting across him. Molly's apartment was dimly lit, but an occasional shadow indicated she and Wallace were still up. Hunt watched without seeing anything specific and growing more annoyed with himself that he was so curious.

He was oddly relieved "Spider" Wallace was Molly's brother; it was less disturbing than the alternative. One can't choose a sibling but one very definitely chooses a lover. His image of Molly as young and sweet and vulnerable was once again solidly in place.

Nevertheless, he was puzzled. Since he'd never heard she even had a brother, had Molly deliberately kept Wallace a secret? Possibly. Having a brother who contracted to kill people for bucks was hardly campus small talk. Yet she hadn't acted nervous when Hunt appeared. In fact, she'd been upbeat and excited. She knew Hunt was an ex-cop—that in itself should have made her wonder if Hunt might recognize Vern. Surely if she'd feared a confrontation or a barrage of questions, she wouldn't have insisted the two men meet.

And the last names. McCulloch and Wallace. Since he knew Molly had never married, had Wallace changed his name? Or maybe they had different fathers. Hunt made a mental note to call his ex-partner, Sean Sullivan, in Boston and ask him to pull Wallace's record. Once he had a few answers, he'd be satisfied. Just a natural curiosity. Molly with a hit man would make anyone curious; he was just lucky he had the contacts to get information. Comfortable, cooler now, he folded his arms across his chest and dozed.

Later, in the dark, he awoke suddenly, blinking. He'd heard something. Then he heard it again. Someone was knocking on his apartment door.

Rising, he shoved a hand through his hair and rubbed his eyes, squinting at his watch. It was nearly ten o'clock.

He pulled open the door just in time to see a retreating back.

"Molly?"

She turned, gripping a midsize window fan as if it were a piece of luggage. "Oh, Hunt, I woke you, didn't I? I'm sorry. When I knocked the second time and you didn't come, I realized you'd probably gone to bed."

"Here, let me take that." He set the fan down near the door. "I was on the balcony trying to cool off. Guess I dozed off."

She'd changed to white shorts and a roomy blue T-shirt with a Narragansett, Rhode Island, logo of a sailboat in full sail. On her feet were navy tennis shoes and low-cuffed socks. The outfit gave her an athletic look of good health and clean living. When she drew close, her scent was light and delicate, like a distant meadow of wildflowers.

Hunt stared in unabashed enchantment, propping his shoulder against the doorjamb in the shadowy light of the hall.

"That's the fan I promised you," she said awkwardly. "I meant to give it to you this afternoon, but you left so quickly...then I forgot until Vern said something about being too warm and...uh, anyway, you have it now." She was backing away as she spoke. "I'm sorry I disturbed you." Her voice was nervous, her hands clasped, and when she looked at him, she quickly glanced away.

Hunt guessed that, she too, had been caught by the tension that seemed to come out of nowhere. It startled Hunt and reminded him once again why he'd avoided her since that courtyard collision.

"Thanks a lot, Molly. It will at least move the air in the bedroom." Though it was the perfect opportunity to say good-night, he didn't want her to go. "So, how's the visit with your brother going?"

Instantly, she grinned. "We're catching up. It's been a long time."

Hunt nodded. "Yeah, I know what that's like. I have a kid brother in the Midwest. We don't see each other often and when we do, it's a lot of late-night gabbing."

She relaxed a little. "Luke, right? The doctor?"

"How did you know?" It was weird that she knew about his family and he knew nothing about hers.

"Denise brags about him just like she brags about you. When you agreed to do the lecture series, she was so excited. She talked and talked about her brother the cop."

"Ex-cop."

She took a step toward him and that scent of wild-flowers wafted pleasantly around him. "I'm planning on sitting in on your lecture series. Being a cop must have been exciting and dangerous."

"Dangerous, sometimes, but most of the time it's not as exciting as it looks on TV."

"Are you sorry you retired?"

"No." He straightened. "Listen, we don't have to stand out here in the hall. Do you want to come in? I have beer and soda, and I think I have some cranberry juice."

She hesitated, and for a moment he thought she would say yes. "Can I take a rain check? I mean that sincerely. I'd love to get better acquainted, you know, maybe become friends…find out what it was like for you being a cop, but right now I want to get back. Vern is only here for the weekend. I wanted him to stay longer, but he said he has to get back to work."

"Hey, I understand. Sure. We can get together another time." Hunt was stunned by his disappointment. Now that it was her turning *him* down, he didn't like it much.

But instead of leaving, she came closer. Hunt's breath caught and he cleared his throat.

"About the fan—" she began. Her eyes, he decided, were more lavender than blue—soft, compelling and mysterious.

"I'll return it tomorrow."

"No, no, that's not necessary."

Hunt moved to the side while she indicated the speed switch. "It has three speeds, but the middle one doesn't always work. I just wanted to warn you."

"Probably the contacts are dirty."

She shrugged. "Since I have AC, I never got it repaired. In fact, I'd planned to put it in a local rummage sale, but I've had it a long time and you never know when you'll need a fan—"

"Like tonight."

"Yes, like tonight."

"I'm glad you had it."

She swallowed. "So...am I."

Hunt found his own breathing shallow and difficult. Somehow she'd made discussing a fan sexy and seductive. They stood very close, and Hunt felt as if a vise were closing them together. The pressure increased making his blood pump with enough heat to bead his back with sweat.

Their eyes met, and Molly's gaze quickly slid

away. Hunt hadn't moved, but he had a powerful urge to slide his hand around her neck and draw her closer. Here, at this moment, kissing her struck him as the most natural thing in the world. His pulse sped up and his heart began to pound with all the intensity of a trip-hammer.

Molly stayed stone still, and the invisible vise tightened.

Ignoring what was happening was ridiculous. Besides, since Hunt had no intentions toward Molly—honorable or otherwise—he decided the best approach to killing the tension was to face it head-on.

"Remember when we bumped into each other that night in the courtyard?" Hunt whispered.

She looked momentarily taken aback by the remark. "Uh, yes, I do."

"I felt some things for you, Molly, that, well…they were things I didn't want to feel. Physical stuff." Hunt grimaced at his own tenuousness. Usually he was blunt; this sounded so wishy-washy he wanted to start again.

"Physical stuff? You mean sexual?"

"Yes. That's why I've been avoiding you."

Her eyes widened, and despite the hall's dimness he was sure he saw pink rise in her cheeks. "Oh."

"I didn't mean to embarrass you."

"You're very straightforward. I like that. And I'm relieved I didn't do anything to offend you. I thought I might have when you were ducking me."

Hunt chuckled. "Well, now that we know what

we're dealing with, you understand where I'm coming from in being honest with you.''

He expected her to nod and then retreat, but she tipped her head sideways and said, ''I do have to say that you're different from the other professors.''

''Probably because I'm not really a professor.''

''In a way, I believe you'll be better. You'll be teaching from your own experience rather than from theory and textbooks. And you *are* different. The other professors are more...'' She paused a moment, as if searching for the right word. ''More regular. Yes, that's it.''

''Which makes me what? A misfit?'' He found the conversation amusing and interesting.

She grinned, touching his arm lightly, but the coolness of her fingers made Hunt want to press them there forever. ''Not really. It's just that the men around here aren't like you. Perhaps because you're attractive as well as streetwise, and that makes you somewhat of a maverick. Most of the professors are staid and serious in tweed jackets with leather patches at the elbows. Their biggest risk in clothing is a yellow oxford shirt. I mean, even in this hot weather, none of them would wear cutoffs or answer a door with no shirt. I don't mean that as criticism. The ones I know well are wonderful and kind, but—''

''I know. Not like me.'' He squeezed her hand reassuringly. ''It's good that we're being so honest with each other.''

She was quiet, her eyes cast down, her hands fiddling with the bottom of her T-shirt. ''Yes, of course it is.''

For reasons he couldn't begin to explain, he wanted the conversation to continue.

''Well, I'd better go. Vern will wonder what happened to me.''

''Yeah, have a good visit. And I appreciate you bringing the fan.''

She turned and hurried down the short hall. Seconds later, he heard the outside door open and close.

Hunt closed his own door and leaned back against it. He was hot; his loose cutoffs suddenly felt tight. His chest rose and fell as if he'd run up a steep hill.

Swearing, he glared at the fan before yanking it up and carrying it into the bedroom. He set it in the window facing the bed, plugged it in and listened to the whirl of the blades. Air blew across him, and he sighed at the cooling effect. Unfortunately, it also blew his lecture papers off the bed, where he'd been sorting notes. Clearly, staying cool and studying weren't going to be compatible tonight. He tried to convince himself his lack of concentration and the heat were to blame.

The truth was that Molly McCulloch had rattled him badly and managed what no other woman since Kristin could do.

She'd made him want her.

SHORTLY BEFORE MIDNIGHT, Hunt had dropped off to sleep, his mind floating into a carnal fantasy that had him making love to Molly in a house he'd never been in and on a bed with slippery sheets. She kept sliding away from him, and he kept pulling her back. Then, just as he had her snug beneath him, his body poised to enter hers, a siren went off. The wail went on and on, clamoring in his mind so loudly he awoke with a start.

He looked around wildly, but there was no Molly, no lovemaking, just the whirl of the fan and that goddamn siren.

Naked, he got out of bed, stumbled over a pair of sneakers, went through the living room and out to the balcony. The siren wail wound down and stopped. The emergency vehicle was parked in front of Molly's building, its red lights flashing. A police car halted, and two officers emerged. Lights came on in the darkened apartments, and Hunt's eyes focused on Molly's windows, where he could see frantic activity. The two officers he'd just seen outside the building entered the apartment. Hunt didn't wait to see any more.

Pulling on jeans and sneakers, he grabbed a shirt, tugging it on while he hurried out of his apartment and onto the street. Turning right, he passed neighbors who'd emerged in night wear or hastily donned clothes to see what was going on.

"Maybe someone had a stroke or something," a man said as Hunt sprinted past.

In Molly's building, Hunt took the stairs two at a time and was stopped by the police officer stationed at the open doorway of her apartment.

"Can't go in there, sir."

"What happened?" Hunt strained to see inside.

"Who are you?"

"I'm a friend of Molly McCulloch. I just saw her a few hours ago. Is she okay?"

"She's okay."

Hunt's heart lifted in relief.

"Her brother?"

But before the officer could answer, Molly appeared and saw Hunt. "Oh, Hunt! Thank God you're here!" she cried. The officer stepped aside and Hunt went in.

Molly was in his arms, her voice breaking with sobs that made her words difficult to understand.

"Tell me what happened," he said in a soothing tone while he rubbed her back and tucked her closer to him.

"I don't kn-know. I was in bed reading and I heard this loud thump from Vern's room. I hurried in and he was on the floor. His hand was pressed against his chest and he could barely talk. I called 911.... He has to be okay.... He has to be...."

She shuddered, and Hunt eased her to the couch, where he made her sit down. He took tissues from a nearby box, and she smiled her gratitude as she dabbed her eyes.

"They wouldn't let me stay in the room, and no

one said anything and...oh, poor Vern. This is so unfair.''

"Let me see what I can find out," Hunt said softly. "Stay here. I'll be right back."

Hunt made his way in the direction of the disturbance and was stopped once again. The EMTs had loaded Vern onto a stretcher. They were monitoring his blood pressure, his breathing and his heart rate as they wheeled him out. Hunt had witnessed similar scenes when he'd done patrol, but the victims were usually much older.

"Heart attack, huh?" he said to one of the cops.

"Yeah."

"Bad?"

He shrugged. "No heart attack is good. The doctor will have the answers. You a relative?"

"Friend of Ms. McCulloch. I'll take her to the hospital."

Molly had thrown on some clothes and was hurrying after the stretcher when Hunt stopped her.

"I'll take you." He fished her keys out of her purse, made sure her door was locked and then took her arm and led her outside.

The ambulance was pulling away, sirens wailing. Molly's car was parked nearby, and Hunt bundled her into the passenger side and slid behind the wheel.

Madison General Hospital was a tall rectangular building with an ivy-covered facade. Hunt and Molly were directed to the third floor, where the intensive care unit was located. Molly immediately headed toward a nearby nurses' station. She explained who she was and that her brother had been sent to ICU.

The nurse looked up and said, "The doctor will want to get him stabilized before you see him. Why don't you have a seat and we'll let you know. There's coffee and soda machines to the right of the elevators," she added as she turned away to take a phone call.

Hunt took Molly's arm. "Let's get some coffee and sit down. Is there anyone I can call for you? Parents? Relatives?"

"No. No one. She lowered her head, her voice ragged. "Oh, Hunt, I want him to be okay."

"He probably will be. They didn't say how serious the attack was. Maybe it was just a minor one."

"It didn't look minor. He was in a lot of pain."

"At least you called 911 right away. It was the best thing you could have done."

They got coffee and returned to the waiting room. She sank onto the soft couch, and Hunt sat on the low table facing her. He sipped his coffee while she simply stared at her cup.

"He has to be okay," she murmured fervently. "He has to be."

Hunt set his own cup down. Taking her hands, he folded them in his. "You're imagining the worst. From what I saw, he looked pretty healthy. Does he have a history of heart problems?"

"I don't know."

"He probably didn't want to worry you. Or maybe

it was a guy thing where he didn't want to look weak in front of his kid sister.''

"You don't understand. I didn't know because I didn't know my brother.''

Hunt frowned in confusion. "I know you said it had been a while since you two got together, but—''

"I was nine when I last saw him.''

Hunt stared at her in disbelief. "You're kidding.''

"I wish I was. I've been trying to find him since I was sixteen. I finally did a month ago.''

"Wait a minute. You lost me. Why were you separated from him for so long?''

She leaned back and closed her eyes. Still holding her hands, Hunt felt her body tighten. In a flat tone, she said, "It was my fault for not knowing what he was doing for me. The McCullochs were reluctant to take two children. Vern wanted to make sure they chose me because he'd learned that they were leaning toward him. So he acted surly and nasty and waved a knife that I didn't even know he had....''

"Hold it.'' Hunt pulled her forward and made her look at him. "Molly, I haven't got a clue what you're talking about.''

She curled her fingers around his wrists as if he were a lifeline. "No, of course you don't. Oh, Hunt, do you have any idea what it's like to want something so badly that when you get it, it's the most precious of gifts? Then to be gripped by the terror of losing it all over again... I'm sorry. It's just that I've lived with these emotions about Vern for so long and I've never really told anyone about them.'' She searched his face. "Are you sure you want to hear all this?"

"Only if you're comfortable telling me."

She was thoughtful for a moment. Then she said, "Vern was ten and I was six when we were left alone for three days in an apartment while our parents gambled and drank in a neighborhood bar. There was a fire and they both died. Vern and I found out when a social worker found us."

Hunt stared at her, shocked and astonished. "My God, Molly..."

She leaned forward, rocking a little, her eyes filled with tears that she struggled to keep at bay. Her voice trembled. "They didn't love us as much as they did drinking and gambling. They left us like we were things, like we were nothing, like we were never part of their lives."

Hunt drew her into his arms, "Sweetheart, I'm so sorry."

She sniffled. "And if it weren't for Vern, God knows what would have happened to me."

Vern Wallace in the role of hero didn't fit what Hunt knew about him, but then, nothing in the past few hours had made a whole lot of sense. Including the deep sense of protectiveness he was developing for Molly.

CHAPTER THREE

MOLLY PULLED HERSELF together and rose to her feet. She was grateful to Hunt for coming with her, but pouring out her life story...

She had mixed emotions. She wanted to tell him, but for so many years it had been her story alone, her mission to find Vern, her obsession to set right their lives. For all that time, she'd kept her past to herself, not because she was ashamed of it, but because she wanted to stay focused and resolute. She didn't want the distraction of good-intentioned opinions or questions she couldn't answer.

Even tonight there were huge gaps in Vern's life that hadn't been explained, and once again, she was grappling with questions, but this time they were underlined with a new fear: would her brother be all right?

She walked to the windows that overlooked the hospital parking lot. Outside, the August night was serene and still. She was anything but, hating the fact that she couldn't do something to help. Never in a thousand years would she have thought that her reunion with Vern would end up like this. She prayed that she'd reached 911 in time, that the doctor would walk into the waiting area and say, he's going to be fine and he wants to see you. Waiting, not knowing—my God, she should be used to it; she'd spent most of her life waiting to hear about Vern. She shivered, suddenly chilled, and then turned and looked back at Hunt.

He had sprawled back on the green vinyl couch, sneakered feet on the magazine-littered table, ankles crossed, his body lean and long and seemingly relaxed. She imagined the posture belied his alertness, his quickness.

She didn't know him, though, not really. Denise had told her he'd lost his wife to breast cancer and that Hunt had been devastated. How they must have loved each other, Molly thought. She envied such devotion and commitment. She'd felt a sisterly dedication toward her brother during the years they'd been separated, but she'd never experienced love and total devotion to a man of her own; she'd never had that kind of faithfulness returned in kind.

Molly had been intrigued by Hunt since Denise had introduced them when he was looking for an apartment. Hunt, she guessed, would never be dull and boring. And now, in the most unpredictable way, here he was waiting with her, wanting to offer support and a listening ear.

A noise in the hall caused Molly to glance at the open doorway. She walked quickly forward, looking for someone to enter and bring her good news. But within a few moments the corridor was once again quiet.

"Molly?" Hunt stood, his dark shirt and jeans giving him the look of a predator in the antiseptic environment. Oddly, she felt safe, rather than threatened.

"I've intrigued you and then left you hanging, haven't I?" Molly asked, anticipating his interest.

"Look, I don't want to intrude. I mean that. Sure I'm curious, but I didn't come with you to force you to tell me your life story."

"I know." She lowered her head and covered her face with her hands. She felt his arms slide around her, and she gave in to the warmth and support of his body. The gesture seemed so natural, given the circumstances, that she didn't even try to pull away. "I don't know where to begin."

"Tell me why you haven't seen your brother since you were nine. Did he disappear?"

"In a way, but he did it for me." She took a deep breath.

"For you."

He sounded skeptical, but then, he probably thought she was some emotional woman caught by her own version of the past.

"Since he's your brother, why does he have a different last name?"

"Actually, I'm the one whose name changed. I was born Molly Wallace."

His silence made her smile. Poor Hunt, he was

trying to figure this all out piecemeal. "Let me tell you what happened, and then I think your questions will be answered."

He led her to the couch, where they both sat down. Hunt once again leaned back; this time he propped one ankle on the knee of his other leg. Molly perched on the sofa's edge, prepared to jump up at a second's notice.

Hunt reached for her hand, and she gladly let him lace their fingers together. The connection soothed her, while at the same time aroused an unexpected physical response that she hurriedly dismissed. He didn't tug her close or urge her into his arms. Molly knew she wouldn't have resisted, but getting too cozy was dangerous. It would be too easy to lean on him, too easy to let herself mistake his touches for something more than comfort. She was extremely aware of him as a man, and had been for a long time, but an inner alarm warned her to be cautious. She was vulnerable now and needed her wits about her.

Taking a shaky breath, but still holding his hand, she began. "After the social worker took us, and the state learned we had no other relatives, we were made available for adoption. The problem was finding a family who would take two older children. Most want babies, so an older child has the best chance if a sibling is under a year old. I didn't have anyone but Vern, and he felt very protective of me, so to the state's credit, they tried to find a way we could stay together. But three years passed and we were still being shuffled around to foster homes.

"Finally Leo and Carol McCulloch came along. They weren't sure they wanted both of us. They had concerns about Vern, even though they'd always dreamed of having a son. Anyway, Vern was thirteen at the time and had a wild streak. Mostly it came from anger at what our parents did, and he used his anger like a shield against getting hurt or abandoned again."

"What about you? Were you wild?"

She shook her head. "Scared mostly, and desperately wanting a room of my own, a Barbie doll and a bed with a puffy quilt. A nine-year-old's idea of happiness, I guess. As long as I could remember, I'd slept on a foldaway cot in the living room. Now, looking back, it seems silly and…"

"Not silly at all. Your brother was dealing with the change in his life in one way and you chose another way. Sometimes tangible things represent bigger issues, such as safety and comfort and being wanted and loved."

She tipped her head sideways, grateful for his understanding. "You sound as if you've studied human behavior."

"I took some courses as part of my training as a police officer, but I learned the most in the everyday routine of watching people and dealing with their problems. Sometimes kids taken from inner-city poverty would attach the greatest meaning to seemingly incidental or simple things. I recall a little boy a few years back who was picked up for stealing flowers from a street vendor. Later we learned that his mother was an alcoholic, but when she was sober she grew flowers in pots in her kitchen. The kid associated the flowers with the positive side of his mother and made the leap in logic that if he brought flowers home she'd stay sober.''

Molly listened, saddened but fascinated. "Did she?"

Hunt shook his head. "She disappeared and the boy is in foster care."

"What about the father?"

"Whereabouts unknown. A deadbeat dad." Hunt squeezed her hand. "Hey, we were talking about you and your brother and the McCullochs."

She nodded, realizing how hard this was to talk about. She'd hoped for a happy ending this weekend, and now... She cleared away the dismal thoughts and reminded herself that her happy ending had just been postponed for a few hours. She had to be optimistic. That's what she'd been for nineteen years, and even a setback like this one couldn't make her give up hope.

To Hunt, she said, "The McCullochs took a long time to decide, because they were worried they couldn't handle Vern. Yet they knew the state wanted to keep us together if at all possible. Carol McCulloch told me this years later. Because most of the questions were about Vern, he got the idea I was going to be left behind. Vern believed he could take care of himself, but he was afraid for me."

"So if a choice had to be made, he wanted you to be the one who got the family," Hunt commented.

"Yes. I didn't know that at the time. Vern told me this evening about that last day and why he acted wild and crazy with the McCullochs. He wanted them to choose me. I remember how stunned I was by his actions. He swore, made surly comments, threatened to run away, and finally pulled out a switchblade and gave some graphic descriptions of how he could cut people up with it."

"Surely the social worker knew that was a lot of bull and bluster."

She shrugged. "Vern was convincing, and it worked. Carol McCulloch wanted no part of adopting him."

"So they took only you."

Her eyes teared at the memory of leaving her brother behind. "It was a horrible day, when it should have been happy. I was losing my brother and I couldn't stop it." Her cheeks dampened and she tried to stem the tears, but couldn't. All the terror of that separation from Vern rushed over her as if it were happening all over again. "Oh, Hunt, it w-was so terrible."

"Shhh, easy, sweetheart," he murmured, drawing her close and rubbing her back. "That was a long time ago. You've found your brother and you're together now. That's what counts. Your persistence and determination...the fact that you never gave up...it's all paid off now.''

But his words, as soothing as they were, weren't enough. The onslaught of memories was too volatile to contain anymore. Perhaps it was finally telling her story for reasons not connected with her search for Vern, but merely for herself, for her own well-being. ''I cried that day and tried to run back to him, but they forced me away. Poor Vern, he'd been restrained by a juvenile officer. But all I saw was that he stood there like a sphinx watching me leave and doing nothing to stop it.'' She sniffled, grateful for Hunt's arms around her. ''I didn't understand why he was letting me go. It seemed so heartless for him not to fight to stay with me instead of pushing me at the McCullochs.''

''Because he loved you,'' Hunt said simply. ''Because he knew what was best for you better than you did.''

Still tucked against the soothing warmth of his body, she said, ''I know that now. But at nine years old, I wouldn't have understood. Vern saw the bigger picture, saw what I needed. I felt only the pain and terror of losing my brother.''

''Did you and Vern keep in touch?''

''I wrote him at the foster home where he'd been placed, but he never answered. And then on his birthday I called to surprise him. No one knew where he was. He'd left his foster home with some friends and never returned.''

"So the day you left with the McCullochs was the last time you saw him until yesterday?"

"Yes."

"That accounts for the nineteen years."

She nodded. "The McCullochs were wonderful to me. They gave me love and lots of things, including my own room and a Barbie doll and a puffy quilt." She smiled at the memories. "I was happy with them, but there was this part of me that was empty because I knew that somewhere I had a brother. I missed him, and as I got older missing him became a crusade to find him. I was still a teenager when I started seriously searching."

"And you finally succeeded."

"Yes, about a month ago. With the help of a search service. He lives in northern Massachusetts."

Neither Molly nor Hunt saw the figure come into the waiting area until he said, "Ms. McCulloch?"

Molly literally jumped to her feet. "Is Vern okay?"

"I'm Dr. Anderson. Your brother's condition has stabilized, so you can see him now for just a few minutes."

"Oh, thank God."

Hunt stood and the doctor said, "Are you family?"

"Just a friend."

"Family members only."

"I know. I'll wait for you, Molly."

She threw him a look of gratitude for his support and followed the doctor to her brother's bedside.

THERE WERE FIVE BEDS in the long, narrow room. Two, besides the one Vern occupied, were taken. Antiseptic smells and the sounds of monitoring life were the only noises in the sobering silence. The room was dimly lit, and each bed had curtains around it that could be pulled. A nurse sat in a nearby chair and nodded as Molly entered.

"The fourth bed," she said.

Molly crept closer, her heart thumping and her own pulse ticking like a time bomb.

Her brother lay so still she had a brief horrid thought that he was in a coma or worse. Then she saw the active heart monitor and was immeasurably relieved. His eyes were closed, and he looked relaxed in a way she'd hadn't seen even while they'd visited.

She brushed her fingers across his cheek and found it cool to the touch. "Vern? It's me, Molly."

No response.

"You had a heart attack, but you're going to be okay."

His eyelashes fluttered and then opened. Her heart skipped joyously, then thudded to a halt when he said gruffly, "Muffin, you always were an optimistic kid."

A huge lump clogged Molly's throat at the childish endearment. She took his hand, holding it with both of hers. "You were, too. You always told me you could make everything okay."

"And you believed me...always you believed me."

"Oh, Vern, we've been through so much...."

He closed his eyes and then opened them. "Muffin, you gotta listen..." He took a breath, an obvious effort.

"You don't have to talk," she whispered, fearing even that expended too much of his energy. She gripped his fingers as if she could imbue him with her own health and strength. He looked pale and weak, his voice was raspy. She leaned close to hear.

"Your boyfriend..."

Molly frowned.

"...the cop."

"Hunt? He's not my boyfriend."

He moved his head back and forth as if her relationship with Hunt wasn't his point. "He won't let you get hurt."

"Hurt?" Molly could barely hear him. "I don't understand. Hurt how?"

He closed his eyes and the nurse touched Molly's shoulder.

"Your brother needs to rest."

Molly straightened, hesitant to let go of his hand, wishing she could literally pull him out of his weakened condition.

"He looks so sick," Molly whispered. "Is he going to be okay? I mean really okay?"

The nurse urged her away from the bed and toward the double doors. "Why don't you go on home and get some sleep."

"I can't leave him. I did once before and... I'm sorry, but you don't understand. When can I come in to see him again?"

"Probably in the morning." The nurse looked sympathetic, but she was obviously following the doctor's instructions. "Dr. Anderson is fiercely protective of his patients. He knew how worried you were and that's why he allowed you these few minutes."

Molly nodded, grateful for the short time with Vern. The nurse and doctor were right. Her brother needed rest more than a worried, hovering kid sister. "I'll be in the waiting room if there are any changes. I couldn't sleep at home."

SINCE MOLLY HAD GONE in to see her brother, Hunt had reviewed in his mind all that Molly had told him. It was such an incredible story of grit, family loyalty and sacrifice that Hunt found himself seeing a side of Vern Wallace that seemed improbable, given "the Spider's" history. How could a man who cold-bloodedly killed people be the kind of person who would sacrifice himself so his sister could be adopted?

Unfortunately, it wasn't a question Molly could answer. Hunt had listened carefully for any clues that Molly knew what Vern did for a living, but either

Molly knew nothing or she was a damn good actress. Hunt's instinct embraced the former.

Then again, they'd only had a few hours together before Vern's heart attack. From the gist of what Molly had told him, Vern had focused on the reunion and his behavior before they were separated.

Wallace wasn't stupid. No way in hell would he come right out and tell Molly he was a hit man. First of all, she was his sister and had an idealistic view of her older brother—only a dolt or total bastard would destroy that picture. Secondly, he realized instinctively, Molly would never have believed him, anyway.

Hunt glanced up as Molly came in. Her smile was tenuous, but it was there, and once again, Hunt saw the optimistic attitude that had fortified her throughout the years of her search.

"How's he doing?" Hunt asked.

"Holding his own. We spoke and he knew me, but he's very weak."

"He's getting the best care, Molly."

"I know and I'm grateful. It's just such a change from a few hours ago, when we were laughing and catching up." She grinned, and Hunt could tell that the few moments with her brother had boosted her spirits.

Despite what Hunt knew about Wallace, there was no backing away from the fact that there was a real bond between them.

"You know what he thought?" Molly said.

"What?"

"That you were my boyfriend." Her eyes were lavender, glistening and rich in color like lilacs in the springtime. Her cheeks were pink, her hair a little mussed, yet they all added up to a confident Molly. The mention of Hunt being her boyfriend apparently amused her, and not wanting to see that emotion lost, Hunt decided to play along.

"Your boyfriend, huh?"

"Yes."

"Hmm. He must have figured out we were having great sex in a dark hallway."

For a second Molly looked confused. "Oh, you mean when I brought you the fan." She laughed. "Of course that's ridiculous, and he probably thought no such thing, but I know what you're doing. You're trying to make me laugh."

"And you did."

She held her smile, nodding. "Yes."

The subject could have been dropped there, and Hunt fully expected it would be, but to his surprise, she continued.

"I know your being my boyfriend was a silly assumption. I told Vern he was wrong."

"I'm sure that reassured him," Hunt muttered.

"Odd, though, that he would mention it, considering how sick he is. I mean, wouldn't you think there would be more important things to talk about?"

"He's probably worried about you."

"And he probably thinks you're okay because you're a cop."

Given that she knew nothing about who Vern was, Hunt allowed the conversation to go on. It didn't mean anything, and more importantly, it was taking Molly's focus off her fears.

"You know, it's been a long time since I've been anyone's boyfriend," Hunt said reflectively. "A husband once. A lover a few times. And when I was in my twenties, my brother used to call me 'The Stud' because I thought I could score with a different girl every week."

Molly's eyes widened with both curiosity and something Hunt couldn't quite define, but it resembled yearning. Maybe she'd never been anyone's girl. Maybe she'd never had a real boyfriend. She was twenty-eight, but by her own admission had spent most of the past years searching for her brother, studying and working. Maybe she hadn't had time for any kind of serious man-woman relationship.

To Hunt's surprise, he found himself wondering about a relationship with Molly. Having her belong to him. Having her as his lover. A woman he could laugh with; a woman who could make him want more than the lonely existence he'd chosen since losing Kristin.

Of course, the whole idea of anything with Molly was insane. He didn't want a new relationship with any woman; his heart had closed when Kristin died, and opening it again held little appeal. He'd known the richest and deepest kind of love with his wife, and that particular emotion died with her.

"Did you?"

Hunt blinked, his mind swirling with thoughts he hadn't had in a long time. Molly's innocence was enough to make him back off. She needed a man with hope, not an ex-cop with an empty heart. "Did I what?"

"Score with a different girl every week?"

He chuckled. "No matter how I answer that I'm not going to come out looking good. But I'll say this. If you'd been one of those girls when I was in my twenties, I would have gladly gone from 'stud' to permanent boyfriend."

"You're teasing me."

"And flirting with you."

"To take my mind off Vern."

"More to ease you away from worrying when worry isn't going to make anything happen faster."

"Like Vern getting better instantly," she mused. "I know. It's just that—"

"He's your brother and you want to be sure he's going to be okay."

She nodded, and Hunt put his arm around her, giving her a squeeze of understanding. He knew what she was going through; he'd felt much the same anxiety and panic when Kristin was so sick. Hunt closed his eyes briefly as those months of waiting and hoping for the best while fearing the worst rushed over him once again. His beloved Kristin...so young, so alive, so beautiful, with all her plans for a house and a huge flower garden and children…plans that were never fulfilled.

Molly had her back to the corridor and didn't see the two nurses scurry down the hall. A door slammed somewhere and wheels on some piece of equipment squeaked in a hurried rumble. Hunt instinctively pulled Molly into his arms. He knew better than to assume all the rushing was because of Vern—the hospital had more than a hundred beds.

"Hey," he said in a heavy whisper. "If I wanted to really take your mind off worrying, I could do this." And before she had a chance to object, question or even wonder at his motive, he tipped her chin up, lowered his mouth and kissed her.

Hunt wasn't prepared for the sweetness, the surprise on her lips, the swell of hunger that rolled through his own body. He angled his head, meeting her mouth more fully, tasting her, memorizing her texture, her scent. Her arms tightened around him, holding him to her as if he were her anchor.

He deepened the kiss, tangling their tongues, and for a few seconds he forgot where they were, forgot she was too young and innocent, forgot he had no room in his heart for a woman like Molly.

Her breathing grew rapid, and Hunt felt the tightness of her breasts against his chest. He moved against her, the stiffening of his own body more than enough reason to halt things immediately. He stilled both their bodies, drawing away.

"Molly..." he murmured, touching their foreheads and pulling back so that he could see her eyes. "I didn't mean—"

She touched her finger to his mouth to quiet him. "Please don't apologize. I could have pulled away." Then, in a lighter tone, she added, "You certainly took my mind off worrying about Vern."

"Yeah," Hunt grumbled. "That was the point." Hunt let her go and backed up a few steps. Damn, he had to be nuts. He wondered what in hell had happened to that vow he'd made to avoid her. Wallace had happened, that's what it was. Nothing more.

He glanced up, his eyes focused on the corridor and the approach of Dr. Anderson. The physician walked into the waiting room, his step reluctant, his tie loosened.

Hunt automatically reached for Molly. She turned.

"More news about Vern?" she asked.

"Ms. McCulloch, I'm sorry. We did everything we could, but your brother's heart was too weak."

"What are you telling me?" Molly whispered, and Hunt gripped her tighter.

"Your brother has died."

CHAPTER FOUR

MOLLY'S HANDS flew up to cover her mouth, but her gasp of pain was clearly audible. She struggled to free herself from Hunt's arms.

"No!" she cried. "It's a lie! I just saw him, I just talked to him. No, please, oh God, please no..."

Hunt gathered her to him again.

"What happened?" Hunt asked the physician.

"Another heart attack. This one was massive."

"You said he was going to be okay," Molly said, accusingly. She sagged against Hunt.

Hunt clearly recalled that Dr. Anderson hadn't said anything even close to that. When Kristin had been so sick, Hunt had learned firsthand that doctors chose their words very carefully. They didn't want the family to lose hope, yet they were careful not to make impossible promises.

"Molly, the doctor said your brother's condition had stabilized."

Dr. Anderson gave him a surprised look, then nodded. "He's right, Ms. McCulloch. At best, your brother has been bargaining for time for quite a while. His heart had been in bad shape for years.

Frankly it's incredible that the attack at your house wasn't fatal.''

She turned, pushing away from Hunt, and went to the couch, where she folded herself into the corner like a tiny animal gripped by pain.

The doctor cleared his throat. "Mr., uh..."

Hunt watched her, his arms feeling suddenly cold. He wanted to comfort her; he wanted to make the hurt and grief less devastating, but he knew from his own experience that was impossible. Getting past the bitter sting of death and loss and moving on took the healing powers of time.

Instead of approaching Molly, Hunt shoved his hands, palms out, into the back pockets of his jeans. "Gresham," he said. "Hunt Gresham. I'm a friend of Molly's."

"Good. She'll need her friends. Does she live with anyone? Parents? A housemate? Another sibling? You?"

"Uh, no. She lives alone."

"Someone should stay with her. What about a neighbor or a female friend? At least for tonight. Her reaction and withdrawal isn't unusual, but she could be in shock. I could admit her, given the circumstances, but I think she'd handle this better at home. Can you call someone?"

Hunt shoved a hand through his hair. It was one in the morning, and he didn't have a clue who Molly's friends were.

As his silence lengthened, the doctor said, "Surely there must be someone. What about you?"

"Me?" Being her neighbor and friend, that he could handle, sort of, but to become an all-night nurse—the idea was ludicrous. Waiting at the hospital and giving a few moments of comfort was one thing, but Hunt had resisted even the possibility of being too involved in her life.

My God, he'd done his best to avoid her for weeks, he thought grimly. And if he'd quashed his damn curiosity about Wallace, he wouldn't be here right now. His insides wouldn't be twisted with angst because he knew things that would be painful for her to hear. What he wouldn't give to be home asleep and oblivious to all of this. But then Molly would have been here all alone, alone while she waited and alone when she got the bad news. Hunt scowled at how she'd managed, without even trying, to worm her way into his thoughts; he vowed she'd get no farther.

The doctor scowled. "Surely this can't be that complicated, Mr. Gresham. One night isn't forever, and you did say you and she were friends."

"Yeah. Look, I'll call my sister. She works with Molly, and they're friends."

"Sounds ideal," the doctor said, not trying to hide his eagerness to be on his way. "Perhaps you and your sister could help Ms. McCulloch get the funeral arrangements started in the morning."

"My sister can handle that."

"Good."

"I'm curious," Hunt said. "Did Wallace tell you he had a heart condition or did you learn it from symptoms?"

"Both, actually. The symptoms were characteristic, but Mr. Wallace told me some of his medical history, which confirmed my suspicions."

"Then he had been seeing a doctor."

"Yes."

"Did he give you a name and where he practiced? The family may want to talk to him."

"Uh, let me see," he said thoughtfully. "I believe the name was Crombie. Mr. Wallace said he practiced in Fernwood."

Hunt recalled that Molly had said her brother lived in northern Massachusetts. Fernwood was northwest of Boston. "Thanks."

The physician walked over to Molly. She'd drawn her knees up to her chin and locked her arms around them. Her face was pale and tear-streaked and an occasional sob broke the rhythm of her breathing.

The doctor laid a hand on her shoulder. "I'm sorry for your loss."

She nodded, dabbing at her eyes with a balled-up tissue. "We'd only just been reunited, and there was so much left unsaid."

"I'm sure," he said, patting her, then adding, "Your brother insisted on talking to you. That and your worry were the reasons I allowed it. He didn't say it in so many words, but I had the sense he was concerned about your well-being.''

Hunt listened, his own knowledge of Wallace from police files giving him insight neither the doctor nor Molly was privy to. Wallace was probably worried that Molly would learn who he really was.

"Vern always worried about me and did things to make sure I was taken care of.''

"Well, it's evident you have a good friend in Mr. Gresham, so I'm sure everything will be fine.''

She nodded, blowing her nose. She slowly stretched out, placing her feet on the floor. Taking a shuddering breath, she rose. Hunt could see her grit and courage return when she lifted her chin and then straightened her shoulders.

Not for a moment did he believe she'd simply accepted her brother's death. No, he guessed she was concentrating on Vern's concern about her while making a valiant effort to show that she could handle this.

In a voice Hunt knew took all her effort, she said, "I'm grateful for what you did.''

"I wish it could have been more," the doctor said gravely. He pressed his lips together, his face looking weary and old, as if fighting the battle against death would be lost almost as often as it was won.

Hunt, once again, was swamped with his own tragic memories. He'd been told something similar when Kristin died, but he hadn't nodded and accepted the sympathetic words. He'd been furious.

Mostly at himself for all the times he'd been apart from Kristin because of his job. All those special details, those boring stakeouts, those weekends he'd worked overtime because the money had been so good and he'd wanted to build Kristin the house she'd wanted. All those moments he could have had with Kristin became lost opportunities that could never be found again. Hunt shuddered. How devastating this must be for Molly. For her, Wallace's death was more than lost opportunities. She was dealing with nineteen empty years, with no one to help her fill in the gaps or find the missing pieces.

Before leaving, the doctor handed Hunt a sample packet of pills. "This is a mild sedative. Give her two when you get home. They'll help her sleep."

Home. He hadn't thought of that word since before Kristin... He cut off his thoughts, taking the packet and tucking it into his pocket. After the doctor was gone, Hunt walked over to where Molly stood staring out at the dark night.

"Come on, Molly. We should go."

"I can't believe all this has happened, Hunt. It's so unfair, so cruel."

"I know. It's frustrating when you're helpless."

She faced him, her expression holding a touch of fierceness. "No, it's not being prepared. Why didn't Vern tell me he had a heart condition? Why would he keep something so important to himself?"

"Probably he didn't want to spend the time he was

with you talking about his health." Or who he really was, Hunt thought.

They made their way to the elevators and rode down to the admitting area. Hunt took her arm as they walked out of the hospital and into the parking lot.

"Or maybe he didn't know," Molly said, picking up the discussion of Wallace's health. "Maybe he never went to a doctor and had no idea his heart was so damaged. I mean, after all, he couldn't tell me something he didn't know. Right?" Her eyes searched his, obviously looking for some affirmation of her own conclusion.

"He knew," Hunt said, unlocking the passenger side of the car. Instead of sliding in, she turned to Hunt.

"Vern knew?"

"Anderson said your brother told him he was seeing a Dr. Crombie in Fernwood."

She was still for a moment, as if gathering all the facts together and sorting them so they made sense. Then she drew herself up and said firmly, "Well, I intend to pay him a visit and find out what Vern wouldn't tell me."

"What good will that do? None of his medical history matters now."

"It matters to me. He was my brother, and what I know about the thirty-two years of his life wouldn't fill four pages. I want to know who he was, who his friends were, what his interests were, if he had any hobbies.''

"Hobbies?" Hunt nearly choked on the word. "Listen to me, Molly. Sometimes the past isn't as we expect it to be.''

"Oh, don't worry. I know he was no saint.''

"That's not what I mean.''

"Don't you understand I need to know?'' Her tone was desperate. "I have to know because he was all I had.''

"Oh, jeez,'' Hunt muttered.

"He told me some things but not enough.'' She got into the car, but when she reached for the door, Hunt stopped her.

"What things?''

"That he's divorced and has a son, for one. I have a nephew—Brandon—out there somewhere. My only blood relative. Maybe Vern's heart condition was hereditary. If so, his ex-wife, Francine... well, she should know in case their son has future problems.''

"Molly, if she was married to the guy, she probably already knows.'' In the back of his mind was a nagging image of a woman who had been connected to Wallace, but he couldn't put a name to her.

"Maybe she did, maybe she didn't.''

Hunt didn't need to ask her intent, he could visualize the wheels turning in Molly mind. The amazing thing about all this was that if Wallace hadn't croaked, Molly would have sailed on believing whatever he'd told her on his occasional visits. Now what would she learn?

"All of this can wait until morning." Hunt said, hoping to buy some time to figure out what to do next. He supposed he was going to have to tell her the truth, but when and how? He closed the door and went around to the driver's side. A quick glance in her direction indicated she agreed, since she didn't say anything further. A few minutes later, they'd exited the parking lot and were headed toward Molly's apartment.

As he drove, it struck Hunt that he could save Molly from what he feared would be some new mission by simply telling her what he knew about Wallace. Yet he remained silent. Truthfully, he didn't want to see the disappointment and horror on her face. She had enough to deal with now; Wallace's checkered past could wait. Destroying her beliefs about her brother moments after he died was unnecessarily cruel.

Then there was a more insidious thought. Hunt toyed with his underlying reason for silence; keeping himself uninvolved in her personal life and therefore her problems. That resolve was becoming more and more difficult.

As they entered Molly's apartment, Hunt pushed away the growing softness for Molly that had wormed its way inside him in the past few hours. He focused on some clear facts. He was no longer a cop and therefore he didn't give a rat's ass about Vern

Wallace. He liked Molly, but no way did he want any personal involvement with her. He didn't want to get lost in her wide lavender eyes, which could set his pulse pounding and send his thoughts racing through a carnival of pleasures. He'd come to Wood-briar to give a lecture series on law enforcement. Other than that, he didn't want to make any decision that was more complicated than whether to drink his beer from a bottle or a can.

Besides, he still loved Kristin. That was the bottom line. *Stay cool, objective and uninvolved,* he reminded himself. *Starting right now.* Thank God for his sister.

"THE POOR THING! Is she all right?" Denise asked anxiously after Hunt told her what had happened. He was in Molly's kitchen, leaning against the counter, the phone anchored to his ear. It was 2:00 a.m. and he'd finally convinced Molly to go to bed. Hunt was anxious to get back to his apartment and do the same. His own eyes were gritty and his head ached. He'd filled Denise in on all that had happened since he'd seen the ambulance outside Molly's building.

"She's gone to bed. The doctor prescribed a mild sedative. Look, Denise, she needs someone to be here with her. Could you come?"

"Well, of course. I can be there by eight. I'll ask my neighbor to keep an eye on the boys."

"No, not in the morning. Now. I need you to come now."

"I can't, Hunt. I can't leave the boys. Did you forget that Clay's away?"

He had. "Damn."

"Look, why don't you stay? You're already there, and it will be daylight in a few hours. With the sedative, she'll probably sleep and you can, too."

No way would he sleep. Not here. Not with this rush of feelings for Molly that had nothing to do with helping her through a grieving period. "How about this? I'll come and stay with the kids and you come over here."

"But that's silly. It's just for a few hours."

"But..." He was losing the argument and he knew it.

"She's just lost her brother. Good grief. You've already been through the worst of it with her. I don't understand why you're making such an issue out of a few more hours."

Because I'm liking being around her too much and my feelings are moving into areas I don't want them to go.

Hunt sighed. Closing his eyes, he took a deep breath.

"Hunt? You still there?"

"Yeah."

"Sleep on the couch, and I promise I'll be there first thing in the morning."

Hunt hung up the phone, switched off the kitchen

lights and walked back into the living room. The couch was a sectional and looked comfortable enough. He could manage this for a few hours.

Before he settled in, he walked down the short hall and stopped by her open bedroom door.

The light from the hallway illuminated her where she was curled up in the middle of a double bed. She'd loosened her hair from the French braid, and it spread across the pillow like cinnamon-colored silk. She'd gotten undressed and now wore what looked to Hunt like a college dorm shirt. It climbed high on her thighs, exposing slender legs and a glimpse of red lace panties. Hunt sucked in his breath and scrambled to put a death hold on his rampaging thoughts.

He stood rigid, his body taut, his heart thumping, barely able to pull his gaze from the sleeping woman. Guilt roared through him for his carnal feelings for Molly at such an inappropriate time. He was reacting more like a voyeur than a friend. He was about to return to the living room when he heard her stir.

"Hunt," she called, her voice husky and low. "Come on in."

He didn't move. "Just wanted to make sure you were okay."

"Please?"

Against his better judgment, he slowly entered the room, lifting a soft cotton quilt from where it had been tossed on a chair.

"You should be asleep," he whispered, laying the quilt over her.

She reached for his hand. "How can I thank you for being such a good friend?"

"You already did."

She laced their fingers together, and Hunt felt a slight tug to draw him closer. The sedative had obviously relaxed her and made her a little groggy. He'd stay for just a few minutes. He carefully sat down on the edge of the bed, making sure his body didn't touch hers.

"I can't believe he's gone," she said, her voice breaking. "Just a few hours ago we were eating and talking, and now..."

Hunt brushed her hair from her cheek. "Shhh. It's going to take time to adjust. And you should call your parents. They will want to know."

"My parents, yes. They've been on a cruise in Alaska. I talked to them after I found Vern. They were happy for me. I'll call them later." She took a shaky breath. "I have so few memories of him, Hunt. If we'd been in contact all these years, then at least I could look back on the good times. I could laugh at the funny moments and even find some wisdom in the not-so-funny ones. I could have gone to his wedding, been there when my nephew was born. We could have shared so much. Instead, all I have are a few bald facts. I don't even know enough to decide if the facts are good or bad." While she talked, she'd burrowed closer to Hunt, so that her cheek lay against his thigh.

Hunt cursed Vern Wallace for his miserable life and the legacy he'd left behind. It was bad enough to lose someone you loved, but then to learn he was part of the mob when you wanted to think he could have been citizen of the year...

"We can talk in the morning," he murmured, easing back and rising to his feet. She still held his hand.

"Don't go."

"You need to sleep."

"Please."

He leaned down and brushed his mouth across her forehead. The gesture seemed natural and right under the circumstances. "I'll be in the living room. I want you to settle down and go to sleep. You have a lot to do tomorrow."

Her eyes were luminous in the lighted shadows. "You know what?"

"What?"

"I wish you *were* my boyfriend." At Hunt's startled reaction, she added, "From the moment I first met you, I thought you were so different. Attractive and sexy and honorable."

"Don't, Molly..."

"Then when we collided in the courtyard, I felt—"

Hunt pressed his fingers against her mouth. "Shhh. You shouldn't be saying those things."

She pushed his fingers away. "Why? They're true."

"And they're dangerous," he snapped, deciding she needed a clear reminder why. "For God's sake, I'm not some tweedy professor who's interested in your relationship theories. And I would hope to hell you don't say that kind of stuff to other men. To a lot of them it would be an open invitation."

She looked at him as if he'd encouraged rather than discouraged her. "I've dated a few guys, but I never wanted to say anything like that to any of them. Just to you."

"Then it's a good thing I'm not interested enough to take advantage of you, isn't it?" He'd stood and planted his hands low on his hips, glaring down at her with an anger he really didn't feel. There was something compelling about such complete honesty. Compelling and risky.

"You're angry with me."

"I'm telling you that it isn't always a good idea to blurt out what you think you feel. Especially now. You've had a shock and a family tragedy. I was with you, so you no doubt feel some gratitude. You're not really thinking straight, plus I think that sedative is making you less cautious about what you're saying."

He backed up, inching his way to the doorway.

"You're not going to leave, are you?"

"I'll be in the living room."

"Hunt?"

"What is it, Molly?" He couldn't keep the exasperation from his voice.

"Here." She reached behind her and then in front of her. "Take one of my pillows and the quilt. I have enough covers."

He came forward and took them only because he didn't want to continue this conversation any further. "Thanks."

"Thank you for staying, for being with me at the hospital."

"Sure. Now go to sleep."

He returned to the living room feeling as if he'd barely escaped a potential disaster. He was sweating, he was hard and he was irritated. He flung the pillow down, stripped down to his briefs and stretched out on the couch. He draped the quilt so that it covered him from the waist down, then laced his hands behind his head and stared at the ceiling. The sweet scent of her was everywhere. The pillow, the quilt, in the air.

Goddammit, Denise. This is all your fault, he muttered under his breath. *If you'd done what I suggested, none of this would have happened.*

But beneath his irritation and determination to stay uninvolved with Molly was a begrudging admiration for her forthrightness. She'd stated her feelings without guile, without any purpose beyond saying what she felt. It surely wasn't her fault that his feelings were so unruly that he couldn't explain them if he wanted to. Which he didn't.

He'd never been one for talking out his innermost thoughts. Spilling his guts because of some emotion-laden situation had always struck him as a weakness. A man dealt with whatever was bothering him and didn't burden the rest of society with it.

Kristin had often accused him of being too much like a clam, but the truth was, Hunt had learned early in life that what you reveal about yourself can be used against you. His father had always talked too much, bragging about his expertise in neighborhood poker games. As a result, some other player would inevitably take up the challenge and beat him, leaving Sammy Gresham to explain to Hunt's mother why he'd lost the rent money.

There had been other times when his old man's talking had gotten him into hot water, and it wasn't long before Hunt got the message. Keep things to yourself and you'll stay in control of your life. And he intended to stay in control.

He smiled into the darkness. In a little while Denise would be here and he'd be history. With that hopeful thought, he drifted off to sleep.

AN HOUR LATER, he jackknifed up, nearly falling off the couch. What had awakened him, he didn't know, but some sixth sense told him something was wrong. He stayed still and then he heard it.

Sobbing. So soft and so muted he was amazed it could have woken him.

He felt around for his jeans and pulled them on,

but didn't bother with the zipper or the snap. He moved silently down the hall and stopped at Molly's room. He could see her thrashing on the bed.

"No!" she shouted. "He's my brother. I can't leave him. Please. I don't want a family without him."

Hunt moved immediately to the bed, sitting down and gathering her into his arms. "Molly, sweetheart, wake up. You're dreaming...."

Her arms went around him and she literally crawled into his lap. "Please, oh, please, make the hurt go away...."

Hunt didn't think about what he was doing, he simply acted. She was clutching him as if he were some barrier against the lonely pain of the night. A pain he understood all too well. He couldn't leave her to deal with it alone.

He eased her back down, but she grabbed at him again.

"Easy, easy... I'm not leaving you...." He pulled the covers up and tucked them securely around her. Then he pulled up the cushioned side chair and settled into it, stretching his legs out. A tiny voice inside him reminded him that this kind of growing attachment to her was exactly what he'd tried to avoid. But no way could he have left her alone to cry.

She burrowed into the covers. "Thank...you for...staying," she murmured, her voice drifting off.

Hunt didn't move from the chair, and within seconds she had fallen into a sound sleep.

Hunt didn't. He lay awake, watching Molly and watching dawn break on the horizon.

Here he was with Molly—where he didn't want to be—and yet… The hell of it was that he couldn't remember ever feeling this content and at peace with himself.

CHAPTER FIVE

"DAD, THANKS FOR offering, but there's nothing you can do here," Molly said to Leo McCulloch.

It was late the following morning and Molly had called her parents to tell them what had happened.

Her parents were involved in foster care with some handicapped children, and Molly knew that for them to come to Woodbriar to be with her would be a strain. It wasn't as if Vern had been their son. Their recent trip to Alaska had been their first vacation in five years, and it would be a hardship for the kids if they were to suddenly leave.

"Your mother and I don't think you should go through this alone," her father was saying.

"I'm not really alone. My best friend, Denise, is here, and her brother has been just great."

"What about funeral arrangements?"

"I made them this morning. The Fernwood Funeral Home is handling things."

"You sound very together, honey. I hope you're not in shock."

"I think I'm numb. But doing these things has helped me not to focus so closely on losing Vern."

"Looking back now, we should have taken Vern...."

"Please don't. You and Mom did what you thought was best. Vern did, too. He knew you would be a wonderful family for me, and you were."

Her father sniffled, then coughed to cover his breaking emotions. Her mother took the line. "I really think we should come and be with you, Molly."

"I'll tell you what. I'll call you right after the funeral so you'll know I'm all right."

"But, darling..."

"I'll be in touch," she said firmly. "I love you both."

After she hung up, she looked over her notes from her talk with the funeral director. He'd been properly sympathetic and not pushy when she said she wanted a simple casket and a graveside service at the cemetery. Since she had no idea who her brother's friends were, she notified the *Fernwood Gazette* with a sketchy obituary. The obits editor assured her it would be printed the following day so that Vern's friends and acquaintances would know of his passing.

The services were set for Friday—three days from now, which gave Molly time to drive to Fernwood to attempt to locate Vern's ex-wife and his son. She'd checked his wallet and found only a small amount of cash, a driver's license and a four-leaf clover. Immediately her eyes misted. She had one that Vern had found for her; she'd pressed it in an old volume of *Uncle Wiggly* that she'd loved as a child. Finding this one gave her a good feeling about those nineteen years of separation. Vern had kept a four-leaf clover as a reminder of her, of the few good times when they had searched for clovers in a park near their parents' home. She sighed and put the lucky clover into an envelope, then placed it in her purse.

There was nothing else in his wallet. No credit cards or pictures or business cards. It was as if he didn't want anyone to know anything about him. It struck her as odd, given that his work involved contact with clients, but since she was dealing with a long gap in their relationship, she knew nothing of her brother's personal habits. With her phone calls completed, there remained only the task of packing up Vern's things.

That would be difficult. Her adult memories of him were limited to yesterday. There were his clothes and toiletry items and a soft leather attaché case, which no doubt held the prospectuses of the companies he'd said he was researching for his clients.

Vern had told her he was an investment analyst; that sounded interesting and important, and Molly had wanted to hear more than the vague explanations her brother had tossed out before changing the subject.

She fervently wished that Hunt was here, and hoped she hadn't scared him away forever. She'd awakened at eight-thirty feeling surprisingly rested, considering she'd had so little sleep. When she'd smelled coffee and then heard footsteps approaching her bedroom, she'd assumed they were Hunt's. Momentary disappointment gripped her when Denise appeared in her doorway, but she was glad for her friend's support, and Hunt had already done more than she had any right to expect.

Molly was still evaluating the twists and turns of circumstances since her brother's unexpected death. Hunt's presence and support had helped her immeasurably. Her only regret now was that she'd probably embarrassed him into never wanting to be alone with her again. No doubt he feared she'd try to cling to him this morning and expect him to become her major source of emotional support.

Now she took a deep breath and vowed she would act like a grown-up and not a blubbering basket case. Poor Hunt. Probably right this minute he was wondering how to avoid her.

Dressed in dark blue cotton slacks and a lightweight ecru sweater with tiny appliquéd pink roses at the neckline, Molly lifted her mug of coffee and sipped the hot liquid. The doorbell rang, but when Molly started for it, Denise appeared and waved her away.

Muted conversation was followed by the sound of the door closing. Denise reappeared, a casserole in her hands, the warm smell of chicken and mushrooms drifting into the room. "I'm running out of space in the refrigerator."

"The neighbors have been so thoughtful," Molly commented.

"Yes, they have. That was Mrs. Oxwill. She said her brother-in-law once worked for a funeral home and if you needed any advice... Well, you know how she is. She has a relative for every emergency."

Molly nodded. "She means well."

Denise took the dish to the kitchen and then returned with her own coffee. She peered at Molly with a mother-hen expression. "I wish you'd come out to the kitchen and let me fix you something to eat. Someone sent a yummy apple coffee cake."

"I'm fine, Denise." She was sure the huge, raw lump in her chest would never allow food to pass.

"Except for your parents, I could have done all that calling for you. That was one of the reasons Hunt wanted me to come over."

"And I appreciate your offering, but I had to do it myself. I knew so little about Vern that it seems the least I could do was make the final arrangements." Molly took one last sip of her coffee and then put the mug aside.

Denise said, "I made your bed and straightened up the kitchen. Your brother's things..."

"Yes, I have to take care of them."

"Hunt said he'd do it."

"He did?" Molly was surprised. Not at the offer but that Hunt would even want to come near her after what had happened. He'd made it clear he had no personal interest in her; surely he had no obligation beyond what he'd already done.

"Didn't he tell you that?" Denise asked.

"Well, no... Or maybe he did and I don't remember."

Denise nodded in understanding. "That's not surprising. You've been through a lot in the past twelve hours."

"Is that all it is? My God, it feels like fifty."

"You poor thing," Denise said sympathetically.

"You know, there's a part of me that wants to clutch every item that belonged to Vern and another part that wants to bury my head and pretend none of this ever happened." Molly took a tissue from her slacks pocket and dabbed her eyes. "Hunt has been wonderful. Staying at the hospital with me, and then when I had that terrible dream..." She remembered the aftermath all too vividly. "I think I embarrassed him."

"Embarrassed Hunt? Why would you think that?"

"He slept in a chair right beside the bed. He must have been uncomfortable, and I'm sure it was the last thing he wanted to do."

Denise, who'd just raised her mug, steadied the tipping container. "He slept in the bedroom with you?"

"I had this awful dream about when Vern and I were separated." She gave Denise a capsule version of what she'd told Hunt. "I was adopted and he wasn't."

Denise immediately put her arm around Molly. "Good heavens, no wonder you're feeling such a huge void. Not seeing him for nineteen years and then this..."

Molly nodded. "Anyway, I guess I must have cried out in my sleep. I don't remember much except that Hunt came in. I didn't want to let go of him. His being there was like some safety barrier."

Denise was staring, eyes wide, mouth slightly agape. "I'm stunned. Since Kristin died, Hunt hasn't had any involvement with a woman. Well, not one that wasn't, uh, strictly physical."

Molly grinned. "Sex but no heart."

Denise's eyes widened. "Why, yes. What a precise way to put it."

"I'm not sure his heart was in it last night beyond feeling pity for me." For an instant, she realized she didn't want pity, she wanted something more, something she couldn't quite define.

"Did he say anything this morning?"

She shook her head.

"Maybe you dreamed it, Molly."

"No, he was comforting and it meant a lot to me. A hundred times more than it meant to him."

Denise tapped her forefinger against her mouth. In a reflective tone, she said, "Hmm. This is very interesting."

"That's the kind of comment that could mean anything."

"Yes, it could, couldn't it? It could indeed."

LATER THAT AFTERNOON, Hunt returned:

Denise sized him up, her eyes twinkling mischievously. She got a raised eyebrow in response. Molly observed this, and a pang of longing gripped her. They were obviously as close as siblings should be; they had the kind of relationship she'd never had with her brother, and now never would.

Denise extracted a promise from Molly that she would call if she needed anything. Once the front door closed and she and Hunt were alone, Molly felt suddenly tense and too warm. Somehow the closeness that had been created earlier now felt awkward.

The weather had turned rainy after a cloudy morning and the apartment took on an intimacy she'd never felt before. Hunt wore tan slacks and a rain-spattered yellow pullover that emphasized his muscular, tanned arms; the same arms that had gently held her at the hospital.

Molly clasped her hands and cleared her throat, determined not to dwell on wanting something more than Hunt could offer.

"I wasn't expecting you," she said, her voice hushed.

"I wanted to see how you were doing, and report that my AC is purring like a tomcat with a basket full of mice."

Molly smiled. "Then Gary kept his word."

"Of course with the rain, I don't need it, but that's the way these things go, don't they? I'll return your fan after the rain stops."

"No rush."

He stood a few feet from her; the room was large and airy, yet Molly felt his dominance. Silence stretched between them. From outside came the far-off blare of a car stereo and the scent of cooking apples. Molly struggled with a caky taste in her mouth that made her wish she had a glass of water. She swallowed and licked her lips, daring to meet Hunt's gaze. When she did, he showed no response that could be construed in any way other than patient sympathy.

Finally Molly said, "Denise said you would help me with Vern's things. Is your offer still good?"

"I always make good on my offers and my promises."

She felt lost in the intoxicating blue of his eyes. "I've packed up most everything, but one of his bags is locked. It's a soft leather attaché case that I think is connected to his business. I know it's silly, because obviously I have to open it.... It just feels as if I'm invading his privacy. I mean, a lock usually means keep out."

Hunt nodded. "I know. When I was taking care of Kristin's things, I came across a small cedar chest that was locked. I knew it contained mementos that were special to her. Going through them felt like I was intruding."

"Yes, that's what I mean," she said, relieved she wasn't overreacting.

He placed a hand on her back and urged her forward. "Then again, Vern's attaché case might be locked because he didn't want to chance losing his papers if it opened accidentally. I lock my briefcase because it's always so stuffed I'm afraid the latches won't hold."

Molly smiled. Hunt managed to make sense out of her chaotic reactions, and for that she was grateful. "You're probably right."

As they passed her bedroom, Molly stopped. "I have to say this, Hunt. I told myself I shouldn't even bring it up, that I should just forget it, but I can't."

Hunt gave her a puzzled look, and she took a deep breath for courage.

"I wanted to thank you for everything you've done...staying with me last night."

He looked decidedly uncomfortable. After a pause that, to Molly, felt like forever, he quickly said, "You're welcome. Now let's get this done."

He tugged her past her bedroom and toward the guest room.

Molly had placed Vern's repacked suitcase by the door. Braided scatter rugs created a colorful accent to the dark wooden floor and the double bed with a white embroidered spread. A vase of summer flowers sat on a pine dresser. The double set of crank-out windows looked out on the street; they were open a few inches, and a cool, damp breeze eased into the room, chasing through a lingering scent of after-shave.

The attaché case lay exactly where Vern had left

it: flat on the floor beside a tan wicker chair with green ivy print cushions.

"I haven't moved it except to note that it was locked."

"Let's have a look."

Molly stood in the doorway, watching as Hunt lifted the case and placed it on the bed.

Hunt kept his back to her, his body a shield between her and the briefcase. Probably he was overreacting or overplaying this, but he wanted an opportunity to examine the contents. His hopes ran high. He might find the names of Wallace's cronies, private correspondence, bugging devices or any number of clues to Wallace's contacts, stuff he would always keep with him because of the damage it could do in the wrong hands.

Yet Hunt acknowledged he was being cautious for another reason. One mob member from a few years back kept photos—souvenirs, he'd called them—of his bloodied victims. After his arrest, a gruesome photo album was found. Hunt didn't know enough about Wallace to know what his personal habits were, and since Molly had left the briefcase opening to him, he wasn't taking any chances.

He glanced over his shoulder to where she waited, her hands locked tightly together in front of her. The urge to sweep her up and carry her away to a place where she'd never be hurt again stunned him with its power. Hunt shook off the feeling as an overreaction.

That's the problem here, he reminded himself

grimly. *You know and she doesn't.* But the deeper reasoning was even more damning—the longer he stalled, the longer she would look at him with that sweetness that had found a small opening in his heart.

Get the attaché case opened, get the truth out and get this stalling over with.

"Hunt? If you don't want to do this..."

"No. It's okay. Tell you what. While I'm fiddling with this locking mechanism, would you get me a beer?"

"Sure. In fact, I also have a lot of food, thanks to the thoughtfulness of neighbors. Would you like me to fix you something?"

Food would take her more time. "Yeah, that would be great."

"I'll be right back."

She walked away, and Hunt's eagerness to get into the attaché case was overwhelming. Just curiosity, he reminded himself sternly. Once a cop, always a cop. Of course. His feelings had nothing to do with Molly.

The closure was a combination of numbers set in four tumblers. He wasted no time in using his pocketknife to deftly slit the leather behind the lock mechanism. He released the side buckles and lifted the lid. Three neatly folded T-shirts greeted him, but when he pulled them away...

"Well, I'll be damned," he whispered, genuinely stunned despite his suspicions.

Two-inch packages of bills held by rubber bands

neatly lined the bottom. He guessed about ten grand. There, in the center, cushioned by the cash and another undershirt, was a gun. Black metal with a long modified barrel, a silencer and a clip of bullets. Hunt didn't touch it, although he'd bet there were no prints. The dull sheen and the faint scent of oil made it evident Wallace took good care of the weapon.

Then he spotted a piece of folded paper peeking out from beneath one of the money wraps. Using his pocketknife, Hunt worked the paper free, then lifted it. Again using the knife tip, so as not to add his own fingerprints, he got the folds open.

Looking at the cryptic scrawl, he scowled.

On it was written "827 BOS."

Just what he wanted, he thought in disgust. A dead hit man who wrote himself notes in code.

He stared, trying to decipher a message. BOS was probably short for Boston, but 827 could mean anything from a flight number to part of a phone number, but why only three digits?

"Here's your beer."

Hunt whirled around. Lost in his thoughts he hadn't heard her footsteps. "Dammit, Molly..."

She held the bottle, her eyes wide as she tried to peer around him. "I didn't mean to startle you."

"I thought you were fixing food."

"It's heating. You can't eat in here. I set the table in the kitchen."

He cursed again. Another step and she'd see the

contents. So much for trying to break the news gently. Now the choice was made for him.

"Tell you what. Why don't we go into the living room. There's something I need to explain to you."

"All right, but first what did you find?" She nodded toward the three T-shirts that Hunt had tossed aside. "Besides those."

She came closer to the bed, handed him the bottle, and when he tried to steer her away, dodged his hand. Hunt braced himself. The gun and money were in plain view and the 827 BOS was nakedly exposed on the spread.

He closed the pocketknife and tried to take Molly's arm and turn her away. "Molly, there's something I haven't told you," he began. But it was too late.

She gasped at the sight of the gun. "My God! No wonder he had it locked."

He closed his eyes wearily. *Just say it. Don't mince words. Tell her.*

"Molly, your brother worked—"

"And all that money. Is it stolen? Did he use the gun to steal it?" Her eyes were glued to the contents of the attaché case.

Hunt said, "I don't think he stole it. At least not in the way you're thinking."

"I don't like guns...." She paused. "Why would my brother bring one when he came to visit me? And what about the money?"

"Did he say anything to you about where he worked or what he did for a living?"

"A little, but it didn't involve guns."

"How do you know?"

She laughed a little self-consciously. "Don't be ridiculous. He was an ordinary man, not a criminal."

"You told me he was belligerent and waved a knife around so the McCullochs would take you and not him. Didn't you ever think that behavior could lead to even more dangerous actions?"

"He was thirteen years old, for God's sake. You even said it sounded like bull and bluster."

Hunt shoved his hand through his hair. "Yeah, I did say that, didn't I? What did he tell you he did for a living?"

"He told me he was an investment analyst."

"Whatever the hell that means," Hunt muttered.

Molly swallowed. "I know one thing. There has to be a good explanation for all this."

"Like he owned the gun and someone paid him a lot of money for something," Hunt said with dry logic.

"Maybe the money and the gun belong to someone else. Maybe he was taking them to someone. Or maybe he was delivering money to one of his clients and brought the gun for protection."

Hunt shook his head. He knew she was trying to cling to her image of Vern any way she could, but he also knew she was doomed to disappointment.

"How do you know? You don't. You're just assuming the worst because you're a cop."

"Ex-cop. And I'm assuming the worst, because the worst is obvious."

She reached out to close the case, as if by doing so, she could put the contents from her mind. Hunt knew he had to say something, and say it now. He grabbed her wrist and turned her toward him. He saw knowledge in her eyes. Oh, not the whole truth, perhaps, but a sense that whatever the contents of the case meant, it didn't reflect well on her brother. He also saw her desperate need to escape that knowledge.

"Let me go."

"You can't ignore this."

"I can! I don't want to hear any more." She tried to twist free, but he held her fast. "You're hurting me."

"I'm not hurting you, and you're going to listen to me," he snapped, and then let out a long breath, easing his hold on her. This wasn't the way he wanted to tell her, and in fact by stalling, he'd made telling the truth twice as difficult.

She stood rigidly, glaring at him.

In a much quieter tone, he said, "I need to tell you something I should have told you yesterday."

He felt her stiffen in resistance. He took a deep breath, guided her around to the other side of the bed and made her sit down. "Tell me again exactly what your brother said about what he did for a living."

"Very little. He said he was an investment analyst and that he had clients. I asked him some questions, and he kept saying it was too complicated."

"Let me ask you this. At the hospital, I recall you said you found your brother through a search service. The kind that works with children looking for birth parents?"

"Sort of. This one specializes in siblings that have been separated either at birth or through adoption. They needed four basic things to search. Name, date of birth, last known address and social security number. Unfortunately I didn't have the last one, so the process took much longer. They used all sorts of reference materials and directories to see how many Vernon Wallaces served in the military."

"How many?"

"Quite a few, but none matched his birth date."

Hunt folded his arms and leaned against the dresser. "Go on."

"It was a slow, arduous process. It almost seemed as if he didn't want to be found. They used a database. They ran the name Vernon Wallace and checked and cross-checked birth dates. There were a lot of Vernon Wallaces, but none of them was my brother. They even went through a database of obituaries, but thankfully he wasn't there, either.

"I was so frustrated, I decided I must have made a mistake on his birth date. I was sure I hadn't, but at that point a mistake was better than never finding him. I checked at the office of vital statistics, and guess what?"

"You'd made a mistake."

"No, they'd misspelled Wallace. So once we used the correct spelling along with the birth date I had, Vern was located in Fernwood."

"So then, out of the blue, you just called him up and said, 'Hi, this is your sister, Molly'?"

"Actually, I did."

Hunt sighed. "Why doesn't that surprise me?" he mumbled.

"At first he denied he was my brother, but I had enough information about our shared past that I finally convinced him."

Hunt was skeptical. Wallace was no fool, and what better way for his enemies to get to him than to find out he'd once had a sister and then set him up?

"How did you convince him?"

"I told him I still had the four-leaf clover he found for me just before I was adopted. Actually, he found two. I saved mine because he'd told me that if I kept it and never lost it, I'd have a happy future."

"And when you reminded him of that, he knew it was you?"

"Yes."

It boggled Hunt's mind that a pro like Wallace would cave in over a four-leaf clover, but then again, it was a convincing detail no one but the real Molly would know. Maybe the guy had needed to find his sister just as much as she had needed to find him.

She glanced back at the open attaché case as if she hoped it had magically emptied or was now filled with innocent business papers.

Hunt said, "Despite the fact that I keep hoping I'll come up with an easier way, there isn't one."

Suddenly she looked queasy, as if the dark side of her brother had flashed before her in ghostly form. She rose, her tone one of closure. "I know enough."

Hunt straightened. No way was he going to delay this any longer. "Do you think this is easy for me to tell you? My God, Molly, I've been wrestling with it since I first saw you in his arms. I wish I'd been mistaken."

She drew herself up as if she'd found some deep inner strength.

Hunt knew it was now or never. "Your brother was a hit man for the mob. He killed for a living."

The truth writhed between them like a nest of disturbed rattlesnakes. Her face drained of color and her legs wobbled. Hunt reached out to steady her, and she swung her arms to avoid him.

"That's a lie!" she cried. "He was my brother. I loved him and he loved me."

"That's not the issue, nor is it in dispute."

"You're wrong. He hated killing. He couldn't even set a mousetrap without getting squeamish."

Hunt tried to draw her into his arms as he'd done the previous night. "Sweetheart, I'm sorry."

She backed away, then went perfectly still, her eyes nakedly perceptive. "All of this, all that you did...all of it was to set up my brother, wasn't it? That's why you've been so nice to me." Her words gathered speed and intensity. "It's why you took me to the hospital, stayed in the bedroom with me and asked me all those questions. It's why you were so willing to help with Vern's things. Damn you!" She flung herself toward the doorway, making a wide sweep away from the money and the gun.

Then she whirled around, and Hunt winced at her pain and disappointment. "I despise you, Hunt Gresham. I want you out of here."

"Molly..."

"Get out!" she shouted, then ran to her bedroom and slammed the door.

Hunt looked at the contents of the attaché case, his earlier enthusiasm gone. He, too, wished like hell that Wallace had been just transporting the items. Or even better, he wished that Vern "the Spider" Wallace had been an investment analyst.

For Molly's sake.

CHAPTER SIX

"YOU WERE THERE when the bastard croaked?"

"I was with his sister."

"Didn't know he had one. Tough telling her, huh?"

"A bitch," Hunt said.

He was back in his apartment and on the phone with Sean Sullivan, his old partner in the Boston Police Department. After Molly's outburst, Hunt put the contents back into the attaché case and took it home with him. A risky move, but no way was he leaving it, considering Molly's anger. For all he knew, she might get rid of it as a final way to protect her brother.

Hunt grimaced, disgruntled by the turn of events. He should have come up with some other way of telling her. The entire debacle was his fault. What made it worse was that he didn't have a clue what the long-run payoff concerning Wallace would be. Then again, what alternative had he had? Saying nothing to her meant that she might learn the truth from some jerk making a move on her for information she didn't have. Either way spelled disaster.

He'd looked in on her before making his exit.

She'd stood, staring out the window at the falling rain. With her back to him, her demeanor was stiff and straight, as if allowing herself to slump would be an admission that Hunt was right. When he said her name, she swung around to present him with a chilling glare, telling him if he didn't leave, she would call the police. That had struck him as ironic, but he hadn't argued and returned to his own apartment.

Now he was sprawled on his couch, shoes off, feet on the coffee table and using his nonportable phone. What he was telling Sean was too sensitive to be heard by anyone; a real drawback to cell and portable phones, which presented a greater security risk.

Wallace's case was open beside him, the 827 BOS note staring back at him.

Sean Sullivan asked, "So who all knows about Wallace?"

"Hospital, of course, and Molly's friends here, but they don't know who Wallace really was. Denise said Molly made funeral arrangements for Friday in Fernwood."

"Damn. We could have used more time. Word's probably already out that he's dead. Why in hell didn't you call when it first happened?"

"Dying isn't a crime, and I didn't know about the contents of the briefcase until now," Hunt said succinctly, restraining himself from commenting that Sean should be damn happy Hunt had made *this* call. Technically, an unloaded gun and a lot of cash in a briefcase wasn't a crime, either. If Hunt hadn't known who Wallace was, he might have bought some innocent explanation. Hell, who was he kidding?

"Besides," Hunt continued, "There were extenuating circumstances. Molly was naturally upset—close to shock, actually. It didn't seem appropriate to say, 'Handle this yourself, kid. I gotta call my old partner and fill him in.'"

"Didn't seem appropriate!" Sullivan exploded. "What in hell kind of reaction is that? You've gotten soft, old buddy. All that nose rubbing with the college types has turned you into some kind of bleeding heart."

"Knock it off, Sean. If I'd done it your way, I wouldn't have gotten within shouting distance of the briefcase. By the way, I can get as soft as marshmallows if I want to. I'm not a cop anymore."

Ignoring that, Sean said, "I get it. You stalled to get a fatter rabbit."

Hunt sighed. "Let's put it this way, I got lucky." Not lucky for Molly, though. He'd found some questionable stuff on Wallace, but at what price? Molly's broken dreams about her brother? Hunt tried to tell himself it didn't matter, since he wasn't interested in Molly in a personal way, but he knew it would be a long time before he forgot the look of hurt and horror in her eyes.

"Listen," Hunt said. "Besides the gun and the money, there's this coded note. If you guys can decode it, you might have an opportunity to make a move on some major mob figures.''

"Yeah, I'll get to the note in a sec. You said she made funeral arrangements in Fernwood. Is she going?''

"I assume so.''

"Excellent. I want you to go with her, and on your way, stop by here with the case—''

"Now wait a minute.

"I'll make some arrangements for an overnight in Fernwood. A friend up that way has a house he's been trying to rent. It will be perfect. This is Tuesday. If you get up here by tomorrow afternoon, all the pieces should be in place.''

"You're not serious.''

"Hell, yes, I'm serious.''

"Then get unserious. At least about me getting involved. I'm in deep enough just making this call. Send someone from the organized crime unit. Anyway, I haven't got any authority to deal with this.''

"You're a citizen, aren't you? Citizens cooperating with the cops was always one of your mantras, wasn't it? In this case, you're a concerned citizen who just happens to have the instincts and insight of an ex-cop. I'd be nuts not take advantage of that.''

"And I'd be nuts to get involved. I'm doing a nice, safe, unstressful lecture series, not playing cop looking for a collar. Doing surveillance for you isn't part of my retirement plan. And even if I were interested, it's not going to work.''

"Why not?"

"Molly wouldn't walk down the same street with me. No way would she want me at her brother's funeral."

"Come on, Gresham. That's a phony excuse and you know it. Tell her what's going on and she'll be begging you to go with her. And there's this—if she goes alone and something happens to her, will you be able to live with yourself?"

"You're a son of a bitch, you know that?"

"So the boys in Southie tell me when they're not calling me other things." Then Sean lowered his voice, his tone near pleading. "I need this, man. The chief has been pushing for some major breaks in the open mob cases. Let me toss some names out to remind you. Pascale. Solozi. Crackston. And those are just for starters. If Wallace's pals are at the funeral, you being there as a mourner would be ideal. Stay with her, keep your ears and eyes open and keep me posted on anything suspicious. I mean, hell, you could do this without breaking a sweat. And the mourning sister will provide great cover."

Sean's last words hit Hunt like a hard fist. A great cover? He could just imagine Molly's reaction if Hunt said that to her.

"It's not like I'm asking you to grill the attendees," Sean continued over Hunt's silence. "All you have to do is go and observe."

"Look, even if I agreed to it—which I have not— I told you she hates me right now."

"She'll get over it," Sean said dismissively.

"I hurt her badly, Sean. She's not going to forget that."

"Then play the friendly neighbor who happens to be an ex-cop. That's what you did yesterday and last night. What's so different about today?"

Good question, but there *was* a difference. Before at least his intentions had been honorable. Now calculation and design and ulterior motives ruled. Hunt swore.

Sean cursed right back.

Hunt scowled. Sean's chilling attitude was one of the reasons Hunt was glad he was no longer a cop. His old partner was so married to his job that he would have climbed over his own dead mother to get results. In police work that wasn't necessarily a bad trait, but it was damn hard to live with over time. Hunt had seen those characteristics in himself.

Then he'd lost Kristin.

Guilt plagued him. Deep, cutting regret for neglecting Kristin and their marriage had wrapped around him with suffocating intensity. He had screwed up a big investigation, and Sean had saved his butt. Still, he had decided to move on to something where his responsibility was only to himself. He'd handed in his resignation.

Now getting involved, even to help out an old partner, unnerved him. Molly was an innocent bystander, but beyond that, he admired her grit and determination in finding her lost brother. Now, instead of having only to deal with his loss, she'd been presented with Wallace's dark side. And Hunt had been presented with a very angry Molly.

Sean again lowered his voice, sounding more like an old friend needing a favor. "Hunt, you gotta do this for me. Remember how we always swore we'd never let each other down? That promotion I want is gonna be history if I don't come up with gold real soon. Just a few days of observation from you, that's all I need. No hold-down, no collar. Remember how I helped you out when Kristin was sick? I mean, that was months, old buddy. This is a few goddamn days."

Hunt closed his eyes wearily. In some deep part of himself he did want to do this. Perhaps to make up for the case he'd screwed up before he retired. And Sean had been there for him. The real source of his conflict was Molly. Getting back in her good graces wasn't going to be a walk in the park.

Hunt finally said. "On one condition. Molly comes first. If it comes down to her or Wallace's pals, she gets the nod."

"Sure, sure." Then, as if that was all settled, he said, "Let's go over the note."

Hunt read what it said and followed with, "The BOS probably means Boston, so the mystery is the 827."

"Okay. Numbers and number sequences. We got phone numbers, locker numbers, combination numbers, house numbers, flight numbers, dates, clock time and that's just for starters. Given who Wallace was, plus the cash and the piece, what's your guess?''

''A down payment for a hit could account for the large amount of cash.''

''Okay. Probably doesn't trust banks. Too much info required, not to mention federal regulations on banking and cash deposit limits.''

''Or if he picked up the down payment on the way to Molly's, that would account for him having it and the gun.''

''Hmm. Let's go with that for a minute. If the note's tied in...'' A few seconds of silence filled the line.

Then Hunt said, ''Oh, hell. I can't believe I didn't think of this.''

''What?''

''It could be August 27th.''

''You're right,'' Sean said eagerly. ''That's next week.'' Sean paused, then asked, ''Why would he be carrying that kind of cash for a week?''

''Wallace liked to bet the greyhounds. Could be he planned a trip to the track after he left Molly's.''

''Possible, but still pretty risky, exposing himself with that kind of evidence. Doesn't sound like Wallace's MO.''

''Yeah, you're right. Anyway, a guy whose job is to kill people wouldn't need to write down the date.''

''Let me get on this and run those numbers. Locker sounds logical, and a flight number, too. If we come up with a flight 827 out of Logan in the

next few days, we could have something. And I
wanna check the street stoolies for info on any
planned hits going down. Might get word of one
planned for the twenty-seventh. I'll look for you tomorrow afternoon. Say around four? That should
give you enough time to get back into Molly's good
graces.''

Enough time, Hunt thought as he hung up the
phone. There probably wasn't enough time in the
next century. Nevertheless, he closed the briefcase
and looked around for someplace to hide it. Finally
he settled it under the books and papers he'd spread
out for his lecture series. With that done, he took a
shower, changed his clothes and within an hour, he
was on his way back to Molly's.

IN HER APARTMENT and once again on the telephone,
Molly checked with her auto club and got the name
of the best-rated motel near Fernwood. After making
a reservation, she opened her desk drawer and took
out the manila envelope that had been her mainstay
while trying to locate her brother. It contained all the
disconnected bits she'd gathered during her search.
Pieces of Vern's history while they were separated,
and yet nothing had indicated what kind of work he
did. If Hunt had been correct, something she found
would have been suspicious, but obviously Hunt was
mistaken.

Pushing Hunt from her mind, she sorted through

the papers, reports and scribbled notes to find Vern's Fernwood phone number.

She knew he lived in an apartment, and Vern had told her he had an aquarium. A neighbor could be picking up his mail or feeding his fish. Someone Vern had known well could confirm what Molly wanted to think about the cash and the gun—at this point anything but what she feared might be the truth.

Questions scurried through her mind despite her determination to believe the best about her brother. If she dwelled on Hunt's words, she'd have questions that scared her; questions without answers she could live with.

Molly wrestled with the empty realization she would never really know her brother. Years of separation, of searching, of wanting to make her family whole again, and now... And, as if that pain weren't enough to deal with, she'd been such a fool with Hunt. Wincing even now at how she'd trusted him, she made herself admit that she'd been used.

Since their collision in the courtyard, he'd been virtually invisible, then suddenly, as of yesterday, when Vern arrived, he was glued to her. He'd even admitted knowing who her brother was from the beginning. Obviously, his attentions hadn't been out of friendly concern, but to get to Vern. She clenched her teeth in annoyance. He'd stuck to her, played out the nice-guy routine, intent on his goal to get to her brother's personal things. He'd even gone to the point of sleeping in the same room with her!

Heat flared in her cheeks at the memory; she'd believed he really cared. She'd believed he meant the things he'd said, probably because her life had been so bereft of relationships. God, what a stupid fool she'd been!

Tears threatened once again, and she impatiently swiped them away. If only she could get relief from the ache in her heart that refused to subside.

She found Vern's home number. "I'll show you, Hunt Gresham," she said as she punched the buttons. "I'm going to prove you're wrong about Vern."

Feeling better, she sat up straight when the third ring was answered. "Uh, yes, hello?"

"Who's this?" growled a man who sounded like he had sandpaper in his throat.

"Oh, uh, this is Molly McCulloch..."

"It's a broad," the man said to someone else. Then to Molly he said, "He ain't here."

"Vern? Yes, I know."

"So why you callin'?"

Not wanting to sound totally dumb, she said, "I'm trying to locate his wife."

"He ain't got no wife."

"Ex-wife. You see, Vern died last night and I wanted to notify her. Are you one of Vern's friends?"

He snorted. "Sure, baby. I'm his best pal."

Molly scowled.

"Better find yourself a new stud."

"I'm not his girlfriend, I'm his—"

"See ya."

"Wait! Don't hang up!"

But he did, and Molly listened to the dial tone for a full ten seconds before putting the receiver down. Just what she needed, some jerk with a smart mouth. She was debating whether to call back or phone the Fernwood police and ask them to check her brother's apartment, when her own doorbell rang.

She didn't need any more casseroles, she thought as she pulled open the door, but instead of a neighbor with a covered dish and a sympathetic smile, she faced Hunt.

She tried to close the door, but he stopped her.

"I have nothing to say you," she said coolly.

He nodded. "I know. You wish I'd rot in hell."

Actually she hadn't been that extreme. And why did he have to look so gorgeous and sexy when it was obvious he wasn't trying to? His clothes were casual and rain-splattered and his hair was charmingly mussed. It fell over his forehead in an almost boyish way. Molly clenched her hands in an effort not to reach up and brush it back.

"What do you want?" she asked, not allowing herself to meet his eyes.

"To be straight with you. To apologize for the inept way I told you about your brother. I am sorry, Molly. Believe me, I didn't set out to destroy your image of Vern."

She drew herself up straighter. "You couldn't do that no matter what you said or what you found in his briefcase. Now, I have things to do, so if you'll excuse me."

"We have to talk."

"I don't want to listen to any more of your lies."

"I wasn't lying about your brother."

She put her hands over her ears and shook her head.

"Molly..." He stepped inside, despite her protests, and closed the door. When she tried to back away, he reached out and took hold of her shoulders.

She squirmed to get loose. "I don't want you to touch me."

But he didn't release her, moving her toward the couch, where he gently urged her to sit down.

He stood above her, appearing large and looming from her perspective. What struck Molly as strange was that his size felt more protective than threatening. Nevertheless, she wasn't giving any ground. "Why did you come back here?"

"I need you to do me a favor."

Suspicious, she frowned. "What kind of favor?"

"I want you to let me take you to the funeral."

She wondered what he was up to. "Why?"

"Because there could be people there who might assume you know things about Wallace."

"I do know things. Lots of things."

"I mean secret things. Stuff his associates wouldn't want you to know or want you to tell anyone about."

Molly immediately thought of the man she'd just

spoken to. He had talked a little strangely, but having a smart mouth wasn't a crime. "Don't you think you're overdoing the cloak-and-dagger business?"

Hunt's face darkened and he gave her an intense look. "Look, I'll make a deal with you. Let me take you to the funeral just to make sure nothing unexpected happens. Pretend you're renting an ex-cop for a few days, an easy method of protection. Nothing personal or complicated between us. The cops will handle the stuff they're supposed to do—"

"And you'll handle me?" She knew she sounded snide and snippy, but she didn't care.

"I couldn't if I wanted to. You've already tied me up in knots, so I'll be just as glad as you to have this all over with."

Now, *that* she could believe. "If I agree to this, it will be admitting you're right about Vern."

"It will be admitting you don't want to go to your brother's funeral alone."

She thought about that for a moment. He was right. She hadn't been looking forward to going alone. She didn't know anyone in Fernwood, nor did she know exactly how to contact her brother's ex-wife, and then there was his apartment... That would have to be cleaned out, and what if there were things there that supported Hunt's version of her brother's life....

For a tiny moment she allowed herself to admit that Hunt could be right, but then she pushed the idea away and pulled her thoughts back to Hunt's request.

Molly realized there was more to his plan than just escorting her to a funeral. Getting information wasn't the issue. It sounded as if he already *had* information. So what was he up to? "And when did you decide to play the role of my protector?" she asked.

Hunt had no intention of not being straight and up front with her. The other way had been a disaster. "I talked to my old partner, and the likelihood that Vern's friends will be at the funeral—perhaps to get a look at you or make a move on you to see what you know—isn't that far-fetched."

"You're obsessed with this hit-man theory, aren't you?"

He looked at her as if she were gripped by denial rather than honest belief in her brother. "Molly, you spent nineteen years separated from your brother and a good part of that time trying to find him. You deserved a happy ending with him and you didn't get it. You're angry and you're directing that at me. That's okay, but underneath that anger and the disappointment and sorrow, I believe you know I'm telling you the truth." When she didn't say anything immediately, he added, "For God's sake, why would I lie to you? What would be my motive?"

"I don't know. I just know that I trusted you. I believed you were with me because you genuinely cared about what I was going through."

"I did care."

"Then why didn't you tell me when you came over yesterday afternoon with that broken air conditioner excuse? Or better yet, when I brought you the fan?''

"Because I didn't know how to tell you without hurting you."

"And you thought it would hurt me less later? It hurt worse, Hunt."

"I know." He paced the width of the room, and from a few feet away, he turned and said, "I didn't tell you for exactly the same reason your brother didn't tell you he knew who I was."

Her mouth dropped open and her eyes widened, then she vigorously shook her head. "No. If he'd known you, he would have said so."

"And if he had, you would have wanted an explanation, and that he couldn't give you. I think Wallace was very happy you found him, and if ever he regretted the life he chose, it was probably when he knew how hurt and disappointed you would be. I didn't know Vern the older brother, so I haven't a clue as to what his intentions were. But I think I'm fairly safe in guessing that he wanted to protect you. That was probably why he was so vague about what he did for a living. No one could get information out of you if you didn't know anything."

She wrapped her arms around herself like a shield to keep away words she didn't want to hear. But there were other words; words she hadn't thought about because they hadn't made sense to her. Now...

Molly swallowed, her voice reedy. "At the hospital when I spoke to him, he thought you were my boyfriend.'' She pressed her fingers to her temples. ''He called me Muffin—that was a nickname from when we were kids.'' Her fingers stilled. ''Oh my God…''

Hunt sat down beside her. ''What?''

''He knew you were a cop. How could he have known? I never told him that.''

''Because he knew who I was,'' Hunt murmured. ''Now do you believe me?''

But Molly didn't really hear him. Her thoughts swirled around her brother's last words to her. Her cheeks felt chilled, her throat icy. ''He also said something just before the nurse told me to leave. He said you wouldn't let me get hurt.''

What at the time had meant little to her now took on herculean meaning. Had her brother known Hunt was trustworthy or were his words some balm he'd used to assure himself she'd be safe? But he'd known Hunt was a cop. If Vern and Hunt knew each other, then they must have had contact at some time or another.

''We never met, Molly,'' Hunt said as if reading her thoughts. ''I'd seen photos of him, and he probably heard my name through his underworld contacts. I worked both vice and homicide, so there could have been lots of opportunities.''

The evidence was mounting, and Molly feared its meaning. She knew she was too close to the situation, too determined to believe the best about Vern to be objective. But a hit man! A hired killer! She shuddered at the mere thought.

Hunt put his arm around her and she didn't object; she was grateful for the warmth and comfort she suddenly realized she needed.

"Hunt?"

"What, sweetheart?"

"It's almost as if Vern kn-knew..." She swallowed, the icy lump in her throat growing bigger and bigger. "As if he knew he was going to d-die."

"Maybe he did," Hunt said softly. "Maybe he waited to make sure you would be safe."

She buried her face in her hands, unable to stop the fresh tears of confusion and pain.

Hunt let her cry, holding her, rubbing his chin across the top of her head. Tears could cleanse the mind as well as release the grief. As he suspected, Molly had believed him about Wallace; she'd just needed some time for the facts to lose their sting.

The afternoon had darkened with the gray, rainy skies. Silence cloaked the apartment, and Hunt leaned back into the couch cushions and pulled Molly deeper into his arms. She curled into him, much as she'd done the previous night, and Hunt didn't discourage her. She needed solace and holding; he knew that need, for he'd craved it himself once. Offering it to Molly now seemed the least he could do. Neither spoke, the only motion the tandem beating of hearts.

Minutes passed before she raised her head, her

lips moist, her cheeks flushed, her eyes luminous. "Please don't say I told you so," she whispered so softly Hunt could barely hear her.

He brushed his thumb across her mouth. "Ah, sweetheart, the only thing I want to tell you is that you are an incredibly strong and determined woman."

She managed a smile before once again curling up against him.

Hunt badly wanted to kiss her. He couldn't deny a desire that came and went with varying degrees of intensity.

He was merely caught up in the moment, he decided, attempting to regain control of his feelings. Loss of control meant complications, and he didn't want those. But there was no denying that Molly was warm and pretty and wholly tempting.

Then there was an even more ominous fact: he'd allowed himself to know more about her than he had about any woman since Kristin. Those seemed to be the operative two words when it came to Molly.

Since Kristin.

CHAPTER SEVEN

THE FOLLOWING AFTERNOON Hunt found what had to be the only on-street parking place in all of downtown Boston. He locked his car, fed the meter and took Molly's arm.

"Hope you don't mind the walk. It's a few blocks to the precinct."

"No, I don't mind."

In his other hand was the attaché case and Hunt couldn't recall when he'd been so jumpy. He'd never carried a briefcase in the city, never mind one with a .357 Magnum and more than ten grand cash. The weight felt awkward and foreign in his hand. But then again, having Molly with him added to his tension.

They'd come to a truce of sorts; Hunt still doubted she'd completely accepted who her brother was. He'd decided to say no more unless she asked questions. Truth was truth, and it wasn't changed by a sister's acceptance or attempt at revisionist history. Besides, if he suddenly learned Denise was running a whorehouse while the boys were in school, he'd be as incredulous as Molly had been about Vern.

Accepting new but painful facts about a loved one

took time. And Molly had no history to speak of with Vern, so he was unblemished, a rediscovered hero from her past that she'd fully intended to turn into an even bigger hero in her future. Until he died.

Now, as they started down the sidewalk, Molly pulled him back when a homeless man shouted expletives at them. She drew closer and whispered, "You're not just going to carry that as if it were papers and a ham sandwich, are you?"

Hunt had deliberately not done anything to call suspicion to the case. "Best disguise is no disguise."

"But if someone just grabbed it, you'd have no chance."

"You sure have a lot of confidence in me," he said grimly.

"I don't want you to get hurt. I mean people shoot people these days for jackets and sneakers. All that cash plus the gun..." She shuddered.

"Except no one knows that."

"A purse snatcher doesn't know how much is in a pocketbook, either."

"Flawed comparison. A purse usually has cash, and as you said earlier, a briefcase usually has papers and maybe a ham sandwich."

She frowned. "I don't know how you can be so cool and calm."

"I'm not. I'm just doing what every other businessman with a briefcase in Boston is doing—walking down the street." When she still looked unconvinced, he said, "I appreciate your worrying about me, but believe me I'm not going to fight to the death over it.''

She looked decidedly unsure, but allowed him to guide her down the sidewalk. Pedestrians flowed toward them and around them. Cabbies honked, trucks rumbled and belched fumes, other vehicles jockeyed for the best position to get them through the city.

''Don't cops handcuff valuable stuff to their wrists?'' At his raised eyebrow, she nodded, ''Okay, don't ex-cops handcuff valuable stuff to their wrists?''

''Not where I worked. If someone made a grab, they'd take my arm with it.''

She thought about that for a moment, then shook her head in resignation. ''It just seems as if you should be doing something.''

''I am. I'm walking down the street with a gorgeous brunette who smells like wildflowers. Never did that one time when I worked up here.''

His words disarmed her, and she smiled. ''What a sweet thing to say.'' After a pause, she asked, ''But what about with Kristin? You were never in Boston with her?''

''She hated the city.''

''Oh.''

''Noise, pollution, crime—all the stuff that makes big cities unappealing.''

''Where did you live?''

''Down near Foxboro. We were renting a place. I worked while Kristin looked at land where she wanted to build. She was very particular. She loved woodsy places with lots of 'nature in the wild,' as she called it. She wanted to live there but she didn't want it spoiled by leveling it or cutting down the trees. Her thing was to integrate the house so that it was part of its surroundings. In other words, a house nestled in nature, rather than nature flattened by a house. I used to tease her that if she was going to really go natural, we should have an outhouse, use oil lamps and beat the clothes on a rock.''

"I bet she loved that," Molly commented, smiling.

"Hmm. I was told lots of nature didn't mean primitive."

"She wanted the best of both, which sounds ideal."

"Yeah." He felt the melancholy float over him and shook it away. He didn't have to say anything more, and he wasn't at all sure why the words suddenly rose to the surface. He'd rarely talked about Kristin since her death; not with Denise, not with Sean, and yet here with Molly the thoughts and emotions stirred restlessly, as if they were searching for release.

"So, did she find the property for the house she wanted built?"

"Kristin had found a piece of land she loved, complete with a small brook, wildflowers and enough birds to keep a bird-watcher enthralled for years. She wanted me to see it. We'd planned to meet after her doctor's appointment. I knew when I picked her up that something was wrong. She was quiet and pale and shaking so bad she couldn't get her seat belt buckled.'' Hunt swallowed the sudden tightness in his throat.

Closing all his emotions down and reciting the words as if by rote had been his habit in the past. But telling Molly felt different. He sensed she would know the pain and horror in a profound way, because she, too, had experienced having someone she loved torn from her.

Molly gripped his arm tighter as they walked.

Hunt continued. ''When I touched her she began to cry, and then she told me. She had cancer and she was going to die. That's how she said it. No leading up to it, or softening it, or trying to find the words....''

''Oh, Hunt, how awful for both of you.'' Then, in a softer voice, she asked, ''She had no prior warnings?''

Hunt shivered, a cold chill penetrating to his bones. The street temperature in Boston had to be close to ninety, but this cold was all inside, icy to the marrow of his bones. ''She'd found a lump some months before, but the doctor said it wasn't serious. Naturally she believed him. She was wrapped up in looking for a place to build as well, and with her doctor unconcerned, she stopped thinking about it.''

''And the cancer grew,'' Molly added grimly.

Hunt nodded. ''She had a mammogram, but it

showed the malignancy had already spread. They did radiation, but the bottom line was that it had progressed too far. I think we both suspected more than we were being told. Denial is easier, but that afternoon, Kristin had stepped beyond her own denial, and she knew. When she told me, it was as if she had to get it all out at once. After that she never used the words death or dying again.''

He paused a minute. "I never said them, either. I insisted we buy the land she wanted and begin construction on the house. She lived long enough to see it completed. The builder knew the situation and worked twice as fast as contractors usually do. After the funeral I sold it all. The house and the land symbolized all that Kristin believed about going after what you want, but for me…" He cleared his throat. "It was a ticking time bomb. I knew that once it was finished she would die. I hated the place, because for every part of it that was completed, another part of Kristin's body grew weaker.''

With the story told, he wanted to abandon the subject for something safe and neutral. The weather, the state of the national debt, the traffic patterns of the Southeast Expressway—anything.

He was relieved Molly didn't feel compelled to spew out words as so many had after Kristin died. He didn't want sympathy, or even understanding, for it changed nothing. He'd lived and Kristin had died; it was the worst kind of hell, because he could do nothing but watch and wait. If there had been a way to exchange places with her, he would have done it.

Finally Molly said, "The hardest part must have been facing the futility of events. Rushing to give her the completed house she wanted so badly and knowing she'd never live in it."

Hunt felt a jolt somewhere in the vicinity of his heart. She was exactly right. "You know, at one point I even believed that Kristin would be magically healed when the house was finished. That some kind of nature-spawned energy would seep into her body and make her healthy again."

"You wanted her to live and have the future you'd planned together," Molly said with vehemence. "We all grasp for those threads of hope."

He stopped a moment, looked at her, and then gently laced their fingers together. "You know about those threads of hope, don't you? Because of the separation from Vern."

"I felt very guilty for years because I was taken and he wasn't. I used to have terrible dreams about him being alone and no one wanting him. It just seemed so unfair."

"It is unfair, and worst of all, it's wrong. Siblings shouldn't be separated. Kids have enough to deal with. They shouldn't have to cope with being forced apart."

"Their intention was good," she said rushing to the McCullochs' defense. "They adopted one child, which was better than none, and they were very good to me.''

"Look, I don't know the McCullochs. Maybe they were great parents, but how they could have decided not to take Vern on such a knee-jerk decision just blows my mind. I'm sure there were support groups and agencies that could have assisted them. And Vern's antics with that knife seemed such an obvious ploy, I can't believe the state or the McCullochs didn't see through them.''

"I didn't, Hunt, and I knew him better than anyone.''

"Sweetheart, you were a kid. They were the experts. They should have seen Vern for what he was. A brother trying desperately to make sure his sister had a family.''

Molly glanced at him, her eyes glazed with sudden tears. "Oh, Hunt, I love you for saying that.''

Hunt swung around and stared at her. "Love me?''

"Yes, for forgetting who you claim Vern was and realizing that he was a real person with real feelings and a tender heart.''

"I never said I didn't think he had feelings or a tender heart for you. It's—''

She pressed her hand against his mouth. "Don't spoil it. For just a little while I'd like to think you and I can agree on one positive thing about my brother.''

He took her wrist, kissed her palm and folded her

fingers around the damp impression. "All right. Your brother sacrificed himself for you because he loved you. I can agree about that."

Her eyes glistened. "Thank you." She pressed her lips together. "It's vital to me that I find out all I can when we get to Fernwood. I'm sure his friends and neighbors will be at the funeral, and they'll be a good starting point for me to sort out the pieces of who Vern really was."

It occurred to Hunt that her life had been so wrapped up in the search for her brother that even now that he was dead, she couldn't stop.

Hunt hated being the negative voice here, but he felt compelled to say, "Probing the past doesn't always result in happy discoveries."

"But there are discoveries. I can deal with the negatives."

Can you, Molly? Hunt wondered, but said nothing.

"And I know there are good things. There have to be." Then, as if she feared an argument from him, she added, "I want you to help me."

"We're only going to be there a few days."

"This time. I can always go back. Don't forget, I searched for years without any idea where Vern lived, and piece by piece I made progress. Now I have a starting point and some people who will know him."

Hunt sighed. He had no doubt Sean would be thrilled by any information he could get on Wallace.

"Let's wait and see how things shake out," he

said vaguely. He wasn't sure which Molly was safest to deal with. The angry Molly who'd thrown him out of her apartment when he'd said Wallace was a hit man, or this more gutsy Molly. If she hoped for information from Vern's pals, she could find herself on his successor's hit list. It was a thought that turned Hunt's blood to ice.

A HALF HOUR LATER, Molly and Hunt were in Sean's office. The glass walls allowed a view of the squad room and all the rush and hustle of the detectives. While Hunt and Sean talked—the briefcase was being checked for prints and the gun examined—Molly sat nursing a cup of coffee and wondering what she would learn about her brother.

"Phone number?"

Molly glanced up, shaking away her thoughts. "Were you speaking to me?"

"Do you know Vern's phone number?"

"Uh, yes." She opened her purse and took out a small notebook. After riffling through the pages, she read. "It's 555-4903."

"So much for that idea," Hunt said.

"What idea?"

"The 827 BOS note. We're trying to pin down what the 827 means. I thought it might be part of Vern's phone number."

"And there aren't any 827 exchanges in the Boston area." Sean leaned back in his chair, his expression frustrated. His black curly hair and vivid blue eyes proclaimed his Irish heritage. Molly watched him for a few moments, picturing Hunt in this scene. Whether it was reasonable or not, she liked the idea that Hunt was no longer a cop. She wondered how Kristin had dealt with all the worry and stress.

Sean said, "We checked locker numbers, flight numbers—there was a flight 827 going to Houston, but that was days ago. The date idea seems to be a dead end, too, at least so far. We're still working on it."

Hunt sprawled in a wooden chair, legs stretched out in front of him, fingers steepled in front of his mouth. Molly thought he looked as if he wanted to abandon the whole plan. In a way she felt responsible for his involvement. If it weren't for the briefcase, she'd be in Fernwood for the funeral and Hunt would be working on his lecture series back in his apartment.

Sean reached for a manila envelope. "Here are the directions and the key to the house. Use a pay phone if you need to call me. Place has been swept, but I don't want to take any chances. You know about the risk of cell phones."

Hunt nodded and then rose to his feet. "You'd better hope something breaks in the next few days. I don't want Molly out in the open too long."

"I cleared this with the chief—you keep your eyes opened and give us a heads-up if you find anything. You're not official, so don't be a cowboy."

"My cowboy days are all over, Sean. Getting this

behind me so I can go back to peace and tranquility can't come too soon.''

Molly put her empty coffee container into the trash.

''I'm sorry we couldn't have met under more pleasant circumstances, Ms. McCulloch,'' Sean said, coming around the desk and opening the office door.

Molly nodded as Hunt touched her back and eased her out the door. Then Sean said something that numbed her.

''Chances are, that hit wasn't made yet, so someone else will get it. That means some dumb bastard out there is contracted to die. If we can intervene and get the shooter and the target, the department will have something to crow about.''

Molly played the words over and over as she and Hunt made their way back to his car.

In one startling moment she realized the truth she'd been denying. Her brother was what Hunt had said he was—a paid killer. Yet following that awful truth was another truth. Vern's replacement had to be stopped; he couldn't carry out her brother's instructions. If she could somehow prevent this one act, there would be one less black mark on his legacy. How she intended to do this, she had no idea.

But there would be a way. There had to be.

CHAPTER EIGHT

IN THE EARLY EVENING, with the sun ruby red on the western horizon, Fernwood, Massachusetts, withered near Interstate 93 like an animal that had crawled away to die. Emaciated grass trapped litter around stumpy buildings. Exhausted houses with rusty TV antennas jutting from sweltering rooftops were crowded together as if seeking solace and support.

Once a prosperous factory town, Fernwood now comprised abandoned brick structures that were smeared with graffiti and dotted with square black holes that had once been shiny lighted windows that showcased buzzing activity.

Despair, Molly thought, was palpable. She'd never before been to Fernwood; she'd wanted to come and visit Vern, but he'd discouraged it. His place wasn't set up for company, he'd told her. Now, glancing around, she wondered if her brother was ashamed of where he lived, but even more bewildering was why he lived here. It was one more odd piece to the puzzle of Vern's life, and as the hours passed, she began to dread fitting those pieces together.

Hunt pulled off the road onto a bumpy shoulder with a twisted guardrail that looked as if it had prevented many a car from careening into the ravine below.

Molly opened the car windows, expecting a blast of heat. Instead she was surprised by a refreshing breeze from the trees beyond. Hunt unfolded the map Sean had given him, studying it for a few moments.

Drawing his finger around an area, he said, "Here's the cemetery in the middle of town. Now that says a lot, doesn't it? Building a town around a bunch of graves is a dead man's town. You'd think they'd have built around a town square, or a statue honoring some reformer or the guy who originally settled the area. But a cemetery... No wonder the place looks so depressing."

"Cemeteries can be quite beautiful and peaceful," Molly said with a sudden sense of defensiveness for the town where her brother had lived.

"Yeah, that's always where I go for beauty and peace."

Molly didn't miss his sarcasm, and she should have let the issue go right then, but she didn't. "You don't have to mock the feelings of others just because you don't agree."

He looked at her. "You haven't said a word since we left Boston. Now I make one comment and you're spoiling for a fight."

"I'm not, but I don't think it's right to condemn a town that's obviously struggling with economic hardship."

"No damn wonder. Who would want to live in a place where the cemetery is the focal point?"

"My brother did."

Hunt swore. "Let's drop the subject, okay?"

Obviously they were both edgy, and it wasn't hard to figure out why. Not only was she adjusting to her brother's death, but to what he'd become while he was alive. Hunt, on the other hand, had been cool and in charge until his discovery of the cemetery. It had to be memories of losing Kristin. Still, it was strange that he'd be so touchy when earlier he'd spoken so freely. But wasn't she doing the same? One moment she could talk about Vern and the next she could barely hold back the tears. Hunt still loved his wife and deeply resented her death. Obviously a cemetery was a too-raw reminder.

Now she regretted her words. "Hunt, I'm sorry. It's been a long day and—"

"Forget it," he said abruptly.

She turned away to look out the window, her inner turmoil over Vern returning. Since they'd left Boston, Molly had wrestled with a truth she didn't like. She had to accept that although she'd found her brother, the intervening years had changed him more than they had her. A sense of chilly numbness had settled deep within her, and she wanted to bury her head and pretend none of this had happened.

On the other hand, the truth had also created a burning responsibility to find and preserve the side of her brother she'd believed in so long. The Vern who'd cared for her when their parents hadn't, the Vern who gave up a chance for a family so she would have one, the Vern who helped her find four-leaf clovers. She wiped away the tears her memories brought.

Hunt had a whole different agenda. He wanted to prove Vern had been on his way to kill someone, and their opposing goals made for a tenseness that only promised to get worse. And complicating everything further were her unwanted feelings for Hunt. She recalled their conversation at his apartment hours before Vern's heart attack. She'd commented on how different he was from the professors at Woodbriar College. Then she'd been thinking about her own fascination with him, how attractive he was; she had even contemplated the excitement of a relationship with him. Obviously a hopeless fantasy.

It was bad enough that every time she looked at Hunt, she was reminded of who her brother really was, but now Hunt's comments gave her another reason to squelch any feelings she might have for him. Kristin might be gone, but it was clear she still commanded Hunt's mind and heart.

She heard the rustle of paper.

"Greenwich Street is a few miles north," he commented, referring to the place where they were to stay. He handed the map to Molly. "Sean marked where your brother lived."

"Ludlow. Yes, I see it here." She refolded the paper, suddenly wishing she could avoid the task ahead. There was something unseemly about probing into his personal things when he was no longer able to explain or defend himself.

"We can get settled and then go take a look at his apartment," Hunt said as he pulled back onto the road.

Molly flinched at the idea of Hunt searching and rummaging through Vern's property. "I don't want to go until after the funeral," she said flatly.

He didn't miss a beat. "Fine. Then that will mean spending a few more days here."

"A few more days together, you mean." Her pride reared to the surface. "I can handle things. You don't have to stick around."

"True. I could just leave you here and let you hitchhike home."

"Don't treat me like a child. I'm perfectly capable of taking care of myself. I've been doing it for a quite a number of years."

"I drove you here and I'll drive you home."

"Maybe I don't want you to drive me home. Maybe I want to do this my way instead of your way. I'm sure buses exist in Fernwood...." She thought for a moment, then added, "Or I could ask one of Vern's friends."

"His friends?" Hunt said with a snort. "They're a bunch of goddamn killers."

Molly narrowed her eyes and snapped, "And you, of course, have only saints for friends. Sean would never step out of line to nab a criminal."

"Right now he's a contact, not a friend."

"And so am I, aren't I? A contact to find out about Vern."

Silence beat through the car like the *thump-thump-thump* of a drum. Hunt stared straight ahead, then finally said in a low, cautious voice, "That's not true, Molly." Then, under his breath, he muttered, "I wish it were."

She wanted to believe him and yet she was afraid to. Afraid that if she allowed herself to understand his view of her brother, she'd be abandoning her meager memories of Vern.

Molly continued, "All you have is a police file. That's not his whole life. People are more than what one person says they are."

"Molly," he said calmly, too calmly. "I know this has been tough and you probably need an outlet for your anger and frustration. And if you want to dump on me, that's fine, but let's not get ridiculous. I came with you and I'll leave with you. End of discussion."

Molly's independence, her sense of self and a certain resentment of his "take-charge" attitude came rushing together. She swung toward him, her expression fierce. "Don't patronize me. And don't tell me what I'm going to do and what I'm not. You have no right. I'm perfectly capable of managing the next few days without you hovering over me as if I'm going to be carried off and murdered by some criminal type."

He took a deep breath and slowly released it.

"In fact, I didn't ask you to come with me in the first place. You invited yourself."

"Not by choice, believe me."

"I don't know if I really believe that, Hunt. Oh, not because I think you want to be with me. I know you don't. You and your old partner are all enthusiastic about solving the mystery of the note. Maybe you even regret retiring, and this taste of police work has given you a chance to be a cop again."

He cursed under his breath using a word she'd never heard before. She didn't even want to think about what it meant and that it was probably directed at her.

She'd been pushing the edge of their fragile civility since this conversation began. The practical side of her said to let it rest here, but she ignored that.

"You're only supposed to be taking me to the funeral for some sort of protection that sounds more like TV drama than reality. You're an ex-cop, as you've reminded me a number of times, therefore you have no authority to investigate my brother. Which is the only reason I can see that you would want to go to his apartment."

Again he slowed down, but this time he turned into a short, unpaved driveway lined with scraggly hedges in need of shaping. He turned the engine off, and without looking at her, he snapped, "Are you finished?"

"Not until you understand that I have some rights and I intend to protect them."

He tapped his fingers on the steering wheel. "Okay, okay. What precious rights of yours have I threatened?"

She lifted her chin and gave him a direct look. "You want to use me to get into my brother's apartment."

"Oh for God's sake!" Hunt said in exasperation. "Didn't we already dance to this tune? Back when you accused me of using you to get to your brother's briefcase?"

"Well, why else would you mention going to his place?" Her body tightened with dread at his answer, and she braced herself.

"Because I thought you might like some support in dealing with his personal things. It's hard going through stuff knowing that the person will never touch it or you again."

Molly blinked, her anger and frustration draining out of her. The only sound in the car was the *click-click* of the cooling engine. She heaved a sigh and tried to speak, but no words came.

Hunt swore, started to open the door and then swore again as he turned back to her. "Dammit, Molly..."

He reached for her, hooked one arm around her neck and pulled her against him. Her mouth fell open in surprise, but he allowed no words to escape before the onslaught of a consuming kiss. Molly was so startled, she didn't resist, but she doubted he would have noticed if she had.

He angled his head, his mouth crushing hers as if he wanted to drive away all her words, all her questions, all her mistrust. Her arms were trapped between them, and she could feel the pounding of his heart. He swept his tongue around hers in a carnal, possessive foray. Then, pulling away a fraction, he murmured, "Put your arms around me."

She did what he said and the motion brought her breasts against him; a deep ache she had never experienced before grew inside her. Her nipples tightened and sought relief; she rubbed herself across his chest to ease the sweet pain.

He groaned and shifted slightly. "I'm gonna regret this...."

"Hunt, this..." A new arrow of pleasure swept across her. "Oh... Oh, Hunt...this wasn't suppose to happen...."

"I know...I know..." He framed her face with his hands, and the hot intensity of his blue eyes turned her misgivings to ashes. "One more kiss and no more..." Clearly he was struggling to keep them both under control, but Molly suddenly realized she liked being uncontrolled; she liked following this burst of passion within her. She'd never felt so alive and eager and wonderful.

"I like this...I mean kissing you, having you against me."

"Oh, Molly, don't tell me that." But his mouth once again took hers.

Molly couldn't get enough, and when his hand

cupped her breast, his fingers folding and unfolding, his thumb nudging her nipple into an ache that became pain, she shuddered with the power of it. The arousal traveled lower, seizing her with an intimacy that made her try to get even closer to him. She tightened her arms and pressed her mouth more firmly against his until finally, he pulled back and held her by the upper arms to keep them separated.

She stared, her cheeks hot, her mouth tingly. She licked her lips, feeling their fullness. She wanted to tell him how she felt, how he made her feel.

"No words and no declarations, sweetheart," he whispered, as if reading her thoughts. "I don't want to hear them."

She lowered her lashes to hide her disappointment. "You still think I'm too young for you, don't you?"

"I'm no good for you, Molly. Not in this way."

"You keep saying that, but you don't tell me why."

"Because I have nothing to give you. I'm empty and hollow inside, and you need a man who's as eager to be happy as you are. I had my happiness with Kristin. Reaching for that again..." He looked at her mouth and then away. "I can't reach again, Molly. I can't..."

Molly was stunned by the despair of his words, the utter and total hopelessness that seemed to swallow him so totally.

Hunt opened his door, then released the trunk latch. He took their bags and walked up a narrow front walk. Three cement steps led to the door. He inserted a key, pushed the door open and disappeared inside the house.

She sat for long silent seconds, astonished at how quickly he could shift gears. She was numb and irritable and frustrated and hurt. "Dammit, Hunt Gresham," she muttered in the empty car. "You don't want to reach out again, and you don't want to feel anything with a woman because you won't, not because you can't."

Wearily she pushed open her own door and made her way to the house. It wasn't large, but it had a cozy cottage look, and she could envision fresh paint and flower boxes filled with impatiens. Inside, it had a stale but sterile scent that said it had been a long time since anyone had lived here.

Hunt stood very still with his back to her, his hands low on his hips as he faced a shadowed doorway. Their two bags sat in the middle of the living room. The bath was next to the room Hunt faced, the kitchen to Molly's right.

She started to say something about how tiny the rooms were when Hunt swung around. Even in the dying light of early evening, she could see him keeping his fury restrained.

"What is it?" she whispered, and wondered why she had.

"There are two bedrooms, but one doesn't have a bed. That's what it is."

For a second she missed his point, then it hit her. "Oh."

He lifted the bags and came toward her without really looking at her. "Come on. We'll find a motel.

She stepped around him and peered into the room. "Wait a minute."

"For what? Another bed to appear? Let's go."

Seizing the opportunity to prove she could be just as cool and uninvolved as he could be, she said, "You don't have to do that for me. I'm really very adaptable. I know you're tired, and frankly, I didn't see any motels I'd want to stay in. We passed the one I made a reservation in before I knew you were coming. It looked like the pits. We can stay here. At least they're twin beds."

He looked at her as if she'd grown another head. "You're not serious. In the car you were on your high horse about my dark, deceptive motives. Then I kissed you enough to make my ears ring, and now you suggest we sleep in the same room?"

Molly flushed, hating the reaction that in turn made her even more determined to prove to him she'd put their kiss in perspective. In a breezy tone, she said, "The same room isn't the same as the same bed."

"Bull."

She grinned, amused by his bluntness and a little flattered that the arrangement had caused him such turmoil. Suddenly he seemed vulnerable to her, and for Hunt, she guessed, revealing his inner agitation wasn't a pleasant experience. "You're afraid, aren't you?"

"This isn't a joke, Molly. We'll be together for a few days, and that means a few nights. Staying in the same room would be outright stupidity."

"It will test your resolve not to get involved in any kind of intimate relationship with me."

He muttered, "Just what I need at the end of the day. An endurance test for the night."

She took her bag from him and walked past him into the bedroom. Switching on a bedside lamp, she glanced around. The light seemed to shrink the room, and the beds now looked too close together. He was right: this was stupid, maybe insane, but for the first time since Vern died, she felt as if she'd seized upon a situation, assessed it and made a decision.

She glanced back at the doorway, where he now leaned, arms folded, face set in an unreadable expression.

"I'll take the couch," he said flatly.

She glanced beyond him, seeing the overstuffed sofa for the first time. Of course it was the best decision. Of course it was the right decision. Still, she was vaguely disappointed.

"You're right. I don't know what I was thinking to suggest we sleep in the same room."

"I know what *I* was thinking, and that's why I won't." He sighed, straightened and set his bag beside the couch. "You get your stuff settled. I'm going to check the kitchen. Sean said the owner set us

up with some basics. I hope one of them is whis-
key.''

"PUT THIS ON, it will answer questions just by its
presence.''

"A ring? I don't understand.''

"If the people attending the calling hours think
we're married, you won't have to explain my presence.''

It was the following afternoon, and they were in
the car, just about to enter the Fernwood Funeral
Home. Hunt had made a note of license plates for
Sean to check out. A number of mourners were scattered around in small groups, chatting, but he didn't
recognize any of them.

He'd been up before dawn, and while Molly slept,
he'd gone to a nearby convenience store, bought the
local newspaper and discovered that Wallace's death
was not only in the obits, but it was a news story on
page two:

Vernon Wallace, a onetime henchman of mobster Olaf Pascale, died in Woodbriar of a heart
attack. Wallace, who had a reputation for silence and precision, broke with Pascale years
ago for undisclosed reasons, and went to work
for John Solozi, a mobster who ran a money-
laundering operation out of central Massachusetts. News reports on Wallace, somewhat of a
lone wolf, are sketchy, and the Boston police,

when contacted about his death, had no comment. He is divorced, and the whereabouts of his ex-wife and son are unknown. Services, arranged by his sister, Molly McCulloch, are being handled through the Fernwood Funeral Home.

Hunt snapped the newspaper closed and swore. The only thing missing was where Molly was staying. He called Sean.

"Yeah, the Boston papers are carrying the story, too," Sean said. "Not much info, but the word is definitely out. Molly's name must have been released by the funeral home."

"At that point she wouldn't have thought to tell them to keep it from a reporter. What's screwy is that everything else in the piece is vague or unknown—like where his ex-wife is. But Molly is right there for all the world to see."

"Good thing you're with her," Sean said. "Oh, by the way, we got a search warrant for Wallace's apartment. Someone was there ahead of us. We didn't find anything that would shed light on the 827 BOS note."

"Terrific," Hunt said grimly.

"Hey, you're no stranger to dead ends." Then, in a lighter tone, Sean asked, "So, how's the cottage?"

"Small."

"The owner calls it cozy. He said he'd had some

weekly renters recently—a couple looking for a cheap honeymoon.''

It was the last comment that had given Hunt pause. Not about honeymooning with Molly for real, but using marriage as a way to eliminate curiosity or questions from Vern's pals during the stay here. Besides, posing as her boyfriend or lover hadn't felt right from the beginning. Molly looked more like orange blossoms and white lace than black garters and see-through bras.

Hell, if she didn't, he'd have slaked himself last night. But she wasn't that kind of woman, and Hunt had no intention of widening her education in disappointment and pain by allowing himself to get serious with her.

Thinking about being married again wrung what emotions he had left so tight he could hear them squeal in protest. But a fake marriage—that would make their being together natural to anyone who cared to look or ask. The ruse was the kind of thing that in his old police days he would have thought of in the planning stages. *Good thing you got out, Gresham, your instincts are rusty as hell.*

He'd found a ring in a pawn-shop across the street from the convenience store and waited until the last minute to present the idea, so Molly would have no opportunity to protest.

Now she was staring at the gold-colored band he held, her own hand clenched.

"Why would I have to explain anything about

you?'' she asked. "You're a friend and you came with me.''

"Or I'm a cop sent to check out Vern's cronies." He was quiet a moment. "Look, I don't want you to get huffy or alarmed, but some of the people here today aren't going to be members of the Fernwood Angelic Society.''

"Is this part of protecting me?''

"Yeah, you could say that." He relaxed her fingers and slipped on the ring. The sunshine caught the gold with a soft shimmer. His fingers lingered for an instant before he pushed open the car door.

"Where did you get it?'' she asked, her head bent as she turned her hand this way and that.

He suddenly wanted to tell her he'd found it in a jewelry store, where he'd lingered over an assortment displayed on black velvet until he found just the one she would like. "A pawn-shop," he said finally, the three words feeling as if he'd besmirched the entire institution of marriage.

She glanced down at it, and he wanted to tip her chin up and tell her that someday a man would slip another band of gold on her finger, one that he'd bought with love and commitment.

"It's...okay," she said, faltering. "I mean, it's not like this is real. Nothing between us is real—except your wanting information about my brother.''

"So the sooner we finish this up and get back to our regular lives, the better.''

He got out of the car, walked around to her door

and opened it, helping her out. She wore a navy blue tailored dress with low-heeled shoes. A navy straw hat shielded her eyes and gave her a sophisticated demeanor. Though it was entirely inappropriate, Hunt was struck by how desirable he found her in the sedate outfit. She carried herself with shoulders back, her step firm and her emotions solidly in control.

A man wearing a black suit with a white rosebud in his lapel glided over to Molly once they were inside. "Ms. McCulloch? I'm Ezra Hopper, the director here at Fernwood," he crooned in an unctuous tone that made Hunt clench his teeth. "I'm so sorry about your loss. Details have been arranged as you requested. And I must say the casket spray is impressive. Haven't seen one like that since I worked in Boston."

Molly scowled. "Yes, well, I appreciate you handling everything. Oh, this is my husband."

"Ah, Mr. McCulloch..." Hopper ushered them forward, toward the room where the body lay in a blue-lined coffin surrounded by hundreds of flowers.

Molly hesitated, her hands trembling. Hunt slid his arm around her, bending close. "Sweetheart, I'm right here."

"I don't want to go over there. I don't want to remember him like that."

"You don't have to. Come on, let's stand by the door, where we can get some fresh air. The flowers are pretty strong."

A short, heavy woman shaped like a fireplug and dressed in dull maroon polyester came up and placed her ringless hands over Molly's. "My dear, I'm so sorry. Had no idea Vern had a sister—God rest his soul—until I read the notice in the newspaper."

"Thank you for coming, uh..." Molly said.

"Name's Myrtle Baker." She peered at Hunt, her eyes the color of overcooked baked beans.

Molly said, "This is my husband."

She said it with such ease, Hunt was amazed.

"Humph. I had one of those once. Nothin' but grief and trouble." Then, in an abrupt change of tone, she added, "But how nice that you have someone to comfort you in your hour of loss."

Hunt rolled his eyes. God, she sounded like a cheap sympathy card.

"Well, my dear, Vern rented a place from me, and he was the sweetest man. Always paid his rent, never caused no trouble."

"I'm glad to hear that. I'll be sorting things out at his apartment once the funeral is over."

"You take your time getting his things cleared out."

"Thank you."

She waited a few seconds and then, in a slightly sharpened tone, she asked, "About how long, do you think?"

"Uh..."

Hunt said, "By the weekend."

"Good. Got a new tenant wants to move in early

September. And just so you know..." She pointed toward the foot of the casket. "I sent the Rest in Peace arrangement over there by the wall. Hopper stuck it in the back, but I moved it so it could be seen. Cost me a month's worth of lottery tickets, and I want it shown."

"It's lovely. Thank you."

She strolled away and Hunt muttered, "Good God."

Molly shuddered. "What an odd woman."

They watched as she walked toward the door, spoke to two men standing nearby and then left.

The first hour passed. Molly was talking to a young woman who claimed Vern had purchased his aquarium at her store. Hunt stepped outside for some air. The cloying flowers had saturated his lungs. So far he'd seen nothing notably suspicious. He walked the grounds, finding an arbor of bushes a gardener had shaped. Through the arbor was a lily pond, stone benches and babbling water over stones. The serenity was designed to be soothing, but the enclosed area felt obviously contrived to reflect quiet grief and sympathy.

He spent some time looking around and then walked back through the arbor to the main grounds. The first thing he noted was a black car he hadn't seen before.

Scowling, he wondered if it was Solozi or one of his men sent to pay their respects. Hunt covered the distance back to the funeral home's entrance in wide strides. But when he entered, the dimness over-whelmed him. Blinking and squeezing his eyes closed to force them to adjust, he berated himself for spending so much time outside.

Ezra Hopper appeared and Hunt snapped, "Where's my wife?"

He gave Hunt a distasteful look. "She was over there speaking to that poor troubled child who so admired Mr. Wallace."

"Cut the funereal pose, Hopper. I asked you a question."

His face reddened. "Please, sir. Your behavior is very distressing. Perhaps she went into one of the prayer rooms."

There were two of them, but Molly wasn't in ei-ther one. Hunt opened every door that was closed, including a broom closet, and went back outside, thinking she may have gone out a side door for some air.

But she wasn't outside, and the black car that had arrived while he was walking the grounds had just slid around a corner.

Hunt felt blindsided and stupid and furious. But more than any of those things, he felt a coiling terror.

She was gone.

CHAPTER NINE

INSIDE THE BLACK SEDAN, Molly's panic began to build as the car picked up speed.

Just a little while ago, she'd been discussing unusual types of tropical fish and then she'd thought—stupidly—that she was just accepting some pictures from a frail old man. Molly shuddered as she recalled the past twenty minutes.

"How can I ever thank you for these pictures, Mr. Pascale," Molly had said in an appreciative voice. She glanced through the snapshots, her heart catching at the ones of her brother with his son. Others were of Vern and his wife before they were divorced. There were also photos of Vern on a tennis court. She, too, played, and was struck by the fact that even though she and Vern had been separated for many years, they shared a love for the same sport. "I didn't know he played tennis."

"I'm sure there are many things about your brother you'll discover from his friends. How sad that his death came so unexpectedly."

After Olaf Pascale had introduced himself to Molly, he'd requested a private moment. He wore a chalk-striped gray suit, white shirt and pearl gray tie.

His frame was so gaunt, Molly was sure a good stiff wind would have blown him away.

"You and Vern were good friends?" she asked.

"I'd known him many years," he said, not really answering the question. "This was an effort for me, getting these pictures to you."

"And I appreciate it so much." She wished she had a better light. The dimness of the room made a close study of the pictures difficult.

"I have more pictures."

"More?"

"Yes, in my car. Some albums. There were too many to carry. I'm not as limber as I used to be. Arthritis. But if you'd care to walk outside with me, I'll be glad to give them to you."

"Oh, I'd love to have them."

"And I know Vernon is happier knowing they'll be yours."

He took her arm, stopping her when she started for the entrance.

"No, I'm parked closer to the back. There weren't any spaces left near the front." He offered his arm in a courtly manner. Molly glanced around for Hunt, but evidently he hadn't come back inside. She knew he was uncomfortable here, if only because it was a reminder of Kristin's funeral. She looked down at her hand and the thin wedding band, knowing it represented the phoniness between them, yet part of her wanting it to be reality.

When he'd slid it on her finger, her thoughts had

momentarily embraced all a wedding ring represented. Commitment, love, devotion, a true relationship between a man and a woman. But Hunt didn't
want any relationship with her, never mind a committed one. He'd made it clear he didn't want her at
all.

So why did her heart keep wanting him? Why did
her thoughts keep plunging into blissful fantasies?
Surely she was only suffering from infatuation or a
fascination with a sexy man. Her own love life was
bereft—the dating she'd done had never been very
serious—so perhaps that accounted for her feelings
for Hunt. If anything, she was probably falling in
love with the idea of being in love.

"Is something wrong?" Olaf Pascale asked, peer-
ing at Molly.

She shook off the unwanted thoughts. "No, no. Of
course not. Just let me tell my husband where I'm
going."

He gripped her arm a little too tightly, then immediately loosened his grasp. "I need to be getting
along, Molly. I'm going to be late for my appointment as it is. Surely you can come outside for a few
moments without permission."

His choice of words made her feel like a child,
and her pride balked. What harm was there? As an
ex-cop, Hunt was suspicious of everything and
everyone. Molly understood a wariness of Myrtle,
the landlady, but Mr. Pascale was a frail, old man
with pictures of her brother. If on the bizarre chance

he was some weird character, she'd thank him for the pictures and return to the funeral home.

"Lead the way, Mr. Pascale." Molly tucked the photos he'd given her into her purse. They were an unexpected treasure, and with the addition of the albums she could begin to put her brother's history together. Pictures meant friends of his she could contact, places she could go where Vern had been, and best of all, pictures of her nephew—now her only blood relative.

They crossed the lawn to an area with a few scattered cars in the distance. A black sedan waited, its paint gleaming with polish in the afternoon sun. Tinted windows gave it an air of mystery, and Molly felt the first inclination not to go any farther.

You're being silly and melodramatic, she scolded herself. There was no one around, and once she had the albums she would thank him and leave. Hunt might be annoyed at first that she'd disappeared for a few minutes, but when she showed him the pictures, she had little doubt his irritation would turn to excitement. Then, back at the cottage, when he was poring over the photos for clues, she'd remind him that if she hadn't spoken to Mr. Pascale, there would be no photos.

The two front car doors opened at exactly the same time. A pair of men in black suits and shoes that were as polished as the car, surrounded Molly. Their expressions were unsmiling, their eyes covered with sunglasses. Molly froze.

"What's going on?" she asked, both frightened and angry.

"Get in the car like a good girl, Molly."

"I certainly will not." She pulled away, but one of the men stopped her.

"Shut up and do as Mr. Pascale says." The man had a bloated, fleshy face, his eyebrows gray-flecked and bushy above his sunglasses. His mouth ticked up at one corner, as if practicing a deadly snarl.

The other man, a cadaverous column, stood sentry, with his legs apart and his arms folded, daring her to escape.

It had all the reality of a bad TV movie, and yet there was no doubt about the back door being thrown open and the one with the salt-and-pepper eyebrows pushing her into the car.

She struggled, one foot kicking up, her shoe making contact.

"Dammit!" He doubled over, his hand cupping the front of his pants. Molly took advantage of the distraction and flung herself sideways, trying to get enough footing to scramble free.

"Knock off the noise, for God's sake," Pascale snapped, all semblance of gentlemanly behavior gone. "You wanna bring a crowd down here? Get her into the friggin' car."

"I'm tryin', Mr. Pascale."

"Brewer! Help him."

"Yes, sir."

Brewer grabbed her, clamping a hand over her

mouth while the other man grasped both of her ankles. Her suit skirt hiked up, and she bucked and twisted in an effort to free herself, but in the next second she was unceremoniously dumped into the back seat.

She fell against the leather, her heart clamoring, her pulse pounding and terror clutching at her. She breathed in deep, gulping pants.

"Check her purse," Pascale snapped.

Brewer rifled through it. "Nothing here. Just female stuff and a wallet."

"Look again. This would be so much easier if she had it."

Molly glared at him. "Had what?"

Her question ignored, one of the henchmen leered at her. "Maybe she's stashed it in her panties. I can check those out."

Pascale gave him a withering look. "Get in the front and drive. I'll deal with Ms. McCulloch."

Her purse was thrown at her, and she wished she could have magically turned it into a gun. All her life she'd been an advocate for gun control, but right now, trapped and fearing for her life, all her theories became empty rhetoric.

Pascale slid into the car, the door closed, and Molly felt a deep and genuine terror. She'd ignored a primary rule of life; never go somewhere with a stranger—even a seemingly harmless one. She'd not only been stupid, but not telling Hunt meant he'd have no idea where to start looking.

Once the car sped away from the funeral home, Molly was convinced Hunt would never find her. Just as she was trying to absorb that awful reality, Pascale brought her thoughts back to the present. "You could make this very easy, Molly, if you'll just tell me what you've done with the notebook."

Molly scowled. "I don't know what you're talking about."

Pascale sat relaxed, as if time was of no import now that she was in the car. Then he reached out and pushed a hidden lever on the console, revealing an array of expensive decanters.

"Have some brandy. It will relax you and we can forget any unpleasantness you're feeling."

"Who are you?"

"A man who doesn't like to see pretty young women roughed up. And you are very pretty indeed. Your husband—" He hesitated, as if he knew their relationship was a ruse. "He's a very lucky man." He poured two snifters and held one out to Molly. She didn't move.

"You didn't answer me. Who are you?"

"Exactly who I said, and you will ask no more questions." Then the car stopped, the engine left to idle as the two thugs got out.

Molly looked out the window but saw only trees and bushes.

"A pity we can't just chat casually, but this is the time for you to be giving me answers. Answers that will keep you from getting hurt."

Molly reminded herself to think, to be cool and objective despite her growing panic. She shuddered in spite of herself. She'd gotten herself into a mess and she'd have to figure a way out by herself.

"What do you want to know?" she asked, deciding her first step was to let Pascale believe she would cooperate.

"Ah, now that's a question I like." Again he offered the snifter. This time she accepted it.

He smiled, relaxing a bit.

"You tricked me," she said, not wanting to appear too willing to talk. "There are no albums, and the pictures were to distract me."

"The pictures are yours, and to show my good faith..." He reached down and brought up an album, handing it to Molly. It was a little wider than a hardcover book, and the outer cover was solid and rough, like imitation leather. Molly clutched it. It felt like a photo album, but she knew it might be just as phony as Pascale's demeanor.

"Now, in the world where I come from, one good turn deserves another. I've given you pictures of your brother, and it's time for you to return the favor and tell me where the notebook is."

"What notebook? I don't know anything about a notebook."

"You're making this very dangerous for yourself," he warned.

Molly felt perspiration break out beneath her clothes. Her mind raced with random thoughts of escape, but how? Physically, she didn't have a chance against three men.

Pascale leaned back, crossed his legs and folded his hands around his nearly empty snifter. His voice bordered on the nostalgic. ''I was once fond of Vernon. He did his job and he knew the rules, but a dying man can forget codes of silence and be gripped by a need to confess. What I want to know from you, Molly, is what he told you to do with the notebook.''

''He didn't tell me anything.''

''Come, come, there's no need to lie.''

''I'm not lying. I saw him only for a few moments. He was in intensive care and drowsy. I was worried about him and I wanted him to get better. What he did with any of his belongings was the last thing on his mind or mine.''

''Your stubbornness makes this very difficult for me.''

Something told her the real difficulty would be hers. She had to say something. Pascale wanted information, and judging from his actions, she felt he would go to extreme means to get it. Floating in the back of her consciousness was the fact that Hunt had warned her that there could be people at the funeral who would believe she knew things about Vern. Dangerous things. But Pascale knew things, too. And more important, he wanted some notebook she knew nothing about.

A new determination raced through her. She had to get away. Hunt needed to know, and maybe, just maybe, the man her brother was supposed to kill could be warned. Then Vern's death would in effect have saved someone else. Molly latched on to that thought. With some calculated thinking and more than a little luck, her contact with Pascale might be the break Hunt and Sean needed.

Stay cool, stay controlled; Pascale thinks you're stubborn, not smart.

"There was one thing," she ventured.

He leaned forward a little. "What?"

"He said he had an appointment in Boston later in the week. He was worried about not keeping it."

Pascale swore, muttered a few things under his breath. "Did he say who he was meeting?"

"He said he was going to call and change it in case he didn't get out of the hospital." She lowered her head, mentally asking her brother's forgiveness for using his death as a tool against Pascale. "Since he died, he never had a chance to change it."

He studied her for a few minutes. "You're a god-damn liar, Molly," he said with an icy calm. "There's no Boston meeting. You must think I'm a fool."

Her heart plummeted.

Pascale leaned forward, his thin lips twitching menacingly.

Molly shrank back.

"You have two minutes to tell me where you've put the notebook, or Jock and Brewer will apply some extra pressure to make you talk."

His words had lethal potency, and Molly had no recourse. She couldn't give him information she didn't have. She had a choice of getting beaten up or fighting back. In an odd way, Pascale's threat tipped her over some edge between fear of what they'd do to her and the cold reality that she had nothing to lose.

A deep, thick resolve formed within her. She had to make her move before he called Jock and Brewer.

In a brisk voice, she said, "I've told you what I know. You don't believe me, so that's your problem. I've had quite enough." She paused, taking a small sip of the brandy. "I want to leave."

He laughed. "First lies and now bravado. You are an amusing broad."

She poured the brandy on the plush carpet, then broke the snifter, grinding the toe of her shoe on the glass.

For a few seconds Pascale stared at the mess, slack-jawed. Then his face turned red with fury. "You bitch! You ruined my carpet!"

He leaned forward to examine the floor, and Molly lifted the album and brought it down with all her strength on Pascale's head. He slumped forward instantly, and for a horrified moment she wondered if she'd killed him. For a few seconds she literally couldn't move. But then she took a deep breath, gathered her purse and the album and worked her way over Pascale's sprawled form to the door.

She eased it open, expecting one of the men to be

standing there, but both were at the front of the car, leaning against the grill, their backs to her. They were laughing and smoking, listening to a ball game on the radio, and Molly sent up a prayer they wouldn't turn around.

Slipping through the door, she closed it so that it made no noise and eased her way to the back of the vehicle, where she crouched to get her bearings. She didn't want to run flat out; if one of them turned and saw her, they'd shoot her. She'd have to do this in short bursts.

Molly spotted a huge rock across the road. If she could get to that...

She took deep breaths, peeked around to see if they still had their backs turned, then moved in quick silent strides to the rock. She snuggled behind it, almost wanting to hug it for its size and presence. Step one completed.

She searched for the next stopping place and spotted a bush. Molly was headed west, and the black sedan was heading east. The car would have to turn completely around before it gave chase. If the two men took after her on foot, the farther away she was, the bigger the advantage. Once again she checked on Jock and Brewer before moving. She ran silently, then dropped into a crouch behind a bush the shape of an open fan. She was nearly giddy with her progress.

About to try for a third shelter, she saw a convertible approaching with a woman and a child buckled into a car seat. The vehicle was moving toward the black sedan. Molly's instinct to stand and cry for help nearly overwhelmed her, but she made herself stay hidden and let the car pass her. To flag them down would risk innocent lives if Jock and Brewer spotted Molly.

But the car did attract Brewer's attention. He flung his cigarette away and turned toward the passenger side of the black sedan, walking toward the door Molly had just escaped through.

Molly's mouth went dry. If he knocked on the glass or opened the door...

She shrank lower, feeling exposed and vulnerable despite the camouflage of the bush. She wasn't far enough away yet. Brewer stopped, turned to say something to Jock, then made an obscene gesture. Jock laughed, the sound carrying in the light wind. The convertible had disappeared and still Molly didn't move.

Then Brewer twisted around, standing near the door, staring at the handle. Then, as if empowered by rocket fuel, he flung the door open, yelled for Jock, who raced to his side, and both men burrowed inside.

Molly shoved her purse and the album under the bush; she couldn't afford to have anything slow her down now. She stood, and ran faster and harder than she ever had in her life. The road curved to the left. If she could get around the corner, they'd never see her. Legs pumping, she sprinted.

A shot exploded, shattering the summer innocence of birds twittering and leaves rustling. Then came another shot, followed by a ping as the bullet struck a stone to her right.

Instinctively she ducked.

Her heart leapt so fast it felt as if it had jammed into her throat. She didn't stop; a moving target was harder to hit. Besides, if she stopped, she'd surely be dead.

Another shot, this one whizzing past her.

Still she ran. Patchy asphalt twisted out ahead of her in an unending strip.

Tires squealed behind her.

Oh God, they were turning around. No way could she outrun a car. Her legs ached, her lungs burned. She didn't know where she was going, or even if there was a place to get to.

She darted sideways, intent on flinging herself into the culvert and rolling down the embankment. Then, to her horror, another car appeared, and it was headed right at her!

Frantically, she sprang to the road's shoulder, literally throwing herself into the scruffy grass. The driver must have seen her, for the car braked, swerved and spun in a half circle as if out of control before coming to an abrupt stop.

It blocked the road sideways so that Molly was looking at the entire length of the passenger side. Horrified, she heard the black vehicle coming; her vision was blocked by her position on the ground and by the other car, but she braced herself for the collision.

Tires squealed like a thousand pigs. Engine roaring, the black car reversed as fast as it had come forward, then, spinning around again, it raced away, heading east.

Molly lay in the grass, her hands digging into the dirty tufts as if they were handfuls of safety. Dust and perspiration coated her face. Her body was numbed from exhaustion and fear. The silence roared in her ears, but slowly, and with agonizing effort, she got to her knees, then to her feet. Somewhere she'd lost a shoe, her hat was long gone, too. A stone was digging into the heel of her stockinged foot.

No one emerged from the stopped car, and she slowly made her way forward. Whoever was inside had inadvertently saved her life twice. First by braking in time, and then by preventing the black vehicle from getting to her.

Molly cautiously approached, looking into the rolled-up passenger window. The vehicle was empty. She stared in puzzlement. Where was the driver? She started to round the car and then stopped, backing away. Was this a trick? Was it all a backup plan by Pascale on the off chance she escaped?

Molly stumbled backward, her body shaking, her weariness now so pervasive she could barely put one foot in front of the other.

A hand touched her shoulder.

She whirled around, a scream catapulting from her throat.

"It's me, babe, it's me."

"Hunt! My God....my God, it really is you..."

And in the next second she was in his arms; she would have climbed into his clothes if that had been possible.

"It's really me. Molly, Molly..." His hands roamed over her as if feeling for anything broken. Her hands were so tight around his waist, he had to literally tug them away.

"Oh, Hunt." She looked up at him, and if ever she'd had any doubts about his being the most wonderful man in the entire world, those doubts were now gone. "H-how did you f-find me?"

"Shhh. Plenty of time for questions. Let's get you back to the cottage." He opened the passenger door. Suddenly she felt weak as a kitten, and she gratefully sank into the seat. Hunt climbed in, started the car and headed back in the direction he'd come, when Molly said, "My purse... I left it and an album under a bush."

"What bush?"

They all looked alike, and she was so tired and hot and thirsty, she didn't have the energy to concentrate. But Hunt would want the pictures. "A bush shaped like a fan just beyond that big rock."

He pulled to the side of the road and got out. After ten minutes of searching under a number of bushes, Hunt found the items.

Molly sagged back in the seat and closed her eyes. By the time Hunt pulled into the funeral home parking lot, she was asleep. Hunt touched her cheek and allowed his fingers to rest against the beating pulse in her neck. Life had never felt so good to him. "We'll be back at the cottage in a few minutes, sweetheart."

Hunt got out of the car and walked over to a pudgy man with a receding hairline. He was pacing back and forth where Hunt had left him after borrowing his car.

When Hunt had seen the black vehicle disappear and one of the funeral attendees had mentioned Olaf Pascale's name, Hunt had raced for his own car, only to find it blocked in by two others. Desperate, he was about to hot-wire a foreign-made car that was in the clear when a late arrival pulled in. Hunt had waved the car down and asked the owner if he could borrow it, saying that it was an emergency. The man, who must have noted the panic in Hunt's eyes, agreed, and in a few seconds, Hunt had rounded the corner where the black sedan had disappeared.

Now Hunt offered his hand and the man shook it.

"Thanks for letting me use your car, Mr.... uh...?"

"Sanderson. Norman Sanderson. What was that all about, anyway?"

"I'm not sure yet. I haven't had a chance to talk to my wife," Hunt said vaguely. Sanderson looked harmless, but Hunt knew that didn't mean anything.

Obviously Pascale had looked harmless to Molly or she wouldn't have gone with him.

He unlocked his own car and rolled down the windows to let out some of the heat.

Sanderson peered at his vehicle. "You didn't dent or scratch it, did you?"

"Good as when I borrowed it." Hunt gave him a quick smile, took some bills from his wallet and said, "But it could do with a car wash, and your gas gauge is low. Here. It's on me. Uh, my wife is asleep in the front seat. I want to get her home, where she'll be more comfortable."

"Your wife? That's who you went after?"

Hunt nodded, reaching into Sanderson's car and lifting Molly into his arms.

"My God, what happened to her?" Sanderson's eyes widened, and he rushed over to help Hunt. "She should see a doctor."

For the first time, Sanderson scowled. "Say, who did this to her? You beat her up or something?"

Hunt couldn't blame the guy for being suspicious; to be honest, he would be, too, given the circumstances. Just then Molly stirred, her arms going around Hunt's neck. "Oh Hunt," she whispered, her voice hoarse. "I wasn't dreaming. You really did find me.... You really did."

Hunt brushed his mouth across her forehead. "Yes, sweetheart, I really did find you."

She settled against him, content. Sanderson looked confused.

Hunt said, "I know this all looks weird, but I promise you I didn't hurt her and I never would."

"Well, she sure doesn't seem to be trying to get away...."

Hunt carefully put Molly into the front seat of his own car, buckled her seat belt, returned to Sanderson's car for her purse and the album, then got behind the wheel. "Thanks again," Hunt said, and drove away, leaving Sanderson gawking.

Moments later, Molly stirred, her eyes slowly opening.

"Are we home yet?"

"In a few minutes."

She nodded, closed her eyes and then opened them again. "I'm sorry I did such a stupid thing, going off with Pascale."

"Shhh. It wasn't stupid."

"You're not mad at me?"

"No, sweetheart, I'm not mad. I'm just grateful you're alive and here with me."

She tried a smile. "I love...you."

Hunt felt a jolt deep in his gut. He knew she meant it in a grateful way—it wasn't an uncommon reaction toward a rescuer, even though Hunt had to admit that Molly's rescue had been mostly her doing. She'd acted with incredible daring, given the dangerous circumstances.

At the cottage, he carried her into the house and directly into the bathroom. The room was tiny, and

Hunt had little space in which to get her undressed and into the shower.

"I can do it," Molly mumbled, wincing as she removed her shredded hose. Hunt lowered his eyes as she stripped off rose-patterned panties and bra. She stepped into the shower, and he heard her sigh as the hot water sluiced over her.

"I'll wait outside."

"No!" She flung the curtain back, unmindful of her nudity. "Don't leave me. Please."

Startled by her intensity and the terror in her eyes, he nodded. "Okay. I'm right here."

By the time she emerged, the steam in the bathroom was so thick it made her a blur. Hunt handed her a towel for her hair and one for her body. She wrapped herself in them and then stood as if paralyzed.

"Molly? What is it?"

She sniffled and Hunt stepped closer, seeing the tears rolling down her cheeks.

He brushed a thumb across the dampness. "It's okay. You're just having a delayed reaction."

"I was so scared."

"I know."

"I was afraid I'd never see you again, that you'd never find me...."

"I was afraid of that, too,"

"I need you close to me, Hunt. I don't ever want to be away from you again."

"I promise," he told her, without giving much

thought to what he was saying. "Come on. Let's get your hair dry and get you into bed."

Her hands slid around him, and she sealed herself against him. Hunt was struck by the combination of desperation and desire he felt in her body. It had to be delayed reaction; she'd been in danger and now she was safe. She was grateful, nothing else.

But Hunt couldn't deny his own need to bond her to him, and that thought unsettled him. He, too, must be experiencing a delayed relief that she was all right.

Then she blew a million holes in that theory when she tipped her head back and pulled his mouth down to hers.

In a whisper as delicate as the steam around them, she said, "I want to love you, Hunt. I want to love you tonight."

CHAPTER TEN

HUNT KISSED HER, allowing her to press against him, not objecting when her arms clung like warm silk.

He wanted her, and yet he feared that intimacy with her would take their relationship to a plane that was irreversible. If this were any woman but Molly, he'd dismiss such silly thoughts. Men and women didn't bond for life on the basis of a romp in the sack.

But Molly wasn't any woman, which was exactly why he wanted no intimate involvement. The fact that he knew what he didn't want, and yet responded to her with a desperate hunger...that scared the hell out of him. Her body felt sweet and innocent, and she was too vulnerable for a man jaded by life and little belief in hope and happiness.

No involvement. He'd told her that, tried to practice it. But here, with her clinging and wanting, he was plunging in with a desire that bordered on recklessness.

"Easy," he murmured, unsure if he meant her or himself. He wanted to slow her down, wanted to think beyond the soft feel of her breasts and belly and thighs and what she was offering him.

"I can't be easy. You'll r-run away." Her lashes were dewy, her eyes wide like lavender lilacs and filled with a headstrong insistence.

She was right. He would run; he'd run like hell. The least hesitation on her part and he'd be history. But here he was, at a loss as to how to fight this volatility, the inevitability that had been building between them for days.

Hunt slipped the towel from her head and ran his fingers through the damp strands. "You smell like wildflowers," he whispered, kissing her eyes, her nose, then once again her mouth.

Her mouth wouldn't release him, her tongue smooth and a little desperate, as if she couldn't get enough, as if no matter how deep and how long the kiss, she'd want more. Not just tonight, not just while they were together, but forever. And the thought of another forever kind of woman paralyzed him anew.

One more try, he reminded himself, pulling at the last threads of his weakened resistance. Hunt gently tugged her away, holding her so that she had to look at him. "Molly, listen to me."

She shook her head, the damp strands of her hair brushing his jaw, clinging to his shirt collar. "No…no. If I listen, you'll say we can't, and tonight, I don't want you to say that."

Hunt swore. He didn't want to say it, either, but he had to. He sighed and put his arm around her. "Let's start by getting out of the bathroom."

She let him lead her out, but when he turned toward the living room, planning to distract her, to talk about what had happened this afternoon with Olaf Pascale, she balked.

Then Hunt glanced at the sofa, where he'd slept the previous night, and hesitated. Truthfully, sleeping there had been a joke; he'd tossed and turned and cursed feelings for Molly he didn't want to have.

Molly saw his hesitation and believed his resistance was real; she had little doubt he truly didn't want to make love. Tomorrow, she'd make their relationship the one he wanted—two people brought together by arrangement.

Tomorrow she'd be businesslike and distant.

Tonight she wanted to make love to him.

Tonight she would die without him.

Molly tugged him toward the bedroom. "I want to go to bed with you."

His body instantly reacted, and he shuddered. "I know you do."

"And you want me," she said with the same assurance that the sun would rise in the morning. "Maybe you don't want to want me, but you do." She touched the front of his pants, and it took all his resolve not to press her hand around the hardness.

"Ah, hell," he muttered with a sigh. "You're beautiful and desirable, and having you practically beg me to make love to you is..." He let his voice trail off, wishing he had answers. Making love to her was what? More than he deserved? More precarious than with another woman because he feared he'd want Molly again and again?

"Tell me." She kissed his jaw, his neck, blew into his ear, and he didn't have to see the delight in her eyes to know she realized she would win.

He pulled away, arched a brow and asked, "You love seeing me in turmoil, don't you?"

"Mmm. I'm going to love having you." The sudden husky vampishness in her voice was deliciously seductive.

Hunt was fighting a losing battle. Despite the complications that "afterward" would create, he wanted her. His body pounded with his need like an overworked bass drum.

Then, as if she knew exactly how to push him over the edge, she released the towel she had wrapped around herself. It dropped in a damp pool around her legs.

"Oh, Molly." He squeezed his eyes closed, but he wanted to look and to touch and to taste. Desire overcame him with a sharpness that was close to pain.

Her skin had a pink ivory richness that deepened into rose on her nipples. Her breasts were small and high, her tummy flat with a small beauty mark just above the downy amber triangle. He took in her long legs, and suddenly the need to have them around him pushed aside any resistance that lingered within him.

She kicked the towel away, took a step toward him and he could fight her no longer. Dragging her against him, he crushed his mouth down on hers. Their tongues danced and tangled with an intimacy born of desperation. His hands went to her bottom, and he lifted her against him. Molly wrapped her arms around his neck, and with the grace of a gazelle, she brought her legs up and locked them around his hips. She felt light and airy, and the heat of her burned through his clothes—clothes he wanted to be rid of.

Without letting her go, he moved into the bedroom, but when he tried to untangle her, she resisted. Her eyes were huge, her mouth wet and ripe from the long, deep kiss.

In a husky voice, she whispered, "You're not going to run away, are you?"

"I can't, babe.... I can't...."

She smiled, a triumphant, seductive smile that seemed to say that she had fought the battle, and winning him was her reward. "I want to be with you.... I want to give you my heart and soul and..." Then, in a fierce voice that spilled from deep within her, she murmured, "I don't ever want to be out of your arms again."

"Oh, Molly, don't. You're offering too much. We'll make love as many times as you want, but..." What he was saying amazed him. His heart, usually so hollow and bereft, now ached for far more than good sex.

"But I want to tell you how I feel." Her eyes were

honest and expectant, the vulnerability so clear, it was painful.

He kissed her then to prevent any more revelations and declarations. Finally laying her down on the bed, he bent low and whispered in her ear, "Shhh. Don't lose your heart to me, sweetheart. You want me, and that's good and healthy, and I'm honored. The heart stuff is for some young man who deserves all your sweetness and hopes for the future."

She didn't argue or attempt to persuade him otherwise, yet the look in her eyes gave him pause. Then he shook it off. Garden-variety desire, that was all. More intense, perhaps. A deeper passion, a confusion on her part because she viewed love in a tangle of idealistic fervor. The events of the past few days had simply brought all her emotions to the surface.

She stretched out, but not with a seductive sexuality. Hunt watched her as he disposed of his clothes and decided that Molly was incapable of guile; she had an honesty of passion that few men ever experienced in a lifetime of encounters. He was truly honored, and he wanted to give her what she expected and more.

Molly stared at him in awe. His body was muscled and lean, his chest hair a rich mat to explore. A concave stomach and tight hips. Molly's eyes sought that part of him that proclaimed him a very aroused male. He was truly magnificent. She lifted her hand and brushed his thigh, then touched him, closing her fingers and then opening them. Her breath caught in wonder at the smooth texture of his sex.

The curiosity of her fingers made him feel like a randy kid. Easing her hand away, Hunt sat down with his hip brushing hers. Moving slowly, he drew his hands down her arms, placing them at her sides. He cupped her breasts, then bent to kiss each of the deep rose tips. She started to reach for him. Once again, he soothed her into stillness with his hands. Her skin was flushed with the beginnings of arousal, and his own body was aching with the primal need to mate.

He moved down the bed, braced his hands on either side of her and realized, in that instant, how much she meant to him. He wanted to please her, cherish her, give her pleasure.

She raised her head from the pillow. "Hunt?"

Pressing his hand to her tummy, he whispered, "I want to make love to you, Molly. Relax..."

Then, before she responded, he placed his hand on the amber curls and she lifted into him like a gift. He leaned down and kissed first one breast and then the other, his mouth lingering long enough at each nipple to taste and memorize the sweetness.

She tugged at him to get him to lie down beside her. "Oh, Hunt, please. You're too far away."

Instead, he kissed her tummy, the tiny beauty mark and finally the amber curls. He urged her legs farther apart and settled his mouth deeper.

Instantly she moaned, then stilled and tried to pull him away. He held her hands, feeling her begin to relax. He kissed her inner thighs, one side and then the other, then again returned to the heart of her.

This time she arched up, with a breathless panting and a swaying of her body that sent rockets off in Hunt's head.

He kissed her deeper and deeper, feeling the rising passion, her body striving toward fulfillment.

"Hunt...no, please...."

He heard a tinge of fear of the unknown. "Trust me. I'll make this good for you."

Molly was lost. She couldn't have pulled back if she'd wanted to. The pleasure enveloped her entirely; the sensation pushed her higher as she opened the most sensitive part of her to his mouth, which promised a release she couldn't escape.

Her climax came in a rush that made her disoriented and dizzy. She clawed at Hunt and then collapsed in a satiated heap, wrung out and exhausted. When she opened her eyes, Hunt was beside her, pulling her into his arms.

She buried her face against him, and murmured something he couldn't understand. Hunt held her, his own body still fiercely aroused, yet he was strangely satisfied at the pleasure and fulfillment he'd felt at her release.

They lay in silence a few moments. Molly against him, one leg flung across his, her fingers wandering across his chest, coasting lower and lower and then stopping. Hunt didn't move. He wanted to give her free rein to explore.

She tipped her head back and then kissed him. "You taste like me," she whispered, kissing him again. "Mmm. I liked what you did."

He grinned. "Yeah, I know."

Then she asked, "Are you going to let me do that to you?" Her fingers folded around him, squeezing lightly.

Arrows of heat hurled deep into his groin. Shifting their bodies, he rolled on top of her, tucking one leg between her thighs and pressing against her. Their mouths came together, their kisses deep and wet. She urged him on, pulling him into her. He nudged himself inside, slowly and with painful control. He was on the verge of exploding and all he wanted was to feel her close around him. Slowly he pressed, hunger for her consuming him.

"Molly, Molly, you're so tight.... You feel so good...."

Her tiny yelp of pain shot through him like a blast of cold air. He halted, his body heaving, his breathing ragged. A second passed, then another and another and another.

He lifted his head, but hers was turned to the side.

"Look at me."

But she wouldn't. Even when he drew her face around, she kept her eyes cast down.

"You're a virgin, aren't you?" When she didn't answer, Hunt cursed. He should have guessed. Her innocence had been all too obvious from the first.

He rolled away from her and sat up, his feet on

the floor, his back to her. He shoved both hands through his hair. Self-disgust swamped him. He never should have let any of this happen. He started to get up.

"No!" She wrapped her arms around his waist. "You're not going to leave me."

He didn't want to. God help him, he didn't. Taking a deep breath, he asked, "Why didn't you tell me?"

"Because you wouldn't want me."

"Damn right," he said bluntly. "None of this should have happened, as I've been saying from the very beginning. But that's not the point now. I could have hurt you. It's bad enough that I was going to do this without a condom, but a virgin! Hell!"

"I'm sorry."

Hunt sighed. What in the world was he doing? Making her feel awful because she hadn't slept around? *Good move, Gresham.* He turned around, and in one smooth motion, drew her down on the bed beside him.

In a fierce voice, he said, "You have nothing to be sorry for. You're a gift, Molly. You're giving me a gift, and I wouldn't want to treat it as ordinary."

Her eyes glistened with tears. "I know you didn't want to get involved with me. I was afraid if you knew I'd never been with a man it would give you an even bigger reason to stay away from me."

"And I would have." At her obvious disappointment, he said, "But I want you, Molly. I know I should get up and walk out of here, but I don't think I can.''

Her face lit up as if someone had turned on the lights. "Oh, Hunt," she exclaimed, hugging him fiercely.

"We're going to take this slow."

"Yes."

"And you tell me when it hurts."

"Yes."

He scowled. "And stop looking like you got what you wanted."

She grinned. "But I did. I got you, and that's always been what I've wanted."

"I am not what you want," he said emphatically. "You don't need to mistake good sex for love." He kissed her and ended the conversation.

He was amazed to find her arousal almost immediate. Nevertheless, he took his time, making her relax, to soften any tension or tightness. Easing himself inside her took a control Hunt hadn't realized he possessed.

She tightened; he felt the resistance and he stopped, then, when she relaxed, he eased a little more fully into her. He felt the thin hymen wall and probed gently but steadily.

"Oh!" Molly stiffened again, and then tried to relax.

"Just a little more, sweetheart." He gritted his teeth and knew that a quick, sure plunge was the least painful. Gripping her hips, he held her against him, and with a thrust, he broke the wall. Her nails dug into his back, and her body closed around him like a long-lost glove.

He tried to keep the rhythm slow, but she clung to him, her mouth fierce under his. Now that he was inside her, his control exploded. He pushed deep, and she welcomed each thrust. To his astonishment, she wrapped her legs around his hips, and in that instant Hunt's control vanished.

His climax roared through him, saturating every pore, pulsing deep into every nerve ending. His mind could focus on nothing but the rush of satisfaction that made the sex act with Molly brand-new and profound and utterly soul stirring.

He lay across her, satiated, numb and astonished by his own feelings. Molly, too, had relaxed, her fingers playing in his hair, her breathing just a little uneven.

"Thank you," she whispered. Then she added, "I'm glad you were the first. I wanted my first time to be because I loved my partner, not because I wanted to have sex."

"You were incredible."

"It was good for you?"

"The very best." He kissed her lightly and then settled her against him. He felt the relaxing of her body, and he, too, drifted into peaceful contentment. He pulled the covers up over them, and from her breathing, he knew she was nearly asleep.

Hunt closed his eyes, thinking that if hope and

happiness—two emotions he considered beyond his reach—were renamed Molly McCulloch, he could be induced to take a chance.

Just the afterglow of good sex, he quickly reminded himself. But a new worry floated into his mind just as the first wave of sleep gripped him.

He remembered he hadn't pulled out before he climaxed.

HER BROTHER'S FUNERAL was the following day, and while Hunt wasn't expecting Pascale to show his face, he did expect a few of his pals. But he saw no one who looked suspicious. Molly had told him Pascale had been looking for a notebook, but since he hadn't given Molly any more information, it was just another unsolved piece of the puzzle of Vernon Wallace's life.

Hunt made a quick stop for coffee at a convenience store. Molly went inside with him, saying she needed to get a few items.

"I'll meet you out at the car. I'm going to call Sean."

"Take your time," she said.

Once he reached his old partner, he heard there had still been no progress on the meaning of the note. Hunt explained the events of the day before.

"Pascale snatched her? Thinking she knew something about a notebook? Now that *is* interesting. For the old man to take that kind of risk, this notebook must be a real problem for him. Our search warrant turned up nothing, but if there is such a notebook, it adds an interesting twist.''

"Wallace had incriminating stuff on Pascale.''

"Sounds that way. A little blackmail. That notebook probably kept Wallace from getting murdered by Pascale. With Wallace dead, Pascale doesn't want it to fall into the wrong hands—namely ours.''

"Why would he think Molly had it?''

"Why not? Pascale is thorough. She was Wallace's sister, and she was the last one to see him before he died. The old guy might think Wallace did a deathbed confess-all.''

"This was supposed to get simpler, and it's getting more complicated,'' Hunt said, unsure if he was talking about the case or his involvement with Molly.

Sean asked, "So how did you rescue her?''

"She got away on her own,'' Hunt replied.

"From Pascale? Did he have Jock and Brewer with him?''

"Yep.''

"Well, I'll be damned. Guess she didn't need you, after all.''

Hunt had hung up feeling a burst of pride that Molly had been so savvy. He was glad she could handle herself in a tough situation, glad she had a cool head. What disturbed him was the contrast to the woman he'd made love to. That woman had needed him, wanted him with a desperation that made her very different from the woman who had outfoxed Pascale.

No wonder he found her so fascinating.

From the car, Molly had been watching Hunt at the pay phone. She guessed he was passing on the events of the previous day. Molly wasn't at all confused by who she was with Pascale and who she was with Hunt. She knew she was falling in love with Hunt—their lovemaking simply confirmed that. Her dilemma now was to keep the feelings she'd so willingly expressed last night subdued in the light of day.

When this was over, Hunt would go back to being her neighbor and a college lecturer; she'd be lucky to see him a couple of times a week. Vern had been correct in saying she could trust Hunt. Trust him to be truthful, yes, but that meant hearing that he didn't want to be involved with her.

She needed to prepare for that; she needed to be cool and distant and show him she could make love and forget it just like he could. Besides, she was here for her brother and for his legacy. Compared to dealing with feelings for Hunt, ensuring that someone else didn't get killed seemed rather straightforward.

Hunt returned to the car, and they drove to the cemetery for Vern's funeral. Molly looked around for Francine and her nephew, Brandon, hoping they'd be there. Since she didn't have their phone number or address, she had no way of contacting them, but the death had been announced in both the local and Boston newspapers, and Molly was hoping Francine would have seen the notice.

After the final prayers were said at the graveside,

the other mourners offered last words of sympathy to Molly before slowly moving away. Hunt and Molly stayed until everyone was gone. The casket was poised to be lowered into the ground, and Hunt took her arm as she walked forward. She laid a single red rose on the coffin and then tucked a four-leaf clover under the flower. She lowered her head in silence, kissed her fingers and pressed the kiss against the wood, then nodded to Hunt that she was ready to leave.

Moments later, they stopped at the edge of the cemetery and Molly glanced back at the site.

Hunt put his arm around her. For the most part he'd followed her lead since they'd awakened this morning. Hunt sensed a shyness in her and took that as a cue; he didn't want to discuss their lovemaking, either. Shyness, however, wasn't his excuse. The entire episode both infuriated him and amazed him. Reckless and dumb were the least of the adjectives to describe his actions. If he'd kept to the self-imposed discipline he thought he'd perfected since Kristin's death, he would have firmly sent Molly to bed and found his own surcease on the goddamn couch.

But it was too late now for second-guessing. Maybe, just maybe, he'd get lucky, she wouldn't be pregnant and they could get on with their separate lives.

"Ready to go?" he asked Molly.

"I guess." She pressed a tissue to her nose and

blew lightly. "I'm just sad and I feel a little lost. I'd hoped Francine would be here."

"Yeah, I was hoping, too."

She turned to the parking area, watching as the last of the cars pulled away. "Pascale and his friends didn't come."

"After yesterday, I'm not surprised."

"Do you think Vern's wife knows he's dead?"

"Maybe she's afraid to come. Maybe she's afraid someone will think she has the notebook."

Suddenly relieved that Francine's absence was so easily explained, Molly said, "You're right. She wouldn't risk herself or Brandon, would she?"

"No, she wouldn't." Hunt, however, had seen a woman with a child in the distance during the service. She'd been too far away for him to do anything but watch her. It was obvious she didn't want to identify herself, and since Hunt couldn't be sure if she was Vern's ex-wife, he'd said nothing.

Molly glanced back to where the workers were lowering the casket into the ground. Quickly, she turned away. "Please, let's go."

At his car, Hunt opened the door for her and then got behind the wheel. "Want to get something to eat?"

She shook her head. She sat straight in the seat, belt buckled, hands clasped lightly around a small purse. She looked straight ahead, her voice emphatic, "I want to go to Vern's apartment."

"Right now?"

"Yes, now. The sooner the better."

Hunt scowled. Since she'd walked out of the bedroom a few hours ago, dressed in black, he'd noted a determination in her manner. He'd been fearful her resolve might be about him and her and their lovemaking, which Hunt didn't want to discuss. Not yet. He still hadn't figured out his own feelings, and he didn't want to get into a conversation filled with Molly's honesty and declarations of love. So he'd deliberately asked no questions about her silence.

Now he wondered if that intense focus was directed toward getting things settled at her brother's so she could return home and get away from him.

That possibility annoyed him, and he cursed himself. He should be pleased if she made the first move to end their involvement. It was what he wanted. Wasn't it? Of course it was.

To Molly, he said, "We don't have to do that today. Tomorrow—"

"Today. There's no reason to postpone it. Vern lived there, and so there has to be more information about him there than anywhere else. Pascale thought I had a notebook that I didn't have. Maybe that's where it is."

"The police already searched his apartment. They didn't find anything. And, by the way, while you were dressing, I thumbed through the album. Mostly they're pictures of his wife and kid. Vern was too smart to leave anything incriminating lying around."

"He was, wasn't he? He was very smart. I just

wish he'd been as smart about his health.'' Molly paused, quiet for a few seconds and then sighed. ''I want my brother to leave a positive legacy, and I'm the only one who can give him that. He certainly sacrificed enough in his life to deserve to be remembered for more than being a hit man. If he'd been hired to kill someone, whoever did the hiring is going to hire someone else. Someone is set to die, and I want to make sure that doesn't happen.''

Hunt glanced over at her. A zillion questions clamored in his mind, most of them reminding him he was totally clueless. Here he'd thought she'd been thinking about him this morning, and instead she'd been concentrating on her brother's reputation. His ego collapsed as if it had taken a direct hit. ''You seem to have it all figured out.''

''Yes, I do.''

''Right up to saving some poor bastard's life. You do realize this hit wasn't contracted on some choirboy.''

She turned toward him, her eyes sharp. ''That doesn't mean he deserves to be murdered.''

''I didn't say that. But the question of making sure nothing happens to him is not your responsibility. Sean and the police will handle it.''

''And what have they done so far?''

''They're doing what they can with what they have, Molly. That's how police work. One step at a time.''

"So far I'm unimpressed. The first time I heard about any notebook was from Pascale."

"Because the police didn't know about it until Pascale tried to snatch you. Besides, the cops aren't trying to impress you. Their intention is to not screw up by acting before they have the evidence."

"Then maybe I can help things along. Pascale wanted that notebook badly, so obviously it's important to him."

"Probably. Since Pascale and your brother had a falling out when Vern crossed over to Solozi's outfit, the notebook may have inside information on Pascale that Vern knew would send him to prison."

"Blackmail?"

Hunt nodded. "Now, with Vern dead, Pascale is desperate to find the notebook."

"Before someone else does," Molly mused. She opened the glove compartment and took out the map they'd studied when they arrived in Fernwood. She glanced at the street sign they passed and then looked back at the map. "Take a left at the next intersection. Ludlow is three streets away."

He followed her directions. They located the apartment house, a well-maintained brownstone in a middle-class neighborhood. Hunt was a little surprised. Not that he thought Wallace couldn't have afforded a nice place, but the encounter with Myrtle had left the impression of some two-floor walk-up with a palm reader's sign in one of the windows.

Molly was out the door before Hunt had a chance

to stop her. But he caught her at the front entrance. "What's the big hurry?"

"I told you, I want to get this done and over with."

"No sale. You're as prickly as a cat who rolled in a buzzy bush."

"I decided that after my encounter with Pascale, I needed to pull myself together and look after Vern's interests."

"Which are?"

"Finding the brother I loved and spent nineteen years looking for. I had him for a few hours, and now all that's left are his things. Pascale gave me pictures—those showed me a side of Vern that couldn't be hired to murder people. He played tennis, he collected exotic fish, and the woman from the aquarium store told me how Vern worried when one of the fish wouldn't eat. Does that sound like some wild-eyed killer?"

"No one said he was a wild-eyed killer."

"But a killer."

"Yes."

She drew herself up. "Are you coming or do you want to wait out here?"

He rolled his eyes. "Lead the way."

Inside, they climbed a wooden staircase, turned a corner and stopped in front of the third door. Molly took the key from her purse and Hunt plucked it from her hand.

"I can do it."

"Humor me, okay?"

He unlocked the door and, keeping Molly behind him, eased it open.

"Son of a bitch." he muttered in disgust.

"What is it?"

"The cops didn't do this. Someone else has been in here."

CHAPTER ELEVEN

MOLLY STOOD FROZEN in the doorway, her gasp of horror and outrage barely audible. Her hands covered her mouth.

Ahead of her, Hunt walked cautiously into the room. He'd left his suit jacket in the car and had rolled back the cuffs of his shirt. His hands on his hips, he shook his head in obvious disgust.

The room looked as if a cyclone had blown through it. Furniture overturned. Cushions slashed. Desk drawers dumped, their contents flung everywhere. An armchair supported a tipped-over brass floor lamp. The parchment shade was crushed and wet under the broken aquarium. Fish lay lifeless and smelly on the hardwood floor.

Hunt opened windows, while Molly turned away, nausea roiling through her stomach. He came back to her side and urged her to sit down in a chair he had moved closer to the breeze blowing into the room.

"You okay?"

She nodded, wondering if she'd ever be completely okay again. At the same time, without Hunt with her, these past few days and past moments would have been impossibly difficult and wrenchingly painful to deal with.

"Stay here while I take a look around." He was gone a few minutes. "Bedroom is the same. Kitchen isn't as bad. Whatever they were looking for, they must have assumed wouldn't be in the kitchen. Here. Found this in the refrigerator."

He handed her a can of ginger ale, and when she made no move to open it, he popped the top. The can was icy, and Hunt urged it to her mouth. She took a sip and the fizziness danced on her tongue, refreshing her sandpapery mouth. She took another drink before handing it back.

He took a long, long swallow and then put the can aside.

"All this time it's been like this," Molly murmured as much to herself as to Hunt.

Hunt was examining some papers he'd picked up. He stopped and looked at her. "All this time what's been like what? What are you talking about?"

"Since Vern died. His apartment has been like this."

"Probably not. The police searched it, but Sean said someone had beat them to it. My guess is this was done around the time Pascale grabbed you."

"I think I interrupted them."

Hunt scowled, righted another chair, then sat down opposite her. "Molly, I'm missing something. You interrupted who?"

In that instant, Molly knew she should have mentioned making the phone call and the odd response. How silly she'd been then. My God, she'd just thought the man was rude when in fact he was probably some goon who'd come to search Vern's apartment.

"Molly?"

Again, she covered her face with her hands.

Hunt pulled them away and cupped her chin, but when he tried to get her to look at him, she wouldn't. "Sweetheart, you're scaring the hell out of me. Interrupted who? What's going on?"

She had to hold him; she had to be in his arms. She needed him to anchor her. She slipped onto his lap and locked her arms around him.

Hunt's hands went to her hips, then her bottom. Molly squirmed closer. He worked his hands beneath the material of her skirt and found the satin panties.

"What the hell am I doing?" he muttered almost to himself before yanking his hands away and pulling her dress back into place. He moved his hands higher. His voice was gruff when he said, "Talk to me, Molly. Come on."

She swallowed. "I called here the morning after Vern died."

Scowling, Hunt leaned back so that he could see her face. "You called this number? Why?"

"I thought Vern might have asked a neighbor to feed his fish or bring in his mail and that I might get lucky and find someone here so I could ask some questions."

"Questions about what?"

She gave him a withering look and got off of his lap. He didn't try to stop her. Molly folded her arms across her chest, unsure whether she was disappointed or hurt by Hunt's lack of intuitiveness. He didn't get it. After all she'd told him about her past, all the angst and desperate sense of isolation she'd felt from Vern. Still, he didn't get it.

"About my brother, for heaven's sake. The brother the whole world knows better than I do."

His scowl deepened, as if he knew what was coming.

"If you give someone the key to your apartment, that means you trust them. I thought if I talked to someone Vern trusted, they could give me some answers about him."

Hunt shook his head. "You hoped some neighbor was going to say he was a saint who bought food for the homeless?"

She stiffened at his obvious scorn. "I don't know what I was expecting. I was having a hard time dealing with Vern's death."

"So you called and chatted with some jerk who was probably connected to Pascale. What revelations did he make?"

"Stop being so snide. The man was rude and hung up on me."

"What a surprise," Hunt muttered, rolling his eyes. "Did you tell him your name or that you were his sister?"

"Obviously I didn't know who they were."

"Did you identify yourself?" he asked, undeterred.

She paced the room, weaving around the items scattered on the floor. When she stopped, a few feet between them, she asked, "How can you make an ordinary statement sound like top-secret information?" When he lifted one eyebrow and stared at her with a "You're stalling" look, she snapped, "All right! Yes, I told him my name."

"Damn!" Hunt raked his hand across his face, looking weary and frustrated. "No wonder Pascale honed in on you like a missile. He had a name, he read the newspapers, figured you had Vern's important things, put two and two together, made his appearance, found you and bingo. You sent him an invitation!"

Molly resumed her pacing, her irritation with him twisting like a corkscrew. She whirled on him, her hands planted firmly on her hips, her eyes furious.

"Well, I'm sorry I'm such a idiot, Mr. Gresham. I should have asked the expert ex-cop exactly what to do. Unlike you, I'm not suspicious of everyone I meet or talk to. Of course, if I were, then your volunteering to protect me would have been much easier, wouldn't it? I certainly wouldn't have gone off with Pascale if I were as brilliant as you. Only a simpleton would have trusted someone because they showed her pictures of her brother."

He reached for her. "Molly..."

She stepped away. "And don't patronize me with platitudes and empty apologies. Might I remind you that without those moments with Pascale, we wouldn't know about this notebook?"

"I can't argue with that," he said softly.

His comment took the punch from her argument. Suddenly she was tired and wishing she could be anywhere but where she was. She fiddled with the ring Hunt had given her, thinking she should take it off and hand it back. Pascale had been clearly skeptical that Hunt was her husband. No one was fooled. The ring was as much of a farce as everything else between them.

Yet last night had felt so real, so wonderful and fulfilling. She shrugged off the memory—an aberration, a few cherished moments with Hunt all wrapped in one night.

Picking up the ginger ale can, she took a swallow and put it back down. "I know you don't understand me or my take on all of this, but you've never had anything like this happen to you. It's just one horrible discovery after another. I'm almost glad I haven't found Francine and Brandon. She's probably some horrible witch who gets pleasure out of hurting people."

Hunt drew her close and, when she tried to push him away, held her fast. Finally she relented. She hated arguing with him; she even hated being at odds with him.

Hunt said, "Shhh. I should have tried harder to

see this the way you do. And I shouldn't have expected you to do things the way I would have. I know this has been rough, but you're trying to re-create an image that—"

She stiffened, gearing up for another defense of her brother. Hunt retreated.

"Okay, okay. Maybe beneath it all, Vern was a swell guy. Obviously he loved you and cared about you. Can't that be enough?"

She wanted it to be, but their separation and her work to find him had been her life. Now her need to know about him was all that she had left. "Is it enough for you that Kristin loved and cared about you? Losing her has changed your life, too."

"That's different."

He tried to pull away, but this time Molly wouldn't let him. "Different only in that your shock and anger were directed at the cancer. You had the answers and couldn't change them, but I bet you tried."

He gave her a hard look, and she knew she'd hit a nerve. Hurrying on, she said, "I bet you insisted Kristin get a second and even a third opinion. I bet you looked into alternative treatments all the while telling yourself you were wasting time, but unable to stop. And I'd even wager you made a few furious phone calls when you didn't get answers. You loved her, and you desperately wanted someone to tell you it was all a mistake, a misdiagnosis, anything that would mean she wasn't going to die."

She took a shaky breath. The paleness she saw in

his face, the raw truth his eyes revealed told her more than words that Hunt had been as desperate in his denial of Kristin's cancer as Molly had been of her brother's career.

"Perhaps that's why you were so determined I face the truth about Vern." Molly pressed her hand against his heart and felt the pound of truth. In that moment she hurt for him and all that he'd gone through, all that he'd lost and been unable to prevent.

In a soothing voice, she said, "Hunt, don't you see? You at least had answers, as cruel and horrible as they were. I have no answers and no way of knowing if they could have been changed. Vern had no time to tell me why he became what he was. So I'm left with endless questions."

Hunt pushed away from her, turning so that she couldn't see his face. His voice was low and bitter and ragged with pain. "I hated her for dying. I hated that I couldn't do anything, that some goddamn medical test was screwed up and Kristin was paying for that with her life. For months after the funeral, I lived in a rage I couldn't shake. It didn't matter how much I drank or how many women I had sex with or how much I was told that my reactions weren't unusual, the fury didn't go away."

Then he sagged into a chair, throwing his head back and staring at the ceiling. "I can't believe I'm saying all this to you." Then, as if he'd broken some self-induced code of silence, he said bitterly, "I never talk about Kristin and what happened."

"We did before," she reminded him gently. "You told me about the house and the diagnosis."

"Yeah, I did, didn't I?" he said, sounding astonished.

Molly felt honored that he'd been so open with her. Even with his sister, Molly knew he'd been closemouthed. "Kristin is an off-limits subject," Denise had told her shortly after Molly learned Hunt's wife had died.

Molly perched on the arm of his chair and placed her hand on his arm. "Maybe it proves that in some fundamental way we are alike. We've both lost people we loved. It's made us angry because it came when we thought life was at its best."

Hunt had noted the change in direction the conversation had taken. In some strange way she had made them emotional allies. Hardly a position of strength for him, nor did it help his denial of anything between them. He sighed. Maybe she was right. "You're wrong."

She gave him a direct look. "No, I'm not, but you don't have to agree with me for me to know it's true." Then in a segue of logic that made Hunt's mind spin, she added, "Like last night, you said you didn't want to make love with me, but I knew you did."

"Yeah? And I suppose that came from your vast storehouse of knowledge about sex."

She reached up and patted his cheek, not at all put

off by his remark. "I know about you and that's enough."

Hunt cursed and moved away from her. The August breeze blew in the smell of someone cooking on a grill, the sound of laughter and a dog barking.

Finally Molly said, "If whoever I spoke to that day had searched here and found what he wanted, then Pascale wouldn't have approached me. You said the police already searched. Pascale's men must have come back here. In fact, since Pascale and Vern were enemies—" She grabbed Hunt's arm, her excitement racing. "I just thought of something."

"What?"

"The pictures. I bet they were taken from here after I called. Once they found out who I was, Pascale wanted something he could use to work on the grieving sister and gain my trust."

Hunt looked thoughtful, then nodded. "Possible. He got the photos and then used the album as the bait to get you to go out to the car with him."

"Yes."

"It makes sense, but what you said earlier also makes sense. They didn't find what they were originally looking for, and you didn't have it, so they returned and really tore the place apart."

"So if there *is* anything, it's still here."

"Let's get started."

Two hours later, Hunt had unbuttoned his shirt and Molly had shed her hose. She sat Indian-style on Vern's bed in front of a fan. She'd opened the buttons of her dress to the lace of her bra, uncaring that she was so exposed. Nor did she care that she'd hiked her dress up so the air could reach her legs.

Hunt's chest was damp and his frustration obvious. "I don't know where else to look. We've combed through everything, and there's nothing even marginally suspicious. Your brother was either brilliant in his ability to hide something or he never hid anything here in the first place."

"He was brilliant."

"Or canny."

"Both."

Hunt grinned. "Okay. So where would a brilliant and canny brother hide something important?"

Suddenly Molly scrambled off the bed. "Oh, my God."

"What? What?"

"Hunt, I know. I know." She danced around like a hundred-million-dollar lottery winner. "Behind the baseboard in the kitchen." She hurried past Hunt and into the tiny kitchen, where she looked for a baseboard. There was none. Counters and appliances covered all the exposed wall space.

"Damn. There has to be some. When we were kids, Vern used to hide money he won playing poker behind a baseboard. It was his secret hiding place and he swore me to silence when I caught him one day. He used that money to buy food when our parents took off and left us. Vern told me to never hide anything in a bedroom—it's the first place a thief looks."

"A baseboard would only work as a hiding place in an old house. New ones have plastered walls or wallboard."

"This is an old house."

"That it is." Hunt opened the pantry door and pulled a light cord. The closet was stuffy and suffocatingly hot, but Hunt pointed to the back wall and the baseboard. "What do you think?"

"See if any are loose."

He moved a few six-packs of beer aside to give him room to work. The tight space plus the pantry shelves made the back wall just barely accessible.

Hunt lay down on his back and twisted to see underneath a low shelf. "Molly, get me a knife, not too long."

She opened drawers and found a table knife. She stooped down and handed it to him.

"Thanks." He picked blindly along the top of the molding. The inaccessibility and the darkness of the area made it impossible to see what he was doing. Molly heard his strained breathing, a few grunts and finally a soft thud.

"You found a loose baseboard?"

"Yeah." He coughed. "Now let's see if there's anything here."

Molly hovered in a stooped position behind him, her hands clenching and unclenching around his thigh, her pulse racing. "Did you find something?"

"Just a sec. I hope no rats took up residence in here."

Molly shuddered, and then in that split second, she remembered that her brother had always kept a mousetrap in his hiding place.

"Hunt, be careful—"

A tinny snap. Then his yowl.

"Dammit!"

Molly flinched, pressing her teeth together in an empathetic grimace. Then the mousetrap skidded past her.

"Nice guy, your brother," Hunt grumbled. "He didn't even trust the mice."

"Is your finger okay?"

"No. It hurts like hell."

She grinned and patted his thigh. "I promise we'll get it all washed and make the hurt go away."

"I'm gonna hold you to— Molly, I found something."

"What is it? What?"

"Scoot back."

She did as he said and watched as he worked his way out of the tight space. Finally he was on his feet, wiping the sweat from his forehead.

Molly reached up and picked some cobwebs from his hair and shirt. In his hand, the same one with the rapidly swelling finger, was a small gray notebook.

Molly grinned, her excitement obvious, and Hunt winked. "We make quite a team. Come on, let's get out of this hot room and see what we've got."

Back in the bedroom, they sat side by side on the bed and Hunt opened his find.

A number of pages were written on, and the writing was in columns. Numbers and letters.

"This is the same sequence—"

Hunt clamped a hand over her mouth, then held a finger to his lips. She nodded.

Hunt continued to stare intently at the numbers and letters. Then his finger stopped at one, but before Molly could ask any questions, he tumbled her back on the bed and kissed her.

His head angled and his body moved against hers. When he lifted his lips, her eyes were glazed, and as much as she hated to admit it, she wanted him.

"Are we going to—?"

"Get outta here," he whispered against her ear. "Should have considered the possibility earlier, but the jerks who trashed the place could have planted a few bugs."

"Oh." She tried to hide her disappointment. "I thought you just wanted to kiss me."

"That, too." He grinned, and unable to resist any longer, he dipped his head and kissed the top of her breasts, where they spilled from the open dress. Her skin was warm and fragrant, and when he nudged one breast from the lacy bra cup, her nipple was too hard and sweet to resist. Molly slipped her hands into his hair holding his mouth against her. He suckled, and her breathless sigh sent him after her other breast. He pressed kisses on her while his hand moved to the juncture of her legs. He touched her and felt the heat of her desire.

With his mouth brushing kisses from her breasts to her cheeks, he murmured, "Want me, don't you?"

"Yes." Her bold affirmation brought a new and deeper hunger into his eyes.

"I do love an honest woman."

"You're supposed to say you want me, too."

"Do I have to say it? Isn't it obvious?"

"I like hearing it as much as I like feeling it."

He leaned closer and whispered in her ear.

Her cheeks burned, but she placed her mouth against his ear and repeated back to him that she wanted the same thing.

Hunt groaned, nestling against her so that their hips rubbed with a sizzling heat. "A few more comments like that and I'm not going to wait until we get home."

She smiled the smile of a woman who knew she was in control and loving it. "Then I won't have to beg and coax you."

"No, ma'am."

He rolled off her, pulling her to her feet, once again holding his finger to his mouth to indicate silence.

She gathered her hose and shoes and purse. Hunt took her arm as they made their way through the apartment. Hunt closed the windows and locked the door on their way out.

"We'll have to come back," Molly said. "I have to clean things out."

Hunt nodded.

In the car, he cranked up the air conditioner, handed Molly the notebook to hold and drove to the nearest pay phone.

"SEAN SULLIVAN," Hunt said, when the precinct desk answered.

"Not here. Who is this?"

"Hunt Gresham. Do you know where I can reach him?"

"Should be back here by four," the officer said, deftly avoiding Hunt's question.

Hunt hung up, dumped some more change in the slot and dialed Sean's cell phone. The phone wasn't on. Hunt stood, his hand resting on the receiver, trying to think where his old partner might be. Then he grinned, dumped in more change and dialed another number.

On the fourth ring, it was answered by the one woman Hunt knew who could wear a feather boa over a leather jacket and not look like she'd stumbled out of a flea market clearance.

"Julie, this is Hunt Gresham. Sean there with you?"

"Why Hunt, honey, is this really you? I haven't seen or heard from you since we had that little old party over in Cambridge."

"Yeah, well, life's just a jungle of missed opportunities, isn't it?" He'd never been to any party with Julie in Cambridge or anywhere else, but to Julie if you were male, then you must have been somewhere with her at sometime.

"Sean is getting dressed." Her voice lowered to a seductive rasp. "So why don't you ever come and see me?"

"And risk my life if Sean found out? Sorry, but I don't have a death wish." In fact, he'd never been interested in Julie Bliss, but it stretched the truth to say Sean would have cared one way or another. Their relationship had been off as much as on, and Sean had made no secret of the fact that she was willing and convenient. Since his divorce, five years ago, he'd sworn off anything with a woman more serious than an afternoon romp in the sack. Julie gave him that.

Now her giggle broke through his thoughts and Hunt rolled his eyes. He glanced back at the car where Molly waited and realized what a profound difference there was between what Sean had with Julie and what he and Molly had done the previous night. Even while Hunt was insisting it was just sex, he knew better. The hell of it was that sex was easy to walk away from; what he had shared with Molly was complicated and tangled. And her giving him her virginity...

"Hunt, how the hell did you find me?"

"Process of elimination."

Immediately on the defensive, Sean said, "I had a couple of hours off."

"Was I asking?"

"Just want you to know I'm not messing around on taxpayers' time."

"You never did, Sean."

"Damn right. So I presume you got something."

"The mother of all pieces to this puzzle." Hunt went on to tell him about finding the notebook and where, the columns and the number and letter sequence. "You remember a few years ago when I worked that case where Rudy Moschetta was gunned down at his summer cottage? The address was 354 Old Beach Drive?"

"Yeah, I remember the case, but the address doesn't ring any bells."

"It made an impression on me because the 354 was part of my old phone number, but my point is that the notebook had a notation 354 OBD. That would be short for the address, and since all the entries are coded in the same way, I figured Wallace must have had trouble remembering addresses so he wrote them down. But he did it so that they wouldn't be easily recognized. There were five entries after that and then the 827 BOS. We're looking in the wrong direction. My guess is that all these entries are addresses."

"Well, I'll be damned. How many are there?"

"A few dozen."

"I don't suppose there's any secondary coding that would clue us in as to towns or cities."

"No such luck, but there are dates, and with a match to past hits that Wallace was contracted for, we should have the Pascale connection. The hits for Pascale and the ones for Solozi."

"My God! We might be able to nail them both and stop the next hit. What about a date on the last entry?"

"None. Wallace must have waited until the contract was complete to date it."

"Okay, we'll use a database and see what we can find. Digging through all the streets in Massachusetts is going to take some time. Got a new guy here we call the cyber cop. He's been working on crimes committed by computer. This isn't his thing, but he might have some ideas on the fastest way to track it down. Thanks, Hunt. This wasn't supposed to be your problem, but sending you off with the sister was a good move."

"Yeah."

"How did the funeral go?"

"The boys were no-shows. After Molly made Pascale and his pals look like three extras from a bad gangster movie, I think they decided to let things cool down." Hunt told Sean about Molly's phone call to the apartment and the search after the police had been there.

"I'll get on this. Staying with her wasn't so tough, was it?"

Hunt reminded himself to stop at a drugstore for condoms. "I'm making sure I'm prepared for anything."

"Good, good. Julie, cut it out. I gotta get back to work." Sean groaned.

Hunt chuckled. "I'll check with you later. Don't forget you're due back at four. Tax dollars don't cover your personal overtime."

"Screw you, Gresham."

Hunt laughed, hung up and went back to the car.

"Well? What did Sean say?"

"I'll fill you in on the way to the drugstore."

"I already bought some at the convenience store."

Hunt scowled. "Bought what?"

She opened her purse and took out an unopened box of condoms.

Hunt thought he was long past being astonished by a woman, but Molly was something else.

"Pretty sure of yourself, aren't you?"

"I was only anticipating. Last night wasn't planned, and I'm sure I'll be okay, but..." As his face grew darker and his mouth grimmer, she said, "You're angry."

"I don't like being maneuvered, Molly. One night doesn't mean more nights."

"But at Vern's apartment—"

"I was trying to keep you from talking."

"We talked earlier and you didn't act worried."

"Before wasn't as important," Hunt said vaguely,

but he knew he simply hadn't considered a bug. Or had Molly flummoxed his thought processes?

"So the kiss was all a diversion. It meant nothing to you?"

"I didn't say that."

"Then what are you saying?"

"That I don't intend to spend the rest of the time we're together in bed with you."

She turned away, and he knew he'd hurt her pride and probably attacked her need to not appear young and innocent. She wanted to be bold and sexy. He really should apologize, but at the moment having her think he was a bastard made it a hell of a lot easier to avoid making use of those condoms.

CHAPTER TWELVE

MOLLY SAW THEM sitting on the top front step.

The woman was waiflike, her complexion pale against her dark hair. Sunglasses shielded her eyes. She wore a gray sleeveless blouse tucked into a blue-and-gray pleated skirt. Clutched close to her was a loosely woven straw bag the size of carry-on luggage. Seated beside her was a small boy in shorts and a T-shirt. A Boston Red Sox cap, worn with the bill backward, nearly covered his hair. In his hands were baseball cards, which he shuffled absentmind-edly. He looked bored, and she looked anxious.

Molly knew exactly who they were.

She had the car door open when Hunt's hand gripped her arm and stopped her. "Be careful what you say," he warned.

Still stung by their conversation of just moments ago, she asked, "Am I allowed to identify myself or should I call myself Ms. X?"

She didn't miss his scowl. "Don't be a smart mouth. We don't have any idea what her connection is or why she's here."

"I'll leave that to you to figure out. She's my sis-ter-in-law, and that's my nephew, and I don't intend to let you make our first meeting an inquisition.'' She slid from the car and closed the door before he could say anything more.

The woman got to her feet, sliding her sunglasses up into her hair. Her eyes were toffee colored and wide, unblinking when she saw Molly. Her fierce determination was an attitude Molly understood and identified with.

The boy peered up at her, lower lip pushed out, his head tipped to the side. She saw the stubbornness in his expression that so perfectly mirrored Vern's when he'd been that age. Molly was awed by the resemblance.

"You're Francine, and this must be Brandon. I recognize you from the pictures," Molly said, her voice cracking slightly with emotion. This was her family…her only connection to her brother. The realization rushed at her with an all-consuming intensity. She had so many things she wanted to ask and say that she had to hold herself in check so as to not bombard Francine.

Behind her she heard Hunt approach, then he stopped, making her think he'd decided to stay back and let her have this time with Francine and Brandon.

"I hope you don't mind me just coming here," Francine said, her gaze sliding from Molly to Hunt and back to Molly.

"Of course not. I've so hoped to meet you. But how did you know where to find us?"

"I followed you after you left the funeral home

yesterday. You were so obviously upset I decided to wait another day.''

Puzzled, Molly said, "I didn't see you there. I would have contacted you, but I had no address. I hated that you had to find out through an obituary.''

"Actually, I learned about it first from a newspaper story. Then I came here to Fernwood and saw the obituary." She adjusted her straw bag on her shoulder. "I was late getting to the funeral home, and there were so many visitors, then the chaos after you disappeared. I didn't go into the viewing room until everyone had left. But I saw your friend outside near the parked cars." She nodded toward Hunt. "He was very upset.''

Molly turned around. Hunt was leaning against the front fender, his own sunglasses in place and his arms folded. He reminded her of some macho bodyguard ready to draw and fire on a split second's notice. His sphinxlike stillness made her feel both secure and nervous.

One moment she thought she knew him, and the next, like now, he was as distant as a stranger. He apparently viewed even reasonable situations, such as this meeting, as needlessly complicated. Obviously police work had jaded him to the point where he took nothing at face value.

Francine continued. "Your friend drove off, and when I asked a man where you were, he said he didn't know but that your friend would be back. So I waited.''

Molly glanced at Hunt again. He'd removed his sunglasses. "Did you see them at the funeral home?"

"At the time, I was more worried about finding you." His words betrayed little emotion, his eyes focused on Francine.

To Francine, she said, "Oh, this is Hunt Gresham. He was with me at the hospital when Vern died. He's my..." She stopped herself, realizing she didn't need to explain. "He didn't want me to come to the funeral alone." She studied Francine. "I don't understand why I never noticed you yesterday."

"Because I didn't want you to." At Molly's confusion, she added, "I wasn't sure how much Vern had told you about Brandon and me. So I went late and hoped to catch you after the others had left."

"And you didn't want her to see you today, either, did you?" Hunt's tone was crisp and suspicious.

Francine looked at him, her eyes not flinching. "It was a moment for Molly to say her final goodbyes to Vern, not for me to appear and distract everyone."

Molly was beginning to think she was blind. She had spoken to the few women who had attended the funeral in hopes that one of them would be Francine. "You were at the cemetery, too?"

"I stayed at a distance."

"Ah, the thoughtful widow," Hunt said in a tone that Molly decided was unnecessarily nasty. "She was mourning all alone near the entrance, ready to run and hide if anyone got too close. Weren't you, Mrs. Wallace?"

"You saw her and never said anything to me?" Molly glared at him.

"I wasn't positive then. I am now."

"How convenient. Could it be that you were more anxious to search Vern's apartment?"

"You were the one who insisted on going to the apartment," he said flatly.

He was right, and that annoyed Molly. "You could have at least pointed her out and let me decide if a lone woman with a small boy just might be Vern's family," she snapped. Molly was fuming at his assumptions and attitude. "What did you think I was going to do? Rush over to her before she disappeared?"

Hunt gave her a direct look. "Yeah, I think that's exactly what you would have done." He resumed watching Francine.

Again he was correct. *My God*, Molly thought, *does he know me better than I know myself?* Of course he didn't. He knew how anxious she'd been about finding them, though. If she'd seen a woman and a small boy at a distance, what other conclusion could he have drawn?

The boy had moved higher on the steps, giving the impression that he would defend his mother if Hunt got too close.

Hunt asked, "Were you sent by Pascale to watch Molly and see what she was going to do?"

Francine visibly shuddered. "No."

"Hunt, stop it!"

He ignored her. "And what about her ride with Pascale yesterday? Did you know about that? Can we expect Pascale and his goons to arrive later, now that you've found us? You got a cell phone in that bag? Did you call Pascale when you saw us coming down the street?" The questions came in a rapid-fire delivery. He straightened and moved slowly forward. Francine tugged Brandon against her, her eyes a little frantic.

Brandon said, "You leave my mother alone!"

Hunt hesitated, his gaze falling on the boy for a few seconds before going back to Francine.

Molly stepped between them, then turned on Hunt, her own eyes narrowed. "Let me have the house key."

He didn't move. He wasn't looking at Molly, either, but still focusing on Francine.

"Damn you, Hunt."

Finally, he stared down at her. His blue eyes locked with hers in a possessiveness she'd never seen before. Not passionately, but with the authority of someone who never took anything as it appeared until he'd weighed every possible consequence. It gave Molly pause, because she guessed he viewed their relationship—as limited as it was—in the same way.

Now, he pulled her close to him, as if he had a secret. He cupped her chin, his hand tense. Molly closed her fingers around his wrist and felt the beating of his pulse. If she moved just a fraction, she could have kissed him. She pushed away the desire and wiped the thought from her mind, scowling at how easily he enticed her.

His voice was low and edged with caution. "You're too trusting, Molly. Pascale knows you're vulnerable when it comes to Vern. Sending a kid with the ex-wife would lure you like fish to bait. No doubt he's still looking for that notebook and might have decided a woman and kid might get info out of you easier than he could. You don't even know if she is who she says she is."

"And you don't know that she's not," she countered. "For your information, Brandon looks exactly like Vern did at ten years old. And I should know, since that's how old he was when we were orphaned."

"I don't like it."

"You know what? I don't care." She stepped back, pushing his hand from her. "Now, are you going to give me the key or do I have to break a window to get into the house?"

He swore and then muttered something she didn't catch, but he fished the key from his pocket and gave it to her.

Molly opened her purse, took out the box of condoms and slapped them into his hand. "Here. You can dispose of these in the garbage can over there."

She didn't wait for a reaction, but swung away and marched up the steps, unlocked the door and ushered Francine and Brandon inside. She let the screen door slam without looking back at him.

Molly invited them to sit down. From the refrigerator, she took a can of soda for Brandon, and fixed iced tea for herself and Francine. Brandon busied himself with the TV, while his mother sat so that she could watch him and still talk with Molly.

Molly perched on the edge of a green ivy-patterned slipcovered chair; her knees were together, her glass between both hands. Now that the actual moment she'd been anticipating was here, she didn't know where to begin.

"I have so many questions," Molly said.

Francine nodded. "Please tell me first how you found Vern. He promised to give me the details after he returned from his visit..." Her voice trailed off, and she was quiet a moment. Both women reflected on the tragic turn of events. Then Francine said, "I never even knew he had a sister until he told me you contacted him. He was always careful about concealing his personal life. But he was so excited about hearing from you, I think he needed to tell someone the good news. He told me about the adoption and the separation."

Molly grasped on to one word. "Excited. Vern was really excited?" At Francine's nod and smile, Molly said, "At first, he seemed uneasy, reluctant about our meeting each other...of course, then I didn't know..."

Francine reached over and cupped Molly's shoulder in a gesture of understanding. "He wanted to protect you. He didn't want you to know what he was. But, Molly, he couldn't wait to see you."

Molly's heart swelled so much, she thought it would burst from her chest. She lowered her head, her eyes damp with tears. All over again, she felt the grief of losing her brother when she'd barely found him.

"I'm sorry if I upset you."

Molly wiped at her eyes and took a swallow of iced tea. "You haven't. Everything has happened so quickly. I've learned so many things lately, some of them not very pleasant."

Francine nodded.

Molly cleared her throat. For the next fifteen minutes, she told about the years she'd searched for her brother, the agencies that had helped her, and her deep terror that she'd never find him. She paused, then asked Francine. "His heart. How long had he known he had a bad heart?"

"A few years."

"Was he taking care of himself?"

"Not as well as he should have been. His doctor, Amos Crombie, moved his practice to Florida in July. In the Jacksonville area, I believe. To my knowledge, Vern hadn't gotten around to finding another doctor."

"But with a bad heart—"

"Molly, you have to understand," Francine said gently. "For Vern a heart attack was the least of his problems. His work made every day he was alive a plus. He simply never thought he'd die in an ordinary way. He had a 'live by the gun, die by the gun' mindset. Death from a heart attack…he didn't think that would ever happen.''

Molly listened, trying to comprehend her brother's logic.

Francine went on, "His doctor and I were the only ones who knew. Vern was very private. If that kind of news became public, it would mean disaster in the world he lived in. His boss would never chance giving Vern a contract in the event that something unplanned happened.''

Like what *did* happen, Molly thought. Vern dying unexpectedly while possessing dangerous information. Pascale and his goons looking for an incriminating notebook. The police on a frantic search to learn when and where the hit would be carried out so they could stop it. Molly wondered if Vern's boss had canceled the contract or given it to someone else. So many involved because her brother had unexpectedly died. Even Hunt.

Wearily, Molly said, "If Vern had been killed in the way he thought he would, he'd be just another mob statistic. But instead, his passing has provoked a lot of people.''

"Yes, it has.''

The door opened, and Molly and Francine glanced up.

Hunt had returned with two triple-scoop ice-cream cones covered with chocolate sprinkles. "Never could resist an ice-cream parlor,'' he said with that heart-jumping smile that Molly found so mesmerizing. "Hey, Brandon.''

Her nephew turned, his eyes widening at the mammoth cones.

Hunt walked up to him. "Hope you like chocolate.''

"Yeah.''

Hunt offered him a cone. "Here. You better lick quick, it's starting to drip.''

Brandon stood and carefully took the top-heavy cone, immediately licking the sides.

Molly stared, amazed at Hunt's transformation. Gone were the suspicion and the guarded eyes. He barely glanced at Francine.

"Think we should go outside so these don't make a mess?''

Brandon glanced at his mother. After Hunt's quizzing of her earlier, she didn't look too agreeable to entrusting her son to him.

Hunt pushed the issue by saying, "I wanted to ask you some questions about your baseball card collection. I've got a couple of nephews who collect, and I'm not sure which are the good cards.''

Ice cream ringed Brandon's mouth. The idea that he could give advice on baseball cards had him standing a little taller and giving his mother pleading looks.

Francine still didn't look too sure.

Molly intervened. "It's okay, Francine. Hunt does

have two nephews who collect cards. Their birthdays are coming up in a few months, and Hunt has been wondering what to get for them. Haven't you, Hunt?"

Hunt gave her a measured look. "It's been on my mind for the past twenty-four hours."

Francine glanced from one to the other, looking a bit confused, but she made no comment.

Hunt held the door while Brandon walked outside. The screen door closed, and she heard Hunt say, "Let's sit here so your mom knows where you are."

Very clever, Hunt Gresham, Molly thought with some amusement. *Act like a nice guy so I'll forgive you, then sit by the door so you can hear what Francine and I talk about.*

She heard Brandon's voice and something about a complete set of the 1967 Red Sox Impossible Dream team. Hunt asked some questions, and within a short time they sounded like two collectors exchanging information.

Molly sat back in her chair, crossing her legs and feeling somewhat content. Hunt, in effect, had apologized; a step she would have thought impossible twenty minutes ago. Francine, too, seemed relaxed, which reminded Molly she still had lots of questions.

"How did you and Vern meet?"

"We lived on the same street here in Fernwood. I worked at the deli in a local grocery store. Vern would come in for sandwiches and we'd talk. Then one night, on my way home, some guy tried to snatch my purse. Vern was coming out of his place and he nabbed the guy. I was so grateful. I'd just cashed my paycheck, and if I'd lost that money I couldn't have paid my bills.''

Her brother helping Francine and her brother being a hit man just didn't fit, but Molly liked it that way. It proved to her that Vern had never lost his way when it came to those he cared about.

"We started seeing each other—dating, I guess you'd call it," Francine said, laughing a little at her own memories. "But Vern didn't want to live with me and he didn't ask me to move in with him." She glanced toward the screen door, where Hunt and Brandon could easily be seen. The cones were rapidly diminishing. In a whispery voice, she said, "We were together, you know, in a sexual way, but Vern was adamant about separate apartments. Later, when I learned what he did, I knew why."

"He wanted you to be safe."

"Yes."

Molly leaned forward. "How, uh...or maybe I should ask why...did he get into the work he did?"

"Money. Vern liked to gamble, and sometimes his losses were big. He ran with a tough crowd growing up, learned to use a knife and a gun. He knew who ran the streets and who to see if you needed anything done. He and Pascale were close. They'd play cards together. Vern knew he did a lot of illegal stuff, but Pascale was nice to him, loaned him money, that sort of thing. He was really sucking Vern into his operation. I think Vern always knew, but when he looked around at his options, a minimum-wage job looked pretty lousy compared to Pascale's offer.''

"Was he with Pascale when you met him?"

"Yes, but more as a gofer. He had to prove that he could be trusted.''

Molly considered that and realized, in the end, Vern had looked out for himself. He hadn't trusted Pascale, as evidenced by the notebook he'd kept. Vern definitely lived in a world of everyone for himself.

Molly continued, "After you married him...was he a hit man then?"

Francine shook her head vigorously. "He was one of Mr. Pascale's bodyguards. After Brandon was born I begged Vern to get out, but by that time he was in too deep. Plus he had gambling debts. Vern adored Brandon. More than he loved me, I think. I sent Brandon to live with my mother up in Maine, hoping that Vern would miss him enough to leave Pascale. But he didn't. The money he made was a huge incentive, ten times more than he'd ever make doing honest work. And by then he'd already done a couple of contracts—sleazy guys, but I couldn't have our son living with a man who killed people to make a living. Deep down, I think Vern agreed with me. He was glad Brandon was somewhere safe. Then something happened...'' She hesitated, and Molly leaned forward.

"I guess it doesn't matter if you know. It was a

long time ago. Pascale had a guy killed for trying to muscle in on a drug-dealing operation. Vern knew the man had been fingered to take the fall for someone else. He did everything he could to convince Pascale, but the old bastard took that to mean Vern was protecting his enemy. They had a falling-out and Vern sent me away. He laid low for a long time and then hooked up with another guy. He was called Weasel, and he was a hit man who worked for Solozi, a rival of Pascale's. But Vern was scared of Pascale. We had a terrible fight. I blamed him for not getting free of them when he still could, and he blamed me for trying to make him into something he wasn't. In the end, the divorce was a mutual agreement.''

"Oh, Francine, how awful.''

"I missed him so much,'' she said sadly, her eyes misty. "We would meet and then Vern would set up some complicated arrangement so he could be with Brandon. But it was always dangerous and tense.'' She shook her head derisively. "When we first fell in love, we had no money but we had each other. Later, I had all the money I wanted, but I didn't have a husband and my son didn't have his father.''

Molly's eyes glistened. Poor Vern. He was always looking out for those he cared for, but at the same time he was doing horrible things. No wonder he had a bad heart. It was impossible to reconcile the two life-styles.

"Did you continue meeting?'' Molly asked.

"No. I stopped it about two years ago."

"What did Vern do?"

"He didn't like it, but I had to get on with my life. Molly, it was like living behind a door I was afraid to open. Brandon needed a normal life where he could have friends. We moved to Wilmington, and I got a job at a discount store. Vern insisted I take some money, so I used it to rent a house in a neighborhood with a park nearby. Brandon made friends and so did I."

"Did you stay in touch with Vern?"

She nodded. "By phone, twice a month. He worried, and he wanted to make sure Brandon and I had what we needed. I guess I should be ashamed to admit it, but I took the money he sent us, even knowing it was dirty. I just felt that Vern had a right to give his son a few comforts since he couldn't be there as his father."

"No one is blaming you for anything."

"Oh, Molly, I loved him so much, and I think he truly loved us, too, but the ties he had to the mob were so deep and tangled he couldn't get free." She paused, her head down, her fingers laced together. Molly noticed a ring on her finger, and when Francine turned it, a small diamond caught the sunlight. She rubbed her finger back and forth on the stone, biting her lower lip.

"Francine? What is it?"

She raised her head and looked at Molly, her expression drawn. "I met a man about six months ago.

He has his own appliance repair business. He's thirty-five and divorced, and he's not as handsome as Vern was, and sometimes he stutters when he talks, but he makes me feel safe and he's wonderful with Brandon...." She paused, again touching the ring. "He asked me to marry him and I said yes."

"Oh." Instantly, Molly chastised herself. "He's a very lucky man to be getting you."

"I dreaded telling Vern. It would have been easy if I hated him or he'd been a horrid ex-husband, but neither was true. When Vern called me about going to see you, he was so upbeat and excited, I thought that it was the right time to tell him about Rick."

Then, with an instinctive insight that stunned her, Molly knew exactly how her brother had reacted. "I bet he wasn't angry at all."

"You're right." Francine laughed a little. "In fact, I was a little put out that he didn't rage about how he wouldn't stand for another man having me." She ducked her head, adding, "Odd, but I wanted him to be jealous, and yet if he'd objected to Rick, I would have been upset at that."

"I understand, Francine. Hunt wouldn't, but men don't understand the way a woman's mind works."

Francine laughed, and the sound eased the tension. "You're right."

"Vern wanted you and Brandon to be safe and to have a normal life. When I was adopted and Vern wasn't, it was because he'd acted up to make sure they took me. He wanted me to be safe and have a family life. As hard as it was to be separated, I think he was being the big brother who was determined his baby sister would have the best. With you, he was being the loving husband and father who knew he couldn't give you what you needed, and so he was happy about Rick.''

''But your brother didn't take any chances. I learned from him that he'd known for weeks I was seeing Rick. Vern even knew about the engagement. He had hired a pal of his to make sure nothing happened to me. His pal told him about Rick.''

''Vern had him checked out.''

She nodded. ''Thank God Rick was exactly who he said he was.''

''Yes, thank God he was.'' Molly and Francine exchanged glances. Both knew what Rick's fate would have been if he had lied or deceived Francine.

''He told me he wanted me to be happy, but he also didn't want Brandon to forget him. I think the long separation from you made Vern realize how much he didn't want that to happen between him and his son. For the two of us, well, we had planned to be together on the Labor Day weekend.'' Her cheeks colored. ''Brandon was to stay with my mother. Vern and I were going to see each other one last time before I remarried.''

''Where did you plan to meet?''

Francine gave her an odd look. ''West of Worcester. There's a B-and-B we've been to before. Why?''

''I just wondered if you happened to know where

Vern was going after our visit. There's a window of time there—never mind. He probably didn't say anything."

"Vern always told me where he'd be. In case there was an emergency."

The screen door squeaked and Molly glanced up. Hunt stood there while Brandon raced over to his mother.

"Gee, Mom, Hunt said I knew more about baseball cards than anyone, but you know what's really neat?" Without waiting for a comment, he added, "Hunt said if I ever come down to Woodbriar, he'd take me to a collector his nephews know who has cards for every Red Sox player since 1955."

"That was very nice of him."

Hunt was staring at Molly, and she was staring back at him. Between them lay Francine's statement—*Vern always told me where he'd be*. Hunt took a step forward, and Molly held up her hand to stop him. Francine was listening to Brandon chatter about his talk with Hunt.

"He's so cool."

"Yes, I'm sure he is. I think we should be going."

Molly had risen to her feet. A rush of feeling for her nephew and for this woman her brother had loved made her even more determined to make sure Vern's legacy wasn't sealed by another death.

With a bluntness that made Hunt raise his eyebrows, she said, "Francine, I need you to tell me where Vern was going after his visit with me."

Hunt crossed to Molly, his hand touching the small of her back. She felt his tension, and she herself was none too calm.

Francine shuddered. It was obvious she had no intention of saying anything upsetting in front of Brandon, certainly not that his father had been on his way to kill someone.

"Grover." She gave Molly a penetrating look that said she'd better read between the lines because she wasn't going to say much. "It's a small town close to the Mass Pike. There's a huge aquarium there, and Vern often visited it when he was in central Massachusetts. We were going to meet around six in the morning for breakfast. His business was always handled before pleasure."

Hunt and Molly exchanged glances.

827 BOS must be located in Grover. And the hit had been set for some time before dawn.

CHAPTER THIRTEEN

"No, Molly, you're not going."

"And why not?"

"Because it's dangerous and there's no reason for you to be there."

"But I want to be. I have to see for myself who my brother was going to..." She hesitated. "I have to know that person is going to be okay. Preventing something from happening to him is why you wanted to know what the note meant, isn't it?"

Hunt turned away. "Yeah."

"Besides, you'll be with me."

"There's no reason why I should be there, either. I planned to turn this all over to Sean and then go home."

"But it's not finished."

"As far as we're concerned, it is. Sean would have my ass if I let you within ten miles of Grover."

That testy exchange had taken place after the departure of Francine and Brandon. Nothing had been said since.

It was nearly five in the afternoon, and they were in the car on the way to a pay phone so Hunt could call Sean. Molly sat with her arms crossed, staring out the windshield. Hunt was tense. His headache threatened to become permanent. Stubborn and single-minded, Molly was obsessed with the idea that her brother was some kind of dispossessed hero who'd had a life of bad breaks. Hunt grimaced. And he'd deluded himself with the belief that it would get simpler once she accepted who Wallace had been. Instead, she'd become even more determined. Molly's idealism apparently had no limits or boundaries.

Molly and her sister-in-law had exchanged addresses and phone numbers with promises to keep in touch. As he'd watched the two women embrace and Molly ruffle Brandon's hair, Hunt had been struck by her willingness to simply accept them as her family. He knew how vulnerable she was, and he flinched at the possibility she might be hurt or used by them or anyone. Yet she'd plunged in with all the faith of a child; no thought that they might not be what they seem. No worry that she might be stepping into a trap.

Even if Francine was legitimate, it didn't change the fact that she had a lot of information about Vern. Information she'd done nothing with; she'd never gone to the cops or the feds, and yet when Molly asked her directly about the hit, she had answered.

In her conversation with Molly, when Hunt was outside with Brandon—a conversation Hunt had listened to with rapt attention—Francine had never mentioned the notebook. From Hunt's point of view, there was no reason why she shouldn't have unless she didn't know about it. And if Wallace had been determined to protect his son and his ex-wife, he would never have revealed the existence of a notebook that could eventually be used as evidence against Pascale and Solozi.

Good God, he was beginning to use Molly's emotional logic. Annoyed that he'd allowed her to invade his usual credo, he wondered just when he'd begun to let down his guard. *A real no-brainer, Gresham. That happened weeks ago on the day you ran into her in the courtyard and spent too damn long fantasizing about taking her to bed. Well, you did that. So, now what?*

He glanced over at her. She'd changed to shorts and a knit shirt that outlined her breasts without being overly snug. He knew her bra was pink and lacy from when she'd opened her blouse at her brother's overheated apartment. He knew it closed in the front. If he were so inclined, he could unhook it with one hand and have her out of it and the shirt in less than ten seconds.

The truth of the matter was that he wanted her, despite his resolution that it wouldn't happen again.

He wanted her.

Again.

And again.

He wanted her more than he wanted to call Sullivan and definitely more than worrying about some sleaze scheduled to leave this earth compliments of a hit man's best shot.

Hunt said, "You're too quiet. Cooking up some new strategy?"

"Not at all," she said blandly. "I know exactly what I'm going to do. You're the one getting squeamish and barking orders."

He swore. "Did it ever occur to you that I might know a little more about hit men and their targets than you do? And is there any chance you might realize that I don't want you to get hurt and taking you back to Woodbriar is the best way to protect you?"

If he'd had any hope she'd get dewy eyed and compliant, her sideways glance killed the idea. "I understand that, and so far, you've done an exemplary job. I'm sure you're pleased and relieved that your involvement with me is nearly over. You can get on with your life and out of mine."

"Nice delivery but no sale."

She gave him a sugary smile. "I'm stating our, uh, situation the way you have so many times. Oh, and by the way—" she opened her purse and took out the ring he'd bought "—you can return this and get your money back." She dropped the ring into the tray on the console as though it were a turnpike token.

Hunt glanced at the gold band, recalling the purchase, and then slipping it on her finger to allay any suspicion about why he was with her. Little good it had done. Pascale still tricked her, and her escape had more to do with her own quick thinking than his.

The ring meant nothing; it was merely an unnecessary prop. Like their relationship.

He parked at the convenience store. His conscience still nagged him about the intimacy they'd shared, and since things were coming to a close, this might be a good time to clean up any misunderstandings. He turned to her. "Molly, about what happened between us—"

"It meant nothing to you. I know," she said quickly and dismissively. She glanced at the digital clock. "Shouldn't you be calling Sean?"

Yeah, he should, but still he didn't move. Her deliberate efforts to distance herself disturbed him. She had said the right words, but they lacked the kind of fervent passion Molly used when something was important to her. And if getting him out of her life was high on her priority list, then eagerness would be—

Hunt scowled. She didn't have to shove him out of her life as if he were some stubborn male determined to possess her. Something else was going on.

He shifted slightly in the seat, one wrist draped over the steering wheel. "Okay, let's quit playing games. You got some backup plan to get to Grover on your own? Is this cold attitude toward me supposed to stop me from worrying about you?"

She turned. "Why were you so negative about Francine?"

"Ah, so we're back to that. I was being cautious. I'm still cautious."

"Even after all she said? Good grief, Hunt, she

practically handed us the time of the hit, and she definitely gave us the place."

"Maybe."

"You're always so suspicious. If it weren't for Francine, I wouldn't know anything about Vern's past. You're the one person who knows how important it is to me to find out about my brother, and yet the one person who knows the most—"

"Hold it. Is this why you're acting so distant? You think my suspicions about Francine are personal?"

"Are they?"

"Oh, for God's sake," he said in exasperation. "Look, I admit she's probably on the level. I just like people to be up front and not sneaking around, magically appearing when they think it's okay."

"Maybe she was scared. She knows how dangerous Pascale was. Maybe she feared putting herself and Brandon in danger. Pascale could have thought she had the notebook."

Hunt shook his head. "If he had, he would have gone after her. Or maybe he already had and came up with zero. You were the target because you were the last one with Vern. If you hadn't made that phone call to Vern's apartment or identified yourself to the funeral director—" He cut off his own words. "There's no point in rehashing that. It's done...all of this is almost done. Thank God."

She heaved a huge sigh, her shoulders trembling slightly. "There are so few people who knew Vern. And those who did aren't people I want to make friends or have contact with. I have nothing but a few old memories.''

"You have Francine and you have Brandon," Hunt said, giving in to the inevitable. At this juncture, he was resigned to accepting them at face value—unless circumstances proved otherwise. To Molly, he said, "Vern obviously cared a great deal about both of them. When Brandon and I were outside, he told me about his dad and how they would look for four-leaf clovers.''

"Like he did with me," she murmured.

"Yeah. Vern apparently tried to convince Brandon he was better off without him. I don't think Brandon bought it, but I was struck by how similarly Vern treated his son and how he treated you. I'm no shrink, but it appears that he used much the same approach. He obviously cared more for you and Brandon and Francine than he ever cared about himself.''

She didn't say anything, and then slowly nodded her head. "He had a good side. He wasn't just some thug. And I do have Francine and Brandon. I've already learned a lot from them.''

"And you'll learn more. I imagine she can fill in the gaps in Vern's life better than anyone." At least the kind of life Molly wanted to know about. "And unless I miss my guess, she has more pictures.''

Molly's eyes glistened, but Hunt also noted the response he'd hoped to see. Her thoughts and concentration had shifted to her new family and away from her crazy idea of going to Grover. Hunt felt more relieved than he had in days. By this time tomorrow, it would be all over.

Now he touched her cheek, his thumb grazing one of her earlobes. "So, am I forgiven for being overly cautious?"

"Mmm."

"Molly," he warned. "Why do I have the feeling you're up to something?"

She turned a bit, her head tipping toward his fingers. Her gaze slid over him, making him suddenly uncomfortable. The tension that had been bubbling between them boiled up like lava from a volcano. A clanging alarm went off in the recesses of his mind when she moved her hand to his thigh and began picking at a ripped place on the denim.

For a few surreal seconds, Hunt just stared at her fingers as they pressed and feathered and smoothed the fabric. His flesh prickled. Not just on his leg, but on the back of his neck.

And then, to his astonishment, she leaned closer, and with a deft motion, she slid her hand across the denim to dip between his thighs. Hunt jumped but she didn't abandon her target; she brushed her fingers over him, amusement in her eyes. "So are you."

Hunt swore and grabbed her wrist before she could surround him. His body's reaction made him furious; he should have removed her hand when it was in safe territory. She wanted to play? Hell, he could do that.

"Come over here," he growled.

"You're supposed to go call Sean."

"He can wait." He pulled her closer, his mouth covering hers in a crushing kiss. Her lips parted like a thirsty flower, and he tangled his tongue around hers. How could kissing one woman send his mind into a tailspin and make his body plead for more? At some level she had a command over him that Hunt had no idea how to deal with; he just knew he wanted her. He moved his hand across her waist, tugging her shirt free from her shorts. He burrowed beneath the knit top, his fingers climbing her skin and unhooking the bra's front clasp. She caught her breath, and Hunt wondered just how far he would go in a public parking lot. *Just this,* he promised himself. *Just this.* He cupped her breast, and it snuggled into his palm as if it had come home.

He wanted to tell her how beautifully responsive she was.

He wanted to kiss her breasts, her belly, all those sweet secret places.

He wanted to put her hand back between his legs.

Instead he pulled away from her, calling on the remnants of his self-control. He gave her a scalding look. "Works both ways, Molly. You want to play? I can play, too."

The moment he'd said the words he wanted to take them back. She lowered her head, and he felt her physically shrink away. He didn't try to stop her.

"It's more than playing, more than just being with

you. It's always been more for me than sex.'' Her tone held a defiance and a ring of truth that Hunt wanted to ignore.

"No declarations, please." He opened the car door, and she grabbed his arm.

"It's not a declaration. It's the way I feel."

"You feel desire. Hell, so do I, but you're twenty-eight and I'm almost forty. This has all the clichés of a horny jerk who should have known better than to mess with a wide-eyed virgin."

"I was never wide-eyed and I'm not a virgin."

You were wide-eyed, Molly, he thought sadly. *Before you knew who your brother really was, before you took on this crusade, before you allowed yourself to get tangled up with me.*

"Yeah, I took care of that virgin thing, didn't I," he said, furious with himself all over again. "But that doesn't mean it will happen again."

"You want me. You said so."

He was about to deny it, but he decided there was no point. He did want her. If she wanted honesty, he'd give her honesty.

He shoved a hand through his hair and sighed heavily. "All right. I want you. Hell, who wouldn't? You're beautiful and desirable and sexy and responsive. I'd have to be dead to deny an attraction. But I also know that you haven't allowed yourself many boyfriends. You play tennis, you crusade against TV violence, you go to work and you have an occasional date. The rest of the time you were involved in finding Vern. Most women your age would have dated dozens of guys, probably slept with a few. I come along at a time when you were vulnerable. We were thrown together, we shared some painful personal memories, and suddenly you thought you'd found the guy you wanted forever.''

Molly was quiet, her head turned away. No protest was forthcoming. Maybe that was all that had ever been needed—just a careful explanation of their situation. Now she understood and probably felt embarrassed.

He watched the late-afternoon light catch some of the amber streaks in her hair. He wanted to tangle his fingers in it and fold her into his arms. But he didn't. Their time together was nearly finished. If he could stay cool and impersonal for just a little longer, Molly would be better off. Eventually she'd forget about him and find some nice unjaded guy.

Don't think about her with someone else, he warned himself. *Think about getting back to your apartment, doing the lecture series and then moving on.* He'd hoped to stay permanently in Woodbriar, now he questioned that plan. Distance from Molly— that was the key.

He got out of the car.

''Hunt?'' She was leaning across the seat. ''I still want to go to Grover.''

He'd seen the look, the determination, the ''I will not be deterred'' fervor. Her passion was back. Once again he'd underestimated her.

"My God, you're not gonna give up on this until it's finished, are you?"

"No."

Hunt slammed the door and went to the pay phone. His back had broken out in a sweat and his hands were shaking. By the time he'd filled Sean in, his voice had just barely lost its gruffness.

"Hunt, this is great news. We know where and when. You say the wife was meeting Wallace, so the hit was probably going to be in the can first."

"There is the chance of a cancel, you know. Solozi may not be too keen on carrying out the original plan."

"Possible. We'll know for sure in a few hours."

"I want to know when you've got the exact address in Grover and the meeting set up."

"Hey, you've done more than I expected. Give it up and take the lady home."

"Call me on the cell. We can set up a code."

"Hunt, are you listening to me?"

"We can use that system we used in the Brackett case in '91."

"For God's sake, you've got your hands full with the sister."

"Tell me about it. She wants to be there, Sean."

"Now wait a minute—"

"I know what you're going to say. Save your breath. She knows what I just told you. In fact, if it weren't for Molly, we wouldn't have that. She's going to go whether I like it or not, and believe me, I don't like it, but we're dealing with a determined sister. Trust me on this."

"This is a mob hit, not a frigging picnic."

"Which is why I'm going to make sure I'm with her."

Sean cursed, argued some more, cursed again. "I don't want to see her there, Gresham. You keep her the hell out of the way or I'll arrest the little bitch for obstruction of justice."

They set up their coding arrangement, and a few minutes later, Hunt was driving back to the cottage.

A few hours. Just what he needed; a few hours with Molly. What was he supposed to do with her? Take her to bed, that's what.

He jammed on the brakes.

"What is it?" she asked, giving him a confused look.

"Your brother's place. I think we should go and get things packed up."

"Now?"

"We can't do anything but wait for Sean's call. Might as well make the time productive."

She frowned. "You're probably right. And it will make the waiting more bearable if we're doing something."

"Exactly my thinking."

AT VERN'S PLACE, they packed the personal items Molly wanted to keep. It was nearly 7:30 when they finished. Molly called Myrtle about the rest. The apartment rented furnished, so Molly paid for the damage. The landlady said she would call a co-op that took household items to pick up the remainder of Vern's things.

"I appreciate that," Molly said, signaling to Hunt to take the boxes she wanted down to the car. "I'd like to have a cleaning service come in. I'll take care of that if you could tell me what's a good day."

"Get them for next Monday," Myrtle said, as if it were the least Molly could do. "Place has been empty too long and I'm losin' money."

"I'll see what I can do," Molly said coolly. "Hunt will drop off the key." She hung up, then did a final walk-through to make sure she hadn't missed anything. Vern had surprisingly few personal things; obviously a sign of a man who wanted few reminders of his life. She wondered if things might have been different if Vern had been adopted with her.

She wiped away the dampness in her eyes. She couldn't change the past; she couldn't change her brother from what he'd been to what she wanted him to be. But Hunt's comments about her brother's relationship to Brandon and Francine had buoyed her spirits. In some ways Vern was honest and had a strong sense of what was right and what was wrong. In some ways he was like Hunt. Fiercely protective.

In fact, all her thoughts seemed to lead back to Hunt. *Oh, Hunt,* she thought dismally. *What am I going to do about you? Why does it have to be so hard, and why do you have to be so stubborn?* She was positive she loved him, but he was being so difficult about their having a relationship, she saw little chance of any kind of commitment between them.

Her problem was that she had nothing he wanted. Telling him she wanted more than sex had scared him off even more. Then she was reminded of his comment about her finding a nice guy. Perhaps she should. She might discover, after dating others, that her feelings for Hunt weren't so intense. Besides, real love could withstand any test. Yes. Once home, she would date others and get more involved in social activities.

"It's late and I'm starved," Hunt grumbled. "We done here?"

She glanced up and her heart turned over. He stood in the doorway, his shirt slung over his shoulder and the cell phone in one hand. His hair was mussed, his cheek was smudged. Sweat glistened on his chest, and his jeans rode low on his hips.

Her mouth went suddenly dry, and she was filled with such longing for him, she ached. She wanted to rush into his arms; she wanted to kiss him and make him want to kiss her back.

Instead, Molly curled her fingers into her palms and glanced around for her purse. "Yes. Let's get something to eat."

After leaving the key with Myrtle, they were once again in the car. They stopped at a fast-food place for burgers and fries and took them back to the cottage.

When they'd eaten, Hunt prowled the confines of the cottage. He'd showered and changed into clean jeans, but hadn't bothered with a shirt. The cell phone hadn't been more than a few inches from him since he'd talked to Sean.

Molly had showered, too, and put on an old dorm shirt over nylon running shorts. She paged through an old news magazine, but her interest was much more focused on the man pacing the room.

She wasn't afraid of her heightened interest in Hunt. Perhaps because she knew he didn't belong to her, that he never would. That gave her a sense of recklessness, a need to get whatever she could before he got away from her for good.

Desperate. That's what she was. Desperate and hungry. Hunt had found a sensual part of her she never knew existed. Now that she'd discovered it...

She shifted and wriggled, her body too warm and tense from watching him move back and forth in those sexy jeans. Her thoughts were racing in directions that should have shocked her, but they didn't.

She wanted to be with him, but she also cared for him deeply, and it was wrenchingly painful to know he didn't want to hear it. Yet she knew he desired her. Molly's desire was just as strong. Their time together was nearly finished. If she offered him what she knew he wanted, without the declarations he didn't want...

"Why in hell doesn't Sullivan call?" Hunt

snapped, checking the cell for the hundredth time to make sure it was working.

"Probably because he doesn't know anything."

"He said a few hours."

Molly glanced at her watch. "It's been a few hours."

"How can you be so damn calm? You were the one so anxious to go to Grover. Now you're sitting there like some college student who knows she'll ace the final."

She grinned. "I always ace my finals."

He scowled. "I'll bet."

"Except the Lose Your Virginity course. I didn't do very well on that."

"Don't start, Molly."

"I was thinking..."

"No."

"You don't even know what I was going to say."

"I don't want to know."

"You'll like this."

He looked at her suspiciously.

"I mean, I plan to cooperate and do what you said earlier in the car. When we get home, I'm going to put you out of my mind and get on with my life. You're probably right. All these feelings I have for you, well, given some time, they'll disappear. We've just been too close these past few days."

He narrowed his eyes. "You've decided all of that, have you."

"Yes."

"Good."

"See? I told you you'd like it."

"I didn't say I like it. I said it was a good idea."

She put the magazine aside. "So, I was thinking…" She rose to her feet and stretched, watching him watch her. He hadn't moved. His arms were folded across his chest in that position she'd seen him use whenever he didn't want her to get too personal. "We could say goodbye in a meaningful way," she continued. "A sort of no-regrets finale before getting on with our lives."

"You want to have sex one more time," he said bluntly.

"I want to make love one more time," she said just as bluntly.

"I tossed the condoms in the garbage. Your request, remember?"

"Then we'll have to be careful."

He unfolded his arms and planted his hands on his hips. He tried to look fierce, but she saw a tiny light of amusement in his expression.

"Walk over here."

She did, standing so close to him she could feel the heat from his body.

He traced a finger down the side of her neck. "You are one determined woman, you know that."

She curled a finger through his chest hair. "And you're a tough man to convince."

He slid his hands into her hair, dispensing with the

combs that held it away from her face. She tipped her head back, her tongue wetting her lips.

Hunt watched the motion and found it sexy as hell. "You have been a major distraction, sweetheart."

"I messed up all your good intentions, didn't I?" She splayed her hands at his waist, tucking her fingers into the waistband of his jeans.

"Yeah, and this is insane and I should be saying no right now...."

"But you can't because you want me."

"Yeah."

A satisfied sigh escaped her lips just as he lowered his head.

"Ah, Molly, Molly," he whispered, kissing her nose, her cheeks, her chin and finally taking her mouth. Just the taste of her made Hunt's heart jump. Desire tore through him like a brushfire. His hands skimmed down the sides of her neck to her breasts, and he knew immediately that she wasn't wearing a bra. He lifted the hem of the dorm shirt, pulling it up and over her head. Her breasts rose, firm and sweetly eager, their color a rich delicate cream. She stood still, a slight flush on her neck and cheeks. He nudged her back against the wall and cupped both breasts.

His thumbs skated back and forth across her nipples and then he lowered his head. Taking first one and then the other into his mouth, he made them wet and hard and hot.

Molly held him there, her head back against the

wall, her pleasure escaping in short pants. His mouth moved lower to her bare stomach and along the elastic band of her running shorts.

In a single move, he tugged her shorts and panties down her legs, and she kicked them away. She stood nude against the wall, her chest pounding, her legs throbbing. The light in the room didn't quite reach this area, giving the shadows free rein to seduce and entice.

Then she felt his mouth like an erotic burn, and she shrank back, but there was nowhere to go. He lingered as if time had no meaning, kissing her again and again, and Molly's breath drifted away. She only needed Hunt and what he was doing to her. Then, when she thought she couldn't endure the pleasure any longer, he pressed his mouth to the insides of both thighs, then slowly rose to his feet.

While watching her, he undid his jeans and dispensed with them. Molly took in every gesture, every part of him, wanting to memorize it all. The broad shoulders, the lawn of hair on his chest that arrowed down and surrounded his hardness. He was fully aroused, and she shuddered with the memory of how he'd felt inside her, of how his body felt over hers, of how he would feel again....

He stepped closer, slid his hand between her thighs and kissed the side of her neck.

"Will you trust me?" he whispered, his finger sending shock waves to some part of her libido she hadn't known existed.

"Yes."

He eased his hand free, then turned her, aligning his body behind her. She felt him slide between her thighs, then position her hips. Molly froze and Hunt immediately soothed her. "Easy, easy..."

"I've never done... Oh!" She panted as a wave of heat sizzled, sparked and then burst inside her. He filled her securely and with an expertise that left her reeling. Her head fell back on his shoulder and she heard him groan. His hands guided her and his whispered words made her shiver anew with need for him.

"You're so beautiful, so incredible.... I want you so much..."

"I want you to love me and never stop.... Oh, Hunt...."

He drew away, and once again turned her to face him. She could barely stand up, and Hunt lifted her into his arms so that her legs locked around his hips. Her hands gripped him, her mouth locking with his in a deep, deep kiss.

In the bedroom, they fell onto the spread, Hunt atop her, sliding inside her with the ease of a man who had been there a thousand times.

Her eyes shimmered as she touched his face, ran her finger over his lips.

"Why did you stop out there?" she asked softly.

His eyes met hers; his were deep and blue and electric with desire. "I wanted to watch you, wanted to see that flush of passion when you come."

She smiled. "You grit your teeth like you're about to blow apart."

"Only with you. I've been trying to put myself back together since I first kissed you."

She hugged him tighter, her legs pulling him more fully inside her. "Oh, Hunt...."

He kissed her neck, his lips brushing her breasts. She arched into him, feeling the heights of her own arousal as he slid full and heavy inside her. "Molly..."

Hunt tried to hold back, tried to pace himself. He wanted this to last forever; he wanted this intensity, this eagerness of her body, this honesty of desire to take him to some magical place where he could throw off all the fears, all the barriers he'd erected since Kristin died. He wanted to find a way to allow himself to have Molly.

Molly lifted into him, her pants of pleasure echoing through him like a chant of joy. Hunt whipped his head back, his own climax rushing, pounding....

No...can't...can't come inside her. Damn fool... don't come yet...not yet....

He gritted his teeth, drawing back, pulling away, but she held him. With more than her body, with more than his thundering desperation, with more than the mating, she held him with something he couldn't name, something he didn't know.

Then he saw her eyes, the pureness of her pleasure, her cry of satisfaction, the sweetness of her body taking from him, giving back in countless measures.

Her climax drenched her and Hunt was lost. Now, pulling away was obscene. He couldn't. The rush made him soar and showed him the inside of his soul, and that secret part of him relished the fact that he'd let down the barrier, that he'd allowed himself to want to be part of her, to simply lose himself in her.

He lay sprawled across her, wanting to tell her things he'd never said to any woman, feelings he hadn't had since Kristin. A ringing pushed through his thoughts. Again and again.

Molly stirred, kissing his ear, nipping the lobe. "Hunt, the phone..."

He blinked. Hell, he'd forgotten all about it. Pressing his hand to her spine to keep her against him, he murmured, "Let the damn thing ring."

"But it's probably Sean."

Hunt was concentrating on the feel of her breast against his lips. It was full and warm, and he hadn't yet had enough. "If I don't answer, he'll figure I changed my mind. I have."

She moved again, this time with more spirit, letting him know she wanted him to move. "But I haven't."

When he raised his head and looked at her, her eyes were pleading, and even in his mellow mood, he knew the plea wasn't for more lovemaking.

"Answer it. Please?"

He rolled from her, rising to his feet and cursing.

She sat up in bed, pushing her hair from her eyes as he left the room.

In a few minutes he was back, his jeans on but unsnapped. He tossed her clothes onto the bed. "It's goin' down in four hours."

"It's almost eleven now." She pulled the dorm shirt over her head and scrambled off the bed. "We have to hurry."

He grabbed her as she rushed past him, pulling her back and making her look at him. In a chilling voice, he asked, "What if the damn phone had rung before you got what you wanted?"

"You wanted it, too."

"Yeah, and I wanted it a helluva lot more than I want to go to Grover."

"Hunt, can't we talk about this on the way?"

He stared at her a long time, then released her, turning away. Molly shivered at the wall of ice that immediately formed between them.

"No more talk. No more sex. No more anything. We go to Grover so you can reinvent your brother's memory into whatever you want it to be. I'm finished."

She reached out to him, and he sidestepped her. "Please, Hunt. You're being unfair."

"*Unfair!*" The word exploded from his mouth. "I'm being unfair? We just made incredible love together, and you toss it all off like I was your hump of the month."

Her eyes widened. Had he said incredible love?

Not incredible sex? What had she done? "Hunt, listen to me. I'm sorry…I just…"

He gave a dismissive wave of his hand. "Forget it. It's over. It should have been over before it even started. Get dressed. I want to be out of here in half an hour."

He stalked out of the room, and Molly sat down on the edge of the bed, her body numb with disbelief. She'd never seen him so angry; she'd never felt so empty. My God, she'd lost him when she'd never even known she'd had him.

CHAPTER FOURTEEN

GROVER WAS RURAL and woodsy with twin strip malls instead of a downtown. A few miles east of the town limits, they passed the Fish House, a large aquarium. Molly recalled that Francine had mentioned that Vern often patronized one in the area. In the early-morning hours a skunk scented the air, and in the distance came the whine of a truck headed west on the Mass Pike.

"I expected something to be happening," Molly said in a low voice. The silence was too eerie.

"Something is. You just can't see it."

Hunt turned a corner and brought the car to a stop. Molly couldn't see anything but a strip of road with a faded yellow stripe, trees and, off to her left, a streetlight that illuminated a cluster of six rural mailboxes. One had its flag up.

With the engine off in the darkened car, the quiet became thick and claustrophobic. Hunt leaned forward and lifted the cartons of coffee he'd purchased moments ago at a twenty-four-hour convenience store.

"Here." He handed one to Molly.

She took the beverage, its warmth filling her

hands. Sipping, she concentrated on her surroundings. In the stillness, Molly listened and watched for anything. A light. Motion. Noise. There was nothing.

Three minutes passed. Five minutes. They both drank; neither spoke. Ten minutes. Then Molly heard a sharp sound like twigs snapping. She focused on the source and saw a meager light.

"Hunt?"

"It's Sullivan."

No sooner was his name spoken than he materialized like a night phantom. He wore dark clothes, but there was no mistaking the shoulder holster. Molly's heart leapt in anticipation. Obviously the police were prepared for a hit man to show up, and intended to make sure he didn't fulfil the contract. A sense of relief poured through her. Vern's death would count for something if his intended replacement was stopped.

Hunt opened the car door and got out. The two men stood side by side against the front fender. Sean lit a cigarette and Hunt sipped his coffee.

He had left the window down, so Molly assumed this wasn't a secret conversation. She slid over to the driver's seat so she wouldn't miss anything.

"Who's the contract?" Hunt asked.

"Horace 'the Horse' Crackston. Once you gave us Grover, 827 BOS translated to mean 827 Burned Oak Street, and we knew Crackston was the target. He's lived here off and on for a few years."

"Crackston...Crackston..." Hunt mused. "Didn't

I read that he's suppose to testify against some banker accused of laundering drug money for Wallace's boss?''

''He's the one. Crackston was a bagman for Solozi until he got picked up on a DWI and the cops found thirty grand in his vehicle. Solozi let him sit in the cell to teach him a lesson about getting arrested for stupidity. Crackston was pissed, and when an ace interrogator questioned him, he spilled his guts. The banker was arrested, but won't talk except to proclaim his innocence. Crackston fingered him and became the state's star witness.''

''And Solozi wanted him dead, so he sent Wallace.''

''Yeah. He still wants him dead—the question is whether Solozi will follow through with the original plan. According to our stoolies on the street, the contract is still a go. We know Crackston is here in the house. From what Francine told you and Molly, we know the hit that Wallace was carrying out was set for sometime before dawn. Crackston apparently plays in a weekly poker game that winds up at about 2:00 a.m. We think Wallace planned to kill him after he returned home.''

Hunt shifted, folding his arms. ''If he's the state's star witness, why wasn't he in protective custody?''

''He was. East of here, in Worcester County. Until he got some flaky idea he wanted to talk to his girlfriend about the good old days. Called her when his guards were trying to figure out how Crackston could draw four inside straights in a row.''

"Good God, who were these guys? Retreads of the Keystone Kops?''

Sean chuckled. "They got too friendly and their instincts got fuzzy.''

"So the broad took the call, cooed about how she much she adored him and missed him. He got a hard-on, blew the cover to meet her, and then she ratted on the poor bastard faster than the phone's speed dial.''

"Don'cha love female integrity.''

"It's a trip, all right.''

Molly scowled. The two of them could have been talking about mindless mushrooms.

Sean said, "Crackston also used to meet with a lot of his pals here, but they quit coming after the cops raided it a couple of years ago.''

"Crackston figured it was safe because it seemed risky.''

"It would seem so.''

"But Wallace knew where he was and apparently knew Crackston wasn't going anywhere anytime soon. He felt secure.'' Hunt was thoughtful for a moment. "So if Wallace had the hit and the address, why the delay?''

Sean shrugged. "Maybe there wasn't a delay, just Wallace's particular timing. He went to see his sister, and from what you got, he planned time with his ex after he did Crackston.''

"At his convenience. Nice. No pressure, no hassle, just do the job and leave."

"Wallace was the best," Sean commented grudgingly. "He never missed and he never screwed up. The big boys knew that when the hour for the planned hit came, it would be done."

"All right. Solozi wanted Crackston dead so he couldn't testify against the banker. Solozi contracted Wallace to do the hit. Flash forward. Word gets back that Wallace died of a heart attack. Solozi had to be freaked."

"Probably. But Solozi didn't get where he is by getting rattled at the unexpected. His bottom line is eliminating Crackston. And since Crackston had been talking to the girlfriend who fingered him for Wallace, Solozi passed that same information on to a new shooter."

"And you're waiting on him," Hunt said.

"Yeah."

The two men fell silent. Molly leaned forward, anticipating the next question—waiting on him to do what? In fact, she had another question: did Crackston know someone intended to kill him? It struck Molly as odd that he'd stay where he was if he knew he was a sitting target. The police must have clued him in. With no answer forthcoming, she could only speculate.

Obviously Hunt preferred to pretend she wasn't there and his old partner must have picked up some signal and agreed. What annoyed her was Hunt's coldness, his shutting her out when he knew how desperately she needed to know what was going on. No doubt he was still angry about what had happened after their lovemaking. She shuddered again, thinking about his furious reaction. Good heavens, it wasn't as if Hunt hadn't known Sean would call. And he had been aware of how important it was to her to be here.

The two men chuckled, Sullivan grinding out his cigarette.

Molly couldn't stand it any longer. "Sean, you said you were waiting on the shooter. Waiting on him to do what?"

Sean didn't answer and Hunt didn't respond, either. Surely they'd heard her. Frowning, she was about to get out of the car when Hunt stepped in front of the door, effectively preventing her from opening it.

"I gotta roll," Sean said, then his voice dropped to a murmur Molly could barely hear. Something about an obstruction of justice arrest.

He walked away and Hunt opened the door. Molly slid back to her own seat, but she watched the path Sean took, and sure enough, in a few seconds she saw the light again.

To Hunt, she said, "Are you going to answer my question? Waiting on the shooter to do what?"

Hunt drained his carton of coffee. "To show up."

"And?"

Hunt stretched his legs, moving to get comfortable. "Depends. Ideally, they'd like to catch him in the act."

"Catch him in the act! The act is murder."

"That's what it is."

His calmness infuriated her. "And you can sit there like this guy is making a social call?"

"Not my job to make a judgment. And no one asked my opinion."

Molly wanted to shake him out of his disinterest. Piqued, she said in a clipped tone, "Oh, yes, Hunt the ex-cop. Heaven forbid I should forget that." She turned in the seat. "Given that you're going to sit here and do nothing, why did you come? I could have come alone."

"No, you couldn't have. Sean would have arrested you for obstruction of justice. You're a civilian. He'd rather take you in than have you get hurt."

"How considerate of Mr. Sullivan," she snapped.

If he'd heard her sarcasm, he gave no indication. Instead, he slid down in the seat, folded his arms and settled back as if he intended to take a nap. "Sullivan will give us the all-clear," he murmured. "Take a deep breath and relax. When it's all over, you can get a look-see at Crackston, and then we can go home."

Arms folded, eyes narrowed, she asked, "Will he be dead or alive?"

He shrugged. "You never know. Crackston might get lucky and the shooter will go down first."

First they wanted to catch the shooter in the act.

Then whoever got lucky was the one who would live. All Molly could envision was her brother: Vern caught in the crosshairs between the cops who wanted ideal arrests and the target who might get lucky.

She sat rigid, her adrenaline pumping like an engine with a full head of steam. She glanced over at Hunt, but he hadn't moved.

Dammit, she hadn't come to sit in a car. She wanted to know what was going on, but most of all, she wanted the man who was supposed to die to live. If he did, then Vern's death would have canceled the contract. She couldn't change what her brother was, but she could change the effect of his death.

The cynicism of Hunt and Sean astounded her. Molly realized that if Vern was indeed the shooter, he would be treated with the same crass dismissal. My God, Hunt, too, would just calmly sit by and wait while her brother was...

Chilled, then hot, then chilled again, Molly determined she couldn't live with herself if she didn't do more than wait for the outcome. Hunt had said Sullivan would give the all-clear, to take a deep breath and relax. Fat chance of that. Right now she was jumpy and itchy. She couldn't just bide her time while all of this was going on.

Molly quietly opened her car door. Hunt hadn't moved. Leave it to him to just fall asleep as if they were parked in Disney World, she thought irritably.

She had one leg out and was about to ease out the other when his hand clamped down on her arm.

"Where the hell do you think you're going?"

"I thought you were asleep."

"I haven't slept since I got mixed up with you. I asked you a question."

Think. Think. Her heart thumped madly. "I have to go to the bathroom, if you must know."

He straightened. "I'll go with you."

Aghast, she said, "You most certainly will not."

"I either go with you or you don't go."

She jerked away him and got out of the car. He followed, taking her arm.

"I can walk by myself." She shook off his hand.

Hunt shrugged but stayed close. The trees and the darkness offered more than enough cover for personal needs. Molly made sure she kept in sight of that tiny light in the distance.

Hunt stood nearby, watchful, and despite her annoyance with him, she grudgingly respected him. He wasn't easily outsmarted. Her only hope was that the blackness of the night would be cover enough that she could gain some distance before Hunt could stop her.

But he had to have eyes like a cat, for when she tried to move deeper into the trees, he grabbed her none too gently.

"Dammit, Molly, knock it off."

"Let me go."

"So you can go down where Sean is? Not likely."

"That man Crackston could die."

"And so could you. Remember how you were roughed up by Pascale and his pals over that notebook?"

"I got away from Pascale."

"Thank God. This time you're staying with me."

Instead of arguing, she stepped close to him, slipped her arms around his neck, stood on tiptoes and kissed him. Her tongue slid deep into his mouth, and he welcomed it with a silent promise to let her have whatever she wanted. His hands gripped her hips, angling her against him, and she felt him swell against her.

"Nice," he murmured.

"I could make it nicer," she said, nibbling on his lower lip.

He drew back, his eyes half shuttered. "Do it all, sweetheart, but you're still not going down there."

She scowled and pushed away from him. "You're supposed to be so swayed by my kisses that you forget everything else."

He chuckled. "I am. But I also know you. You want something, and you'll use any means to get it."

"You make me sound ruthless."

"Just determined."

She dropped her arms and stepped away, heaving a long sigh.

"Guess that means we're not gonna get hot and serious here, huh?"

She heard the amusement in his voice. "I hate you, Hunt Gresham."

"Yeah, I could tell," he said pleasantly.

They started back toward the car when Molly jumped back.

"What is it?" Hunt asked.

"There's a skunk."

"Where?"

"There." Already, she was stepping away from him. "Over there. Just to your left. Do something, Hunt…"

While his attention was diverted, she bolted.

Running back into the trees, dodging limbs, rocks and scrambling over the uneven terrain, she headed toward the source of that light. She ran, fearful of stopping, trying to listen for Hunt's footsteps behind her.

Finally, out of breath, she halted behind a hedge. Leaning forward, her hands on her knees, she took long, deep breaths. Her eyes strained against the darkness, fully expecting Hunt to materialize and grab her.

In front of her was a clearing, then a road. Behind her were the trees, and she glanced around for that tiny light but couldn't find it. Had to be here somewhere. Sean had come in this direction. Cautiously, she moved forward.

A rural mailbox stood by a gravel drive that led to a house. An outside light was on, and she wondered if this was the light she'd seen.

She stood still, hands on her hips. Nothing. No noise. No vehicles. Just a symphony of crickets. She moved over to the mailbox, but there was no name and no number. She opened it and found a few pieces of mail. Feeling as if she'd discovered gold, she took it and headed toward the house and the light.

Seconds later, she read the name, Lympton, and 793 Burned Oak Street.

Molly's pulse rate jumped. At least she was on the right street, and 827 couldn't be too far away. Quickly she returned to the box, replaced the mail and looked in both directions. Crackston's house was on this side. She decided to go forward.

She hadn't walked four hundred feet when she spotted two state police officers. Then she saw a shadowy movement, and another man appeared. Then, with a signal from one of the officers, the man slipped into the denseness of some trees. Sean was probably here, and by this time, Hunt. She worked her way closer, being careful to stay hidden.

She was about to move toward an unassuming house when two men she hadn't seen earlier loomed in front of her.

Molly froze, plastering herself against a tree trunk.

The men blocked her way to the house, and she was trying to see a way around them when one said, "My stoolie says he'll show."

"Unless someone dropped a dime."

"Crackston ain't got a lot of friends lookin' to save his ass. Fingerin' the banker screwed him with

Solozi, but if he could've kept his pants zipped, he'd have probably been okay. Instead he blows his own protection. Jeez, go figure on why he'd trust some broad.''

Low snickers. "So what's your take? Think we'll do them both clean and easy?''

"If Sullivan has any say. Crackston ain't got the brains of a cockroach. My money is on the shooter. Weasel ain't had a lot of misses, and zero arrests.''

"But he's not 'the Spider.' God, that guy could bull's-eye a target on a dark night with his eyes closed. Swear he could smell the scum. Didn't need to see them.''

Molly was appalled. These were police officers and they talked as if they were in awe of both her brother and this Weasel. And here they were laying bets that Crackston wouldn't escape alive!

She moved back and to her left. Then she heard a familiar voice. Hunt. She didn't have to hear the words to discern the fury in his tone.

It was now or never. Obviously the police didn't care if Crackston died, but she cared. Maybe he was scum, but he deserved a chance. No one should be a sitting target.

She carefully moved between some bushes and made her way toward the house. If Hunt caught sight of her, he'd probably handcuff her to him. All she needed was a few minutes. Warn Crackston about Weasel and leave. Simple.

The house was brown; the interior dark. The moon

cast some light as Molly worked her way around to the back. She stood there by the closed door. Now what? *Simple and direct,* she reminded herself. *You're here to warn Crackston, not to become his new best friend.*

She tapped on the door. Even that muted sound vibrated in the night, and Molly had to tamp down her urge to run. No one came and she knocked again. When her second knock was ignored, she had the giddy thought that Crackston had outfoxed the cops. Maybe he had learned of the planned hit and taken off hours ago. Maybe he was smarter than anyone thought.

She was about to turn and leave when she heard a noise inside. She pressed her ear to the door, when suddenly it was opened and she was grabbed by arms the size of tree trunks.

Molly struggled, but a man yanked her inside and slammed the door. The sudden noise reverberated through the stillness like machine-gun fire.

He spun her around and gripped her chin as his eyes bored into her. Molly sucked in a breath. The man was huge, with a sagging, fleshy, full-cheeked face, his mouth turned down. His hair was oily, gingersnap brown and messy. A lurking viciousness shone in his eyes. She swallowed, and swallowed again. She hadn't expected a neighborly grin, but perhaps another Pascale, who at least acted smooth and charming. Crackston neither grinned nor charmed. He was terrifying.

"Who are you?" he snarled.

Suddenly warning him—so important when she was picturing him as a victim—didn't feel so smart.

Her mouth felt dust-dry. "S-someone named W-Weasel is going to try and k-kill you."

He looked at her as if she had mashed potatoes for brains. "What is this? Some kinda screwy trick?" Even as he asked the question, his eyes darted to the curtained window. "Since when do the cops send a broad to do their dirty work? They think I'm gonna fall for that?"

"They don't want anything to happen to you," she managed to say with a croaky voice. Molly wasn't entirely sure that was true, but *she* certainly didn't want to see anyone gunned down.

He let go of her chin, and Molly sagged against the wall. She'd been practically on her tiptoes to relieve the pressure on her throat. She gingerly felt her chin and then glanced around for a way to get out. He moved like a bear, shoulders swaying, arms loose. She learned how deceptively agile he was when she took a step toward the door.

He halted her and swung her so that her back was pinned to his chest. "We're goin' to see just how much you're worth to your pals outside." He gave her a disdainful look. "You ain't got breasts worth getting sweaty palms over."

She didn't flinch and she didn't answer him. He moved with her toward the back door, slid the curtain back and peered out. All Molly could see was blackness. *Good move,* she thought to herself. *Either you like getting into trouble or you're not very good at planning your strategy.* Then she felt a hard poke against her side.

"Make a sound and you're singin' with the angels."

He poked harder, and she chanced a glance and shuddered. The weapon was enormous, and his finger slid across the trigger with a master's touch.

"I TOLD YOU to keep her the hell out of the way." Sullivan's voice was a croaking whisper. "Now I don't have to sweat arresting her because she'll probably be dead."

"Knock it off, Sullivan." But it was Sean's finger shoved in Hunt's chest that infuriated him. "You were real interested in her when she could get you info. I take the blame for the screwup. The issue now is Molly and her safety."

"I got guys who are supposed to be nailin' Weasel and they're searchin' for your girlfriend. If this gets messed up because of her—"

"Because of her you're here, goddammit, so back it off." Hunt stalked away and headed toward the house.

He knew. He didn't have to guess or wonder; she was either in the house or damn close. He should have known by her outrage over how Sullivan was handling this that she wouldn't sit passively by. Hell, maybe he *had* known and hadn't wanted to think about it. From the beginning, she'd been determined to learn all she could about her brother, to make him something he wasn't or find a reason why he'd gone wrong. With that in mind, she'd gone with Pascale and put her full trust in Francine. She'd even agreed to him accompanying her to the funeral. No doubt she'd had an ulterior motive for that, too, he thought grimly.

Which, of course, changed nothing. Hunt guessed that Crackston would be breathing with the devil right now if Wallace had lived. But Molly wouldn't be here, either. She'd be back in Woodbriar, still blissfully naive.

Two cops came out of the darkness. "What do you think, Gresham?"

Hunt knew Oswald and Peterson. Both worked under Sean. Hunt nodded toward the house. "My guess is she's in there."

"She some kind of screwy broad?"

"Most of the time I'd say no. But tonight...never mind. Let's just call her idealistic."

The officers looked at each other and rolled their eyes.

"I'm going to see how close I can get to the back door," Hunt told them.

"Better hold up until we check with Sullivan."

But Hunt had no intention of standing around. He'd already done enough of that.

"Gresham, hey, man, wait a minute...."

Hunt ignored the low-spoken command. He crept

closer to the house, using the darkness, but just as he moved to the side near the back door, a shot rang out from inside.

"You cops better stay the hell back," Crackston yelled. "She don't mean squat to me, but she can stop a lot of bullets."

"Crackston!" Hunt shouted. "Give it up."

"Gresham? That you? You sober or you still playing the cop screw-up. Thought you were history, and here you are on my ass again."

"Crackston, I don't give two shits if you live or die."

"But you care about the woman. You coppers always do. Well, you didn't do such a good job carin' about her if she got in here."

Molly stiffened, a surge of adrenaline pushing through her. She had to do something. Since she couldn't physically get away from him, she began to chatter. "He didn't know anything about this. He didn't want me here and he's probably furious, but you're a fool if you think he's going to—"

"Shut up!"

"I'm telling you, Hunt isn't going to let you leave here with me. He's—"

"Lady, either shut up or I'm gonna gag you."

"But—"

Crackston's hand clamped over her mouth, pushing her lips so hard against her teeth, her eyes watered with the pain. Blinking to clear her vision, she felt as if the breath were being squeezed out of her.

Suddenly Crackston whirled around. "What was that?"

Molly hadn't heard anything.

"Gresham? I wanna see you or I'm gonna start chewin' on this broad."

Silence.

"Gresham!"

Molly's eyes widened as the silence continued. Crackston cursed, then, still holding her against him, dragged her across the kitchen to another room, where she saw sparse furnishings and the remains of a take-out meal.

Crackston spun her around, shoved her down in a chair, tore a drapery cord off the window and tied her hands behind her back. Then he took a long doily off a table, rolled it into a long tube and gagged her. Molly tasted dusty cotton. He hauled her to her feet, shoving her in front of him as he made his way toward a closed door.

Molly had moved beyond scared to terrified. Where was Hunt? If she'd stayed with him, none of this would have happened. In the hospital, Vern had told her that Hunt wouldn't let her get hurt. Vern had been so positive of that, and he hadn't even known Hunt. In effect, her obsession to put right what her brother had done wrong had not only put her in danger, but Hunt, too. Hunt could get killed trying to save her.

Oh, God...

They were moving down a cobwebby stairway that

led to a cellar. Her arms were growing numb and the gag was making her nauseous.

"Move it, lady. Your boyfriend ain't gonna save you now."

Maybe not, but... The idea was implausible, but it could work....

She made a muffled sound, signaling frantically with her eyes. Crackston looked confused, but when she continued to gesture, he untied the gag. "Make it quick, and if you scream I'll hit you."

"My brother will get you for this," she blurted out, thinking it sounded even more implausible when she said it.

"Huh?"

"My brother. Vernon Wallace."

Even in the darkness, she saw the white in his eyes grow larger. Then he guffawed. "First you're tellin' me the Weasel is gonna do me and now you're talkin' about a dead man? Claimin' to be 'the Spider's' sister? You're screwier than I figured."

"It's a trick."

"What's a trick?"

"Vern isn't dead. That was all a lie. A setup." Molly chattered on with no idea if anything she said made sense, but Crackston seemed distracted and disoriented by the information. And that was all she wanted. To throw him off stride so she could escape.

"Shut up! Shut up before I put a bullet through you right now." He regagged her, mumbling about women making lousy hostages, then moved across the cellar to a bulkhead and slid the inside lock open.

Molly eased her way back, trying to use the darkness of the cellar to her advantage. She backed into a cobweb and shuddered at the feel of it on her neck. With her hands tied, she couldn't do anything but shake to keep her arms from going numb.

She moved slowly toward the stairs, intending to try to escape back up them. Just as she was about to take the first step, Crackston swung around and bellowed, "Get over here, you little bitch. Do it now!"

The gleam of the gun barrel aimed right at her convinced her to do as she was told. He opened the bulkhead, looked around, and then pulling her in front of him as cover, climbed the steps from the cellar to the backyard.

No one was around. Not Hunt or Sean or any of the other cops. For a nightmarish moment Molly envisioned Weasel in some nearby tree with her and Crackston in his sights. She felt exposed and vulnerable, and in that moment knew that this was the reason Vern would have never told her anything about what he did for a living. Even if he'd lived and they'd had a close relationship, he would have kept silent. How foolishly naive she was! Her brother probably knew that, too, which was why, on his deathbed, he'd urged her to trust Hunt.

Now it was too late to trust anyone.

The yard was scruffy and banked by trees. Once Crackston had her in the denseness of the trees...

Crackston took no chances. He searched, his eyes moving all the time, turning Molly and turning her again so that she was getting dizzy.

Then, just as they walked into the trees, a man dropped from one of the branches onto Crackston's shoulders while another grabbed Molly and shoved her aside. Feet pounded the ground. Men appeared from twenty different directions. Lights were everywhere. Molly struggled to get to her feet as strong arms lifted her, and she looked into very blue eyes that were terrified and intense.

Hunt untied her hands and removed the gag; she was in his arms instantly. He held her as if tomorrow would never come.

"Please tell me you're okay."

She held him as if she couldn't imagine ever being away from him again. "I'm okay now. Okay now..."

Moments later, after Crackston was taken away, Hunt and Molly walked together to where Sean was finishing up.

"That was one of the stupidest moves you could have made, Molly," Sean said tersely. "You're damn lucky to be alive."

"What about Weasel?" Molly asked, and then from Sean's disgusted expression, she wished she hadn't.

"Thanks to you and all the commotion you caused, the likelihood of getting him is nil."

"But Crackston is alive," Hunt reminded him. "Be grateful for that."

"I'd have been a helluva lot more grateful if she'd never been here in the first place." Sean stepped away for a few moments to talk to another officer, then turned back to them. "Just thought you'd like to know. Crackston told us his girlfriend's name. Nancy Lynch."

Hunt scowled, but Molly was stunned. "I know Nancy. She works at the aquarium where Vern bought his fish. I spoke with her at the funeral home. But Crackston's girlfriend? My God, she looked like a nice quiet young woman."

"Yeah, these days it's the nice quiet types who are the most trouble."

Molly narrowed her eyes at the obvious shot at her, but Hunt steered her around Sullivan and back to where their car was parked.

Once inside, Molly snapped, "You know, I don't like Sean."

"He's got a thing about civilians sticking their noses where they don't belong."

"He didn't have any trouble when he wanted to use me and you to get information."

"And I told him so. He's just doing his job, Molly, the only way he knows how."

"Well, I'm glad you're an *ex*-cop if he's an example of what you used to be."

Hunt sighed, and she suddenly sagged against him,

her body trembling. Hunt held her close, and she clung to him as if he were a raft in a churning sea.

"Oh, God..."

"Easy, easy. You're okay, sweetheart. You're more than okay. You're brave and persistent and unlike any woman I've ever known."

And in that moment, the horror of the past few days slipped away, leaving her with only her feelings for Hunt. She had no doubt she really loved him. She wanted to tell him, but he kissed her again and again, and she guessed that he didn't want to hear any of those declarations. In this, nothing between them had changed. She loved him, but he didn't love her.

CHAPTER FIFTEEN

ON FRIDAY AFTERNOON, two weeks after Molly and Hunt returned to Woodbriar, Molly stood at the windows in her apartment, facing the courtyard. It wasn't yet officially autumn, but the air had sharpened, cutting away the summer's lazy sweetness. For Molly, the change of season usually meant an energized outlook, but not this year. No doubt Vern's death and the events that had followed added to her melancholy, but the end of her relationship with Hunt had made her morose and unable to concentrate.

At work she'd been especially preoccupied. A new complex of off-campus apartments had just become available, and she had a waiting list of students requesting them. In fact, her office desk was piled high with applications that needed to be sorted, and yet her mind had been distracted.

Today, she'd come home early, using a raging headache for an excuse. It wasn't a lie, for her head did indeed ache. As did her heart and her body. She'd given up anticipating that Hunt would call, or leave a message on her voice mail, or stop by her office at work.

She'd spoken to her parents twice since her return. First to fill them in on what had happened.

Their concern had made her wish they were closer, but they must have heard the melancholy in her voice, because a few days later her mother called again, concerned that Molly might not have to come to terms with her brother's death or who he really was.

"I think I have, Mom. In a way, Vern's death helped the police. They have a notebook Vern kept that will be used as evidence to convict some mobsters, and a corrupt banker is probably going to go to prison, thanks to a key witness. His death will count for something."

"More important, honey, is the fact that you were so diligent in finding him. It *made* his death count for something. If you and your policeman friend hadn't worked together... Hunt, isn't it?"

"Yes. His name is Hunt."

"If Hunt hadn't been with you when Vern died, and you hadn't been so determined to find out who he was beyond his criminal side, then perhaps the people who will go to prison would have remained free."

By the time Molly hung up, she felt better about the past weeks. Her mother's call had put things into perspective. Vern had come to see her, and despite who he was and their years of separation, they'd had a bond that couldn't be broken. His death mattered because other people's lives had been affected—Pascale's, Crackston's, Solozi's, hers, Hunt's.

Because of Vern, she'd fallen in love with Hunt.

Once again, she was reminded of her brother's words. "You can trust him."

Hunt's apartment was directly across from hers, and yet not once in the past two weeks had she seen him. Oh, she knew he was around. His lecture series was the talk of the campus; the administration had even moved him from one of the small lecture halls to the largest.

"Gritty," "truthful" and "bold" had been some of the comments Molly had heard around the campus. Administration officials extolled Hunt as an ex-cop who didn't whitewash or sugarcoat or make excuses for police mistakes. The students were mesmerized, and according to Hunt's sister, Denise, she'd had calls from three New England colleges inquiring about Hunt's availability for a future semester.

Molly was happy for him, but in a selfish way, she almost resented that things were going so well. Obviously, he didn't need or miss her when he was Woodbriar's most popular visiting lecturer.

She couldn't even say she'd had her chance with him and blown it. For with Hunt there had never been a prospective relationship. Even their final conversation had been awkward and uncomfortable.

They'd returned to Woodbriar, arriving in the early-morning hours. Hunt had carried her things inside, as well as the boxes they'd taken from Vern's.

With the first streaks of dawn lighting the sky, Hunt had stayed by her front door, his arms at his side. She'd stood just a foot from him, her hands jammed in her pockets.

Neither had spoken, both searching for an appropriate goodbye. Watching him, Molly had been reminded of the afternoon he'd come on the pretense of his broken air conditioner. She remembered how excited she'd been at opening her door and finding him there, of thinking he was handsome and sexy and intriguing. He'd looked so serious, and she'd been so thrilled by her brother's visit, her whole personality had been bubbly.

However, when they returned to Woodbriar, she had definitely not been bubbly. Instead, a go-for-broke attitude had fanned to life within her. She loved him, and that knowledge made her brazen. So when he'd brought her home, instead of simply saying goodbye, she asked, "Are you going to kiss me one last time?"

He'd tipped his head to the side as he studied her mouth. Molly literally held her breath during the seconds of silence that ticked by. When his gaze met hers, he said softly, "I don't think so."

"Are you afraid to?"

"Yeah." He paused, then added, "It will just start something that shouldn't be started."

"Maybe it will end something that isn't finished."

"Molly..."

"I know. No declarations."

He turned to go.

"Wait." She took a step forward, her thoughts tumbling recklessly into words. "We could see each other," she offered hopefully. "I mean, of course we'll run into each other. The campus isn't that big. And I did want to hear some of your lectures. But we could also see each other, uh...other times, uh, on a personal basis, sort of like a..." Molly knew she was babbling and stumbling over the word *date*, and yet the word sounded ridiculously silly after the intimacies they'd shared.

Nor did Hunt try to relieve her distress by saying what he undoubtedly knew she meant.

"There is one thing," he said in a low voice.

"Yes?"

"If you're pregnant..." When she scowled, he said, "Don't look like that."

"Like what?"

"Like it's impossible. We made love twice, and neither time— Hell, you know what happened. I just want you to know that if you are, I'll take responsibility. Money and, uh..."

"Marriage?" she prompted, then decided that she'd taken the word *brazen* to a new level.

He looked at her for a long time, not so much as if he were weighing his answer, but as if he were furious with himself for getting them into this predicament. Finally, he nodded, albeit reluctantly.

"Yeah," he'd muttered. "If that's what you want."

"Gee, what a romantic proposal," she'd said with a bite of sarcasm. Planting her hands on her hips, she gave him a withering look. "You sound as if you've been sentenced to execution. You'll marry me if I'm going to have your baby, but if I'm not pregnant, it's all over. How do you think that makes me feel? How can you possibly believe I'd marry a man who is willing only if I'm pregnant?"

Hunt swore, then shook his head, the situation clearly making him uncomfortable. "I'm trying to tell you I'll do the right thing."

"But reluctantly. Like going with me to Fernwood was the right thing."

"That was different."

"Only because it was just a few days," she retorted, pacing the perimeter of the room. Now that she was hip-deep into this, she had no intention of giving him any advantage.

Stepping around her luggage, she said, "Besides, you were the ex-cop doing a favor for an old partner. Nothing personal in that. Marriage and a child, on the other hand, are personal and forever. And you're not a forever kind of guy, are you? At least you've been making that pretty clear the past few days. Now you want me to believe that forever works if I'm pregnant, but if I'm not, well, it's been nice knowing you?"

"Dammit all to hell," he growled, then slammed the partially open door and tunneled his hand through his hair in frustration.

For a moment she thought he was going to defend himself, but instead he only swore again, this time more fervently. It was obvious that he didn't know what to say to her.

Molly almost felt sorry for him. He looked

stricken and confused. Clearly he'd never encountered this kind of situation. Not Hunt, who always kept his emotions at a distance. His sense of responsibility had kicked in not because of some outside force or devotion, but because, in his opinion, he'd acted irresponsibly by taking her to bed in the first place.

From Hunt's point of view he'd had no choice but to offer money, marriage or anything else she'd need for herself and a child. But he hadn't offered the one thing she wanted. His love.

Finally, he said, "I think we both need a breather. I'll be in touch."

He'd dug his keys out of his pocket and opened the door. He hesitated a moment as if he wanted to say something more, then shook his head and left, pulling the door closed behind him.

Those last four words had stayed with her—a loose promise, a vague acknowledgment that he'd see her. She'd waited and she'd hoped, but the days had passed without any contact.

She'd considered going to his apartment, but she had no reason. Even the fan she'd loaned him had been returned by one of the kids in the neighborhood. "Mr. Gresham said thanks" had been the brief message.

As for begging, pleading, throwing herself at him in some infantile declaration, well, she simply couldn't do it. It would be too humiliating, and what would it accomplish? She couldn't force or talk him into loving her.

Molly turned from the windows with a long sigh. Her eyes glistened and she wiped away the dampness. She needed to stop feeling sorry for herself and get on with her life. Start dating some other men. There was no future with Hunt; she knew it, she hated it, but she couldn't create what wasn't to be.

The phone rang and her heart leapt. But it was Denise asking about her headache, then telling her about some baseball cards Hunt had gotten for her boys and an interview he had the following day at a college in Vermont. She chattered on and Molly half listened, the tears she could no longer contain sliding down her cheeks.

THE FOLLOWING FRIDAY, Hunt paused outside Molly's office door, gathering his thoughts. He didn't look very professorish; he'd just finished a lecture on the dangers and rules of undercover work and had looked the part—grungy jeans, heavy rap T-shirt, leather vest, unshaven and unsavory.

One thing he'd learned quickly was that the students liked the underlying drama of what he did as much as the facts of his presentation. For Hunt, he discovered he really loved to teach. What had begun as a nonstress, low-key endeavor to distance police work had become a source of enjoyment and pleasure. He was eagerly looking forward to visiting other colleges. Already he was booked for the following spring and fall.

Now he glanced down at his dirty clothes. He'd planned to go home and clean up, but he'd heard at lunch that Molly had a date tonight with Bill Ketchum, one of the professors in the history department.

She'd done what he'd been telling her to do; she'd started dating. And to his utter astonishment, he hated the whole idea. Ketchum wasn't dull, tweedy and intellectual like many of the professors. He was younger than Hunt, gregarious, charming and, according to campus rumor, had been interested in Molly for months. All in all, he was perfect for her, and Hunt despised him.

Of course he was being irrational, selfish and arbitrary, but some inner truth that Hunt had refused to deal with since meeting Molly had finally shoved Hunt's objections aside and sprung to life. Hunt had finally recognized his own vulnerability and caring and need to give and get love.

He'd firmly believed that part of himself had died with Kristin; now he knew it had just been buried under his pain and self-protective instincts. Now he knew he didn't want Molly to be with another man. For most of the afternoon, that possibility and all its potential consequences had sliced and diced its way through him like a butcher knife run amok.

Hunt had told himself he didn't want to barge into her apartment when she was getting ready for her date, but the truth was, he doubted he'd get in the door. He knew he'd botched their parting moments badly. Hell, he'd wanted to kiss her—he'd wanted to take her to bed, but going beyond that into something long-term...

Frankly, love and commitment had scared the hell out of him. Because of losing Kristin, yes, but with Molly his fear of involvement had moved into new realms.

She was too young. She needed to find out if her feelings were real or just an intoxicating attraction that was enhanced by great sex. Her giving him her virginity made the issue more momentous; that act had created a crack in his armor he could never seal up again. He'd never slept with a virgin, and even now his head reeled with its significance. She'd chosen to belong to him. She'd entrusted him with the one thing that she could give only once. And when he heard about her date with Ketchum, the thought of Molly eventually having sex with him brought out a possessive side that stunned even him. Irrational, perhaps, even selfish and arbitrary, but he would not allow another man to trespass on what belonged to him.

Belonged to him.... God, he could only hope.

He pushed the door open and stepped inside. Molly's office was across the room and her door was closed.

"I'd like to see Molly McCulloch," Hunt said to a plumpish woman in a red-and-gray dress working at a copy machine.

She turned and her eyes widened, then slid over Hunt as if he'd been left behind by the trash collector.

"Do you have an appointment?" she asked briskly.

"No. Look, I'm sure she's busy, but it's important I see her."

She gathered up her copies and took the long way back to her desk rather than pass too close to him.

Giving him another head-to-toe perusal, she said, "I'll see if she has a minute. What's your name?"

"Hunt Gresham."

The abrupt change in the woman was cataclysmic. Her hands flew to her cheeks and she began gushing. "Why, Mr. Gresham, I should have known. Please forgive my rudeness. My son is in your lecture series, and he says it's the best course on campus."

"I'm glad he's getting something from it."

"I had so much trouble with him last year," she said, gesturing with her hands. "Drinking, parties. But this year, thanks to you, well, it's just wonderful."

"That's great." He glanced at Molly's door.

"He's even talking about changing his major to criminology."

"Well, it's a huge field...." Hunt shifted his weight impatiently. Usually he didn't mind discussing the response to his series, but today his mind was on Molly. "Could you please tell Molly I'm here?"

"Oh, yes, yes." She reached for the door, but at that moment Molly opened it.

She had a file in her hand that she was leafing through. Her head was down, and Hunt took advantage of the opportunity to look at her before she noticed him. Wearing a plum-colored trouser suit with a ruffly beige blouse, she looked sleek, sophisticated and very professional.

Hunt felt a kick of excitement so strong, he knew his nights with little sleep and his days of confused and unwieldy thoughts were more than sexual memories.

Still sorting through the sheaf of papers, she said, "Shirley, I have a student who is—to use her words—'grossed out by her housemate.' She wants to make a switch today if possible. I thought we could move her—" She halted when she glanced up and saw him, and she stared as if he were an apparition.

He stared back, noting her surprise, which was quickly followed by suspicion.

Shirley said, "I was just about to come in and tell you he wanted to see you."

"Really? In reference to what?"

Hunt didn't miss the coolness. He could hardly blame her. He'd made it clear he wanted nothing to do with her and hadn't expected an open-arms welcome. Besides, he reminded himself, her date with Ketchum further confirmed she was getting on with her life—and getting over him.

He didn't have much time.

"In reference to our date later tonight."

"Our date?" She blinked as if she'd missed a cue.

Hunt winked at Shirley. "I've had a helluva time trying to convince her to go out with me. Now, after I finally have, she forgets all about me. Guess I'd better work on my approach."

Shirley smiled, taking the folder from Molly. "I'll get right on this housemate change."

Molly scowled, but Hunt strode forward, took her arm and hustled her back into her office. He closed the door and turned the lock.

"You have a lot of nerve, Hunt Gresham."

"Yeah, with you I need nerve." He ran a finger along the edge of her ruffly blouse. "You look gorgeous."

She pushed his hand away. "You look like a bum."

"Gee, all those women in my class thought I was sexy."

"I can just imagine. What do you want?"

"Besides getting into your panties?"

"Stop it." She stepped away from him. "I don't know what this is all about, but I can do without all the sexual byplay."

"You were supposed to say, 'What are you up to?'"

She narrowed her eyes and studied him for a moment. "The reluctant Hunt Gresham is suddenly doing the sexy come-on? Sorry, I don't buy it."

"It's a new side of me. Light and upbeat." He leaned against the edge of her desk and folded his arms.

"Congratulations on a stellar performance for Shirley. I hope you're very successful with this new approach." She started past him, but he gripped her arm. When he tried to pull her between his legs, she balked. "Look, I have work to do and I have—"

"A date tonight with Bill Ketchum."

"How did you know?"

"Lunchroom gossip. Are you pregnant?"

She looked startled by the question. Then, quickly recovering, she said smoothly, "Ah, so that's why you're here. To gear yourself up for the worst. Well, you'll be happy to know I'm not, so your life won't be complicated by anything messy like an unwanted woman with a baby."

She started to turn away when he stopped her and pressed his hand against her stomach. "You know, when I first saw you with your brother, I vowed to stay uninvolved because I didn't want anything messy and complicated. And yet I'm the one who caused all the complications. And as weird and crazy as it sounds, I think I was happier in the midst of all those chaotic feelings than I've ever been. Frankly, I was hoping you *were* pregnant, because it would force me to make a decision I was afraid to make otherwise."

Still looking unsure, she asked, "A decision about what?"

"About wanting to spend the rest of my life with you."

She blinked in disbelief. "I don't believe that. From the beginning, you said I was too young for you, that you couldn't deal with another permanent relationship after Kristin. And even after we got home, you obviously dreaded me being pregnant. Surely you can't forget that you looked like a condemned man when I mentioned marriage."

"Yeah, well, my stupidity was in full bloom."

"Maybe not. Maybe it's how you really felt."

In spite of her words, he sensed she wanted to believe him, and he drew her closer, resting his hand on her waist. "I want you to break your date tonight."

"Why?"

"Because I don't want to have to convince Ketchum that it's bad for his health if he goes out with you."

She rocked back a little, crossed her arms, her right foot tapping the floor. He knew immediately he wasn't home free yet. "Is this a threat? Do away with the undesirable competition? You have a lot of nerve. You were the one who told me to date. I've just spent two weeks waiting for you to realize we had more than good sex, but have I heard from you? No. Now, when Bill and I are going out, you show up like some outraged ex-boyfriend."

"I love you, Molly."

"Well, you can just forget being outraged, because I don't believe— What did you say?"

"I love you."

She wavered and Hunt steadied her. Her eyes searched his for a long time. "You're serious, aren't you?"

"Yes."

"But when? How? I mean, we haven't even seen each other. We haven't argued or talked or even kissed. Surely you're not going to say something like absence makes the heart grow fonder."

"How about my heart not being the same since I met you." He tunneled his hands through her hair, messing the pinned-up style, loving the familiar scent of her, the treasure of emotions that came to life in her lavender eyes. "I've missed this." He kissed her mouth, then her cheeks and then her mouth again. "I've also missed your quickness and your honesty. I've missed arguing with you and having you curl against me like I'm the safest place in the whole world. I've thought about you every day since we got home."

"Oh, Hunt, I want to believe you, but I don't understand why you took so long to tell me. Why you chose a few hours before I went out with Bill Ketchum."

"Because I was afraid you'd find out what I'd been telling you was true. That there are other men out there more deserving of you than me. Bill's a good guy, and you two would probably have a lot in common. I should be offering you good wishes and watch from the sidelines. I should be thankful I didn't make you pregnant, but instead I was disappointed and confused that you were so unconcerned about it. That ate away at me. Not once did you ever mention it. Why?"

She slid her arms around his waist, and Hunt thought his heart would burst.

Watching him, she said, "For one thing, we were together during a safe time for me, so I knew the likelihood of pregnancy was slim, but beyond that, I knew I loved you. Having your baby would have been a gift."

Hunt closed his eyes, then folded her deeply into his arms. "My God...my God..." Then a thought occurred to him. "Wait a minute. You wouldn't have told me? You would have just had it?"

"Of course I would have told you, but I wouldn't have pushed you into marriage or a relationship you didn't want. I knew how much you loved Kristin, and I knew you'd refused to allow yourself to feel anything for any other woman. I didn't want you if you didn't want me. I loved you, Hunt, but I'm not a martyr, and I certainly wasn't going to use the pressure of a pregnancy or play on the guilt you already had for making love with a virgin."

"And I thought you were too young," he muttered. "I'm the one who needs some instruction on mature relationships."

She grinned. "Only one with me."

"Then I'm forgiven for putting us both through all this indecision and unhappiness?"

"No, but I might give you a few years to make it up to me."

"I'm gonna pay big-time, huh?"

"In spades."

He chuckled.

She laughed.

"But I'm going to have a good time loving you while I'm forgiving you."

"Hmm. Does this mean the date with Bill Ketchum tonight is officially off?"

She gave him an innocent look. "Well..."

"Well, hell!"

Molly hugged him, and he gathered her close for a long, deep and very intimate kiss. He cupped her bottom and positioned her against him. She rubbed her cheek across the bristle on his cheeks as if it were velvet.

"I love you, Hunt. I've loved you for so long I ache with it."

He tipped her chin up and looked into those incredible lavender eyes. "Thank God you didn't give up on me."

"I wanted to, but it's very hard to give up on forever."

"And forever starts right now."

"Yes," she whispered. "Oh, yes."

And once again his mouth met hers with the knowledge that love never abandons those who truly seek it.

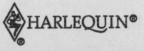

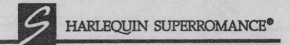

HARLEQUIN SUPERROMANCE®

THE OTHER AMANDA
by
Lynn Leslie

Superromance #735

Who Is She?

Amanda Braithwaite has been found nearly beaten to death in a park. At least, everyone *calls* her Amanda— her aunt, her uncle, her grandmother, her doctors. But Amanda remembers nothing, remembers no one. Except Dr. Jonathan Taylor. He saved her life, and he knows more about her than he'll reveal....

Does she really *want* to know the truth, or is the past too painful to remember?

Look for *The Other Amanda* in April wherever Harlequin books are sold.

Look us up on-line at: http://www.romance.net

HARLEQUIN®
Temptation

and

HARLEQUIN®

INTRIGUE®

Double Dare ya!

Identical twin authors Patricia Ryan and
Pamela Burford bring you a dynamic duo of
books that just happen to feature identical twins.

Meet Emma, the shy one, and her diva double,
Zara. Be prepared for twice the pleasure and
twice the excitement as they give two
unsuspecting men trouble times two!

In April, the scorching **Harlequin Temptation** novel
#631 Twice the Spice by Patricia Ryan

In May, the suspenseful **Harlequin Intrigue** novel
#420 Twice Burned by Pamela Burford

Pick up both—if you dare....

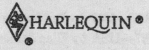

HARLEQUIN®

HARLEQUIN SUPERROMANCE®

A trilogy by three of your favorite authors.

Peg Sutherland
Ellen James
Marisa Carroll

A golden wedding *usually* means a family celebration.

But the Hardaway sisters drifted apart years ago. And each has her own reason for wanting no part of a family reunion. As plans for the party proceed, tensions mount, and it begins to look as if their parents' marriage might fall apart before the big event. Can the daughters put aside old hurts and betrayals...for the sake of the family?

Follow the fortunes of AMY, LISA and MEGAN in these three dramatic love stories.

April 1997—AMY by Peg Sutherland
May 1997—LISA by Ellen James
June 1997—MEGAN by Marisa Carroll

Available wherever Harlequin books are sold.

REQUEST YOUR FREE BOOKS!

2 FREE NOVELS
FROM THE ROMANCE/SUSPENSE COLLECTION PLUS 2 FREE GIFTS!

YES! Please send me 2 FREE novels from the Romance/Suspense Collection and my 2 FREE gifts. After receiving them, if I don't wish to receive any more books, I can return the shipping statement marked "cancel." If I don't cancel, I will receive 4 brand-new novels every month and be billed just $5.49 per book in the U.S., or $5.99 per book in Canada, plus 25¢ shipping and handling per book plus applicable taxes, if any*. That's a savings of at least 20% off the cover price! I understand that accepting the 2 free books and gifts places me under no obligation to buy anything. I can always return a shipment and cancel at any time. Even if I never buy another book from the Reader Service, the two free books and gifts are mine to keep forever.

185 MDN EF5Y   385 MDN EF6C

Name	(PLEASE PRINT)
Address	Apt. #
City	State/Prov.	Zip/Postal Code

Signature (if under 18, a parent or guardian must sign)

Mail to **The Reader Service:**
IN U.S.A.: P.O. Box 1867, Buffalo, NY 14240-1867
IN CANADA: P.O. Box 609, Fort Erie, Ontario L2A 5X3

Not valid to current subscribers to the Romance Collection,
the Suspense Collection or the Romance/Suspense Collection.

Want to try two free books from another line?
Call 1-800-873-8635 or visit www.morefreebooks.com.

* Terms and prices subject to change without notice. NY residents add applicable sales tax. Canadian residents will be charged applicable provincial taxes and GST. This offer is limited to one order per household. All orders subject to approval. Credit or debit balances in a customer's account(s) may be offset by any other outstanding balance owed by or to the customer. Please allow 4 to 6 weeks for delivery.

Your Privacy: Harlequin is committed to protecting your privacy. Our Privacy Policy is available online at www.eHarlequin.com or upon request from the Reader Service. From time to time we make our lists of customers available to reputable firms who may have a product or service of interest to you. If you would prefer we not share your name and address, please check here. ☐

BOB07

HARLEQUIN

More Than Words

"Jeanne proves that one woman can change the world, with vision, compassion and hard work."

—**Linda Lael Miller,** author

Linda wrote "Queen of the Rodeo," inspired by Jeanne Greenberg, founder of SARI Therapeutic Riding. Since 1978 Jeanne has devoted her life to enriching the lives of disabled children and their families through innovative and exciting therapies on horseback.

Look for "*Queen of the Rodeo*" in
More Than Words, Vol. 4,
available in April 2008 at eHarlequin.com
or wherever books are sold.

SUPPORTING CAUSES OF CONCERN TO WOMEN   **☷ HARLEQUIN**

WWW.HARLEQUINMORETHANWORDS.COM

MTW07JG2

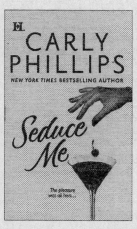

MARGARET MOORE